PRAISE FOR

THE SIBERIAN DILEMMA

"Stellar . . . This is a must for any crime fiction fan interested in the underside of Putin's Russia."

—*Publishers Weekly* (starred review)

"Put Arkady Renko near the top of your list of favorite cynics in crime fiction . . . This is Smith at his absolute best: black humor, brown bears, and gray souls."

—*Booklist* (starred review)

"This is vintage Martin Cruz Smith. Fans of Arkady Renko will be pleased."

—*Kirkus Reviews*

"Arkady Renko . . . returns with style."

—*The Wall Street Journal*

"Smith's lucid prose, surprising imagery, and realistic dialogue, as well as his wonderfully quirky characters, all serve his engrossing storytelling."

— *The New York Times Book Review*

"Rich in atmosphere and suspense, *The Siberian Dilemma* is an interesting and fast-paced crime thriller."

— *The Washington Times*

"*The Siberian Dilemma* is Cruz Smith at his best: ace storytelling with ... umpled but courageous hero."

—*Financial Times*

T0026565

"Those drawn to Smith's mysterious Russian settings will be fully rewarded by the depictions of vast and cold Siberian expanses, monstrous bears, and precious sables (Smith appears to have a special feeling for the last: a sable-smuggling operation was central to the plot of *Gorky Park*), as well as small-time mobsters, big-time oil tycoons, dirty politics, banyas, and vodka."

—*Foreign Affairs*

"Smith may be a fiction writer, but his crime novels featuring the durable, laconic policeman Arkady Renko have over the last few decades supplied some of our most insightful coverage of Russia. Smith, for example, was one of the first Russia-watchers to flag that country's far-right revisionist embrace of Stalin not as a monster but a national hero."

—*The Daily Beast*

"[C]hilling thriller."

—*CrimeReads*

"[A] first-rate crime novel."

—*BookTrib*

"Excellent."

—*Air Mail*

"Martin Cruz-Smith's deftness of touch, lightness of humor, and depth of knowledge are on display as ever in *The Siberian Dilemma*."

—*The Guardian*

ALSO BY MARTIN CRUZ SMITH

THE ARKADY RENKO NOVELS

Gorky Park

Polar Star

Red Square

Havana Bay

Wolves Eat Dogs

Stalin's Ghost

Three Stations

Tatiana

OTHER FICTION

December 6

Rose

Stallion Gate

Night Wing

Gypsy in Amber

Canto for a Gypsy

THE
SIBERIAN
DILEMMA

MARTIN
CRUZ SMITH

SIMON & SCHUSTER PAPERBACKS

NEW YORK   LONDON   TORONTO   SYDNEY   NEW DELHI

Simon & Schuster Paperbacks
An Imprint of Simon and Schuster, Inc.
1230 Avenue of the Americas
New York, NY 10020

This book is a work of fiction. Any references to historical events, real people, or real places are used fictitiously. Other names, characters, places, and events are products of the author's imagination, and any resemblance to actual events or places or persons, living or dead, is entirely coincidental.

Copyright © 2019 by Titanic Productions

All rights reserved, including the right to reproduce this book or portions thereof in any form whatsoever. For information, address Simon & Schuster Paperbacks Subsidiary Rights Department, 1230 Avenue of the Americas, New York, NY 10020.

First Simon & Schuster trade paperback edition October 2020

SIMON & SCHUSTER PAPERBACKS and colophon are registered trademarks of Simon & Schuster, Inc.

For information about special discounts for bulk purchases, please contact Simon & Schuster Special Sales at 1-866-506-1949 or business@simonandschuster.com.

The Simon & Schuster Speakers Bureau can bring authors to your live event. For more information or to book an event, contact the Simon & Schuster Speakers Bureau at 1-866-248-3049 or visit our website at www.simonspeakers.com.

Interior design by Laura Levatino

PHOTO CREDITS:
Baturina Yuliya: viii–1. Nuttawut Uttamaharad: 72–73. alex_aladdin: 270–271.

Manufactured in the United States of America

10 9 8 7 6 5 4 3 2

Library of Congress Cataloging-in-Publication Data has been applied for.

ISBN 978-1-4391-4025-3
ISBN 978-1-4391-4026-0 (pbk)
ISBN 978-1-4391-5320-8 (ebook)

FOR EM

FROM BEGINNING TO END

MOSCOW

1

Sasha's eyes were set in a huge pan-shaped head and he studied Arkady as someone who might share his misery. The bear was a towering beast but his customary roar was weakened by alcohol. His mate, Masha, sat on her rump, a half-empty bottle of champagne pressed to her breast. A plaque on the zoo guardrail read "Sasha and Masha, American Brown Bear (*Ursus arctos horribilis*)." That sounded about right, Arkady thought.

The bears had been released by somebody who had left a poster that declared "We Are Animals Too." Arkady wasn't going to dispute this.

At four in the morning the dark made every fairy-tale feature of the park into something grotesque. Statues became monsters. Shadows spread wings. Lions softly growled and polar bears manically paced back and forth.

Arkady was an Investigator of Special Cases, and if a bear running loose in the heart of Moscow was not a special case, he didn't know what was. Victor, his partner, was an excellent detective when he was sober.

By the time they arrived, the zoo director had tagged Sasha and Masha with tranquilizer darts loaded with barbiturates that, combined with champagne, made a heady cocktail for even an *Ursus arctos horribilis*.

Masha slumped against a stone wall. Sasha's every burp was a foul bubble and each snore resonated like a broken drum. One moment he seemed inert, the next he jerked upright and swept the air with a massive paw. A half dozen young zookeepers held poles like lances and cautiously surrounded the bears from a distance.

They were greeted by Victor's sister, Nina, the zoo director, a take-charge kind of woman dressed in a sheepskin coat and hat. She was toting a tranquilizer gun.

She gave Arkady a firm handshake.

"Did you call for more help?" he asked.

"I don't want police charging around the grounds," she said. "That's why I called you."

"I *am* the police," Victor said.

"Ha!"

So much for Nina's estimate of her brother.

Sasha and Masha were thirty meters away, lurching toward an ice cream cart. Together they shook it until the handle broke, then rocked it from side to side until it fell over. Discouraged, they lumbered back to their stone wall and collapsed to the ground.

Arkady's father, General Renko, had hunted bears and warned him about people who thought they could outrun or outclimb them. "In case of an encounter, do not run; a bear is faster," he said. "If he catches you, play dead."

Arkady hoped that these young zookeepers had been trained to deal with brown bears. He had the feeling that Sasha could knock them over like tenpins.

"Tell me about last night," Arkady said.

"We had a fund-raiser for patrons of the zoo in the main hall and there was a good deal of drinking and celebrating. We feed them, offer them champagne, and while they're in a generous mood, we hold an auction. A cleanup crew put all the empty and half-empty bottles in bins to be picked up in the morning. It appears Sasha and Masha got into them."

"How did they get out of their cage in the first place?"

"There's been a lot of agitation by animal activists lately. It looks to me like an idealistic animal lover snuck in after everyone had gone, released the bears, and put up his poster as a protest. It had to be someone that the bears were familiar with."

A classic inside job, Arkady thought.

"Apparently, one of your keepers has gone soft in the brain," Victor said.

"And what do you auction at a zoo?" Arkady asked.

"The highest bidders are given the honor of having a baby giraffe named after them, or a private visit with a koala bear. Things of that nature."

"In other words, it's a crass display of money," Victor said.

"We depend on wealthy people in high places to support the zoo."

Not bad, Arkady thought. Had President Putin himself attended? He was known to like photo ops with lion cubs.

"Tell me about the bears," he said.

"The female, Masha, is docile enough, but Sasha, the male, can be aggressive."

"Poor bastards. They'll probably be hosed down," Victor said. "At least, that's what they do to me in the drunk tank. Bears should be rambling through the wilds of Kamchatka in all their glory, scooping salmon out of streams and scaring the wits out of campers. Instead, they're an embarrassment to nature."

"Animals don't suffer from the zoo experience," Nina said. "Nothing could be further from the truth. Bears live longer in captivity than in the wild. They don't mind."

"And if you tickle a lab rat, it will giggle," Victor said. "Can you kill a bear with that?" Victor nodded at her tranquilizer gun.

"Of course not," Nina said. "The gun is for the bear's protection."

"Does the bear know that?"

"It's just compressed air and barbiturates." She pulled a dart with a pink pompom at its end. "We call it 'chemical immobilization.' "

"Masha's on the move," a zookeeper called out.

Masha wanted no part of the scene; she stood, sadly turned, and waddled back toward the open door of her caged den. A champagne bottle slipped from her grasp and rolled away. She sighed. The brief excursion had been excitement enough for her.

"She likes her den," Arkady said.

"It's called a habitat," Nina corrected him.

"It's a fucking circus," said Victor.

Sasha was brokenhearted by Masha's betrayal. He got to his feet, moaned, and swung his head from side to side.

"Now what?" Victor asked.

Nina dropped her voice. "It depends on whether Sasha follows Masha or goes to sleep. All we can do is wait."

"How smart are they?" Arkady asked.

"At a guess, I'd say as intelligent as a three-year-old. That's a very unscientific estimate."

"A three-year-old giant with claws," Victor said.

"On that order."

"Let's hope he needs a nap," Arkady said. "Are bears your specialty?"

"Primatology." She swept hair from her forehead. "I study apes."

"Me too," said Arkady.

"You had pets when you were a boy, didn't you?" Victor asked.

"Some." Arkady didn't have ordinary pets like dogs or cats. He had collected geckos and snakes, whatever he could catch on the Mongolian steppe.

"I understood that you have experience hunting bears," Nina said.

"Me?"

"Victor told me that you were a regular big-game hunter."

Arkady turned to Victor. "You said that?"

"Maybe I exaggerated."

"No, I never shot a bear. Maybe a rabbit."

"Then I've been misinformed, as usual."

"I'm afraid so."

Arkady's father had been posted in a number of godforsaken

places in the middle of Siberia. In the wintertime he would enlist a native guide and head into the taiga, with Arkady following their snowshoe tracks. The natives made their living by trapping or shooting sables through the eye, leaving a pelt smooth and intact. General Renko nearly matched the hunter's marksmanship. With a rifle, Arkady was lucky to hit a tree.

"So you have never shot or tagged a bear." Nina's voice sank.

"No," Arkady said.

"Maybe we should just shoot him," Victor said.

"Shooting a bear is the last thing we want," Nina said. "You have no idea how difficult and expensive it would be to find another bear with a clean bill of health. Besides, Masha might reject a new bear."

That was always a possibility, Arkady thought.

Sasha's eyes took on a more focused glint. As he rose to his full height, a rank smell steamed off him. There was a honking and clatter as the surface of the pond rose. Sasha lifted his head and watched ducks and geese rise in formation, then locked eyes on Arkady, took a sly step forward, and extended a paw as if to say, "This way to your table, *monsieur*." This was followed by a roar that shook the earth.

The zookeepers lowered their poles like lances and slowly began to move in.

"Stop!" Victor shouted. "Stay where you are!"

The young men tripped over their feet as they backed up.

Nina cocked the tranquilizer gun. She fired but the dart fell short.

She reached for another dart, inserted it into the chamber, and pulled the trigger again. By this time, Sasha was no more than ten meters away from them. Again the dart fell short. A dud.

Nina's hands were shaking. She shoved the gun into Arkady's hands.

He loaded and fired. A pink plume like an artificial flower appeared in Sasha's forehead. The bear swatted at it once, twice, and was asleep before he hit the ground.

2

After leaving the zoo, Arkady bought a bouquet of flowers and headed to Yaroslavsky Station to meet Tatiana's train. The station was a byzantine creation as frightening as a child's nightmare. It rose up in the middle of Moscow like a goblin, windows for eyes and a dark slanted roof capping a huge entryway ready to devour all who entered.

As the Trans-Siberian Express drew up to the platform, third-class passengers with no time to lose rushed off the train, leaving the pigsties they had made of their cabins. Crumpled wrappers, sausage ends, greasy cheese, spilled beer, and empty bags of potato chips littered the compartments. Oilmen, gamblers, and miners—the sort that never dug grit from under their fingernails—found their wives. Babies howled with discomfort while older children rubbed sleep from their eyes.

Wealthy tourists disembarked from luxury carriages to meet porters who rescued luggage and bags of souvenirs. Tatiana would be riding in the second-class carriage, neither hard nor luxurious but perfectly suited for those doing business in the new Russia.

Hundreds of travelers fanned out across the great hall or ducked into Metro tunnels. Arkady scanned the crowd searching for Tatiana, listening for the decisive tap of her heels on the marble floor. He tripped over Gypsies who were sprawled out on the floor like so many pashas at ease. Babushkas defended sweet-smelling loaves of bread and bottles of homemade pickles from police dogs. Boys handed out fliers advertising local bars, cafés, and strip clubs.

Rather than argue with Arkady about the risks she took, Tatiana often simply left without telling him where she was going. Two months earlier she had disappeared from their apartment, leaving only a railroad timetable on the kitchen table with the route to Moscow from Siberia underlined as if to say, "Catch me if you can." She had circled November 14 and 13:45 as her return time.

As an investigative journalist, Tatiana was the natural target of thugs: a stab in the leg with a poisoned umbrella or sometimes a shot in the back of the head. She never looked for such dangers. She was fatalistic and, oddly enough, light-hearted. When he was with her, he looked for individuals who might wish her harm, who folded their newspapers too tightly or walked too briskly or too slowly.

Arkady went from tunnel to tunnel, back and forth from racks of fashion magazines to the electronic board of departure and arrival times and back again. There was no Tatiana. He dropped his flowers into a metal basket as he left.

• • •

From the train station, Arkady went straight to the prosecutor's office, where Prosecutor Zurin was holding forth on a recent trip to Cuba. Four deputies in blue serge and brass buttons drew their chairs close to give Zurin their rapt attention. His white hair was starting to thin and his features starting to pucker with age, but he still enjoyed the sound of his own voice.

"I conveyed to our counterparts in Havana our profound condolences on the death of our Comrade Fidel Castro."

Arkady remembered Havana Club rum and insinuating music. A dozen years earlier he had investigated the death of a colleague floating in Havana Bay.

Zurin saw his least favorite investigator slipping down the hall.

"Renko, wait—wait, I want to talk to you. Not here. In your office."

Arkady's office was as crowded as a crab pot. Desk, chair, cabinet, coatrack, and file cabinets huddled together. The desktops of other investigators displayed photographs of their wives and children like sworn testimonials of virtue. His was bare by comparison.

Zurin shut the door behind him. "I was there, you know—at Fidel's memorial."

"I didn't know that." Arkady hoped that the prosecutor would notice that there was room for only one person to sit.

Zurin assumed a thoughtful expression. "It reminds us that the Revolution must always be guarded with vigilance. Our statistical success against violent crime should not be taken for granted."

Russian homicides had a high "solved" rate thanks to a judicial system that relied less on evidence than confession. It was easier to beat a confession out of an innocent drunk than to pry it out of a sober killer. Still, Renko had a knack for solving the most difficult cases without resorting to force.

"The annual review is coming up. What should I say about you?" Zurin asked.

"Tell them I could use a larger office."

"I was thinking of mentioning your lack of collegial cooperation. Don't you think collegial cooperation is important, Renko?"

"Absolutely."

"Then why don't you show it? Your colleagues say that at times you even reverse their hard work."

"If the evidence is insubstantial, yes."

"If a man has confessed, what does evidence matter? I've told you a hundred times that the best evidence in the world is a confession. And among colleagues, cooperation. Each man pulling his own oar." Zurin then took Arkady by surprise. "You've been to Cuba?"

"A long time ago."

"So you obviously speak Spanish."

"Very poorly."

"Well, a man of your skills—Spanish, Russian, familiar with the locals, knowledge of the law—would be nicely positioned in the new Cuba. If he had the right attitude."

"We'll never know."

"You'd have to be motivated. I understand that."

Arkady pictured life under a palm tree, ducking coconuts, plucking the strings of a guitar.

"Too nice. It doesn't sound like me."

"Just a thought. There would be suspicions. With you, there

14

is always a cloud of suspicion." As suddenly as Zurin had gone one direction, he went another. "How do you feel about Siberia?"

"It's large and it's cold," Arkady said.

"I have an assignment for you. Nothing could be simpler. Next week you go to Irkutsk, pick up a would-be murderer named Aba Makhmud, take him to a transit prison where you will prosecute him, and see that he gets a good, long sentence."

"'A would-be murderer'?"

"He's a Chechen, a terrorist. He tried to kill a prosecutor."

"I haven't heard about this case."

"It's fresh." Zurin slapped a dossier onto Arkady's desk. "It's all in here."

"Which prosecutor?"

"It happens to be me. You are my investigator and I want you to bring about a swift and proper conviction."

"Why me?"

"Because you're famous for being difficult. No one would say that you're the kind of person who allows himself to be influenced or railroaded."

"What if I decline the case? Or come to the wrong conclusion?"

"You won't. I've finally figured you out, Renko. You think you're so independent, but you're a hostage to fate like the rest of us."

"Meaning?"

"I hear that your stepson is quite a chess player."

"Zhenya?" Zurin had never mentioned him before.

"Yes. He looks like a laggard but apparently on the chessboard he's quite the dynamo."

Arkady's face got hot. Just when he thought he had eluded

the snake, the snake swallowed him a little bit more. Swallowed and smiled, because if State Security had its teeth in Zhenya, it meant it had its teeth in Arkady.

Zurin put the dossier in Arkady's hands. It was tied shut with a red ribbon. "I think you're in for some fascinating reading." Satisfied, Zurin returned to his deputies and his visit with Fidel.

3

The next morning Arkady visited Sergei Obolensky, publisher of the news magazine *Russia Now*. With steel-rimmed glasses and rolled-up sleeves, he was the picture of a crusading journalist, and Tatiana was his lead writer.

Commendations and awards were displayed on the shelves, and stacks of newspapers were piled on the floor. A rubber-tree plant languished in its pot. A suckerfish lurked in an aquarium.

"So you went to pick up Tatiana at the station yesterday and she wasn't on the train. And because of this you're worried? I'm surprised at you, Arkady. She is one day late. I can tell you from experience that Tatiana has missed plenty of deadlines before. You've obviously never worked with writers. How does the nursery rhyme go? 'Leave her alone and she'll come home wagging her tail behind her.'"

Arkady was so frustrated, he found it hard to speak. "Is it such a fine distinction to you whether a person is dead or alive?"

"Said like a real investigator." Obolensky stared into the murky fish tank as if it were a crystal ball. "I'll admit, she should have checked in by now. I haven't heard from her since she left."

"Didn't you give her the assignment?"

"She makes up her own assignments. That's what makes her unique. I think this one is about the oligarchs in Siberia. Have you heard from her?"

"Only this." Arkady took out Tatiana's train schedule and pointed out the underlined connection to Moscow from Irkutsk. "This was, I believe, her schedule."

"There you are. So she missed yesterday's train. She'll catch one today or tomorrow."

Arkady knew that Obolensky loved Tatiana; that's what made his equanimity all the harder to buy. "Has she been threatened lately?" Arkady asked.

"Lately? Do you know how many death threats Tatiana receives in a week at the magazine?" Obolensky opened a desk drawer and pulled out a stack of letters. "Take your pick. These are threats made against her just this month from Kaliningrad because she exposed the radioactivity of the Baltic Fleet. And from Moscow because she wrote a sidebar about the president's new dacha. That's what makes her such a target. It's more dangerous to be an honest reporter than a dishonest policeman, wouldn't you say?"

"But you're not worried about her?"

"I'd just say you have an investigator's paranoia."

"Maybe."

The door to Obolensky's office was open and his staff found reasons to look in as they passed by. They were young and earnest about the truth but suspicious when it came to police investigators. Arkady did not blame them.

"So you'd say these letters mean nothing," Arkady said.

"That's right."

Arkady scooped up the letters and timetable and stuffed them in his overcoat. "Then you won't miss them."

4

It turned into the first real snowfall of the year, full of pillowy flakes that settled gently on statues and pedestrians alike. Men slouched. Women walked as straight as ramrods in fur hats.

Zhenya was a tall, weedy boy but he always had a new girlfriend. They would sit motionlessly in cafés to watch him play chess as snow packed against the windows. His latest conquest was Sosi, an Armenian girl with purple hair and dramatically scalloped brows who watched his games so intently, she didn't seem to breathe. She wore a scarf wrapped three times around her neck and gloves cut off at the fingers.

The café had well-worn sofas instead of banquettes, tables with scars, and enough players with high chess ratings to lend the place authenticity.

"Would you like something to drink?" Arkady asked Sosi.

She shushed him and pointed to a chessboard where Zhenya's opponent was on the brink of extinction. As the man recognized the hopelessness of his position, he toppled his king and slunk off.

Zhenya couldn't totally suppress a smirk.

"That was magnificent," Sosi said.

"You two were made for each other," said Arkady.

At seventeen, it wasn't clear whether Zhenya was a prodigy or a scam artist. He had become Arkady's responsibility years before, when Arkady had taken him out of a children's shelter just for a day, then for a second day and a third. Even at five years old his only interest had been chess, and since then he had developed a reputation as a sort of chess pirate.

Zhenya lit a cigarette and sat back. "That was an easy hundred dollars. See what Sosi made me?" He slipped the money into the new false bottom of his backpack. Velcro and velvet could make anything disappear.

"You could make twice the prize money if you entered a tournament," Arkady said. "And you wouldn't have to hide it."

"Sure. But my way, I play when I want to."

"And who you want to. You're going to run out of marks."

The one thing that stung Zhenya was the insinuation that he ducked the best players.

"Anyone I play, it's their choice," Zhenya said. "I can't help it if I'm better than they are. Sometimes I play a rook or a bishop down. What could be fairer than that?"

"They never know what hit them," Sosi said; her eyes grew as round as moons. She looked like the perfect fanatic to encourage a leap into a volcano. She rolled a rook back and forth on the

Formica as if she were gathering an electric charge. "Zhenya can turn any game into a slaughter."

It was like visiting the Macbeths, Arkady thought. He wiped the condensation that clouded his windshield and watched a tram climb a back street. The opposite wall was yellow. Moscow was a yellow blur.

5

As swallows darted back and forth along the Kremlin's walls, the sky went to purple, then to black, and still Tatiana had not called.

Arkady called Victor.

"We had to count every fucking animal, starting with 'aard-vark,'" Victor said. "My sister hasn't changed. Did you know that the cute little platypus has a poison fang?"

"Everyone does. How is your sister?"

"The Jungle Queen? I'd watch out if I were you. She likes you."

"Did you figure out who freed the bears?"

"Do you think I care? Dear God, may I never see another bear in my life." Victor hung up before Arkady could.

• • •

Windshield wipers thudded back and forth and Arkady felt like a pilot looking for a landing.

Backtracking sounded good. He knew he would probably get nowhere at Yaroslavsky Station itself. The attendants on the Siberian Express were probably halfway back to Irkutsk by now.

Five o'clock was the hour when many Russian men got thirsty, especially men who had reached the retirement age of sixty-five and had little else to do. Of course, they weren't totally retired. They washed cars, collected bottles and cans, or tutored unappreciative students. On holidays they brought out their good suits and caps and chest boards full of medals, then curled up with the cat and drank. Maybe drank moonshine raw enough to make a man go blind. There were exceptions. Riot police were allowed early retirement at forty-five, and in recognition that the state would collapse without him, the president had the option of living forever. Imagine that. Living forever with Putin. When Arkady got close to Yaroslavsky Station, he darted into a grocery store and picked up a bottle of vodka.

While he waited to pay, he heard a dismissive snort from the woman behind him. From her pink fur hat and coat to her felt-lined boots, she looked like a sugared pastry.

She eyed Arkady's bottle and asked, "Is that for a female acquaintance?"

"As a matter of fact, it is," Arkady said.

"Then do yourself a favor and go first class. Not Stolichnaya. You want Russian Standard vodka."

"I do?"

"Get a bottle with a ribbon on it. Take my word for it. It will pay off in the long run."

"Good to know." Arkady switched vodkas.

The cashier waved him forward. "If you want an informed opinion, Svetlana Maximova is the person to see. She's seen the world."

"That's true," the woman admitted.

Arkady added a box of chocolates and paid. Outside, the snow was getting thicker. Men slouched while Svetlana slid by as smoothly as a magnet. She had problems, however. One of her plastic grocery bags tore and threatened to spill its load of canned goods, dried fruit, and instant noodles.

"Where are you going?" Arkady asked. "Maybe I can give you a lift."

"And get into a car with a stranger and a bottle of vodka?"

"Well, it's your choice."

"I'd be an idiot."

"What floor is your apartment on?"

"Six." That tipped the scales. "Very well, but I'll have my eye on you."

The stairs in her apartment building were narrow and the lights flickered on and off. Svetlana was ahead of Arkady, when a can dropped from her broken bag and began rolling ominously down the steps until he extended his foot and blocked it. Another can rolled free and he blocked it with his other foot.

"Brilliant," she said. "Only now you can't move."

Arkady heard a meow and saw a cat at the top of the stairs. It purred and started to ooze down the steps.

What next? Arkady couldn't help but laugh.

She delivered a forceful "Scat!" and the cat bolted. "My name is Svetlana," she said.

"Arkady."

"Arkady, I think you jumped higher than the cat."

"I'm sure I did."

"Well, I don't want to be held responsible if you collapse. Sit down."

Arkady guessed that Svetlana was about forty, with an attitude between flirtatious and demanding. Her walls were covered with travel posters for Omsk, Novosibirsk, and Irkutsk, all Siberian cities. The chairs were covered with red pashmina shawls and the air was heavy with perfume.

"Who's the lucky girl you were buying this vodka for?" she asked as she put away groceries. One cabinet held two bottles of the otherwise despised Stolichnaya. "A little wife at home?"

"No."

"You're just a man of mystery who goes around offering free rides to stranded women?"

"That sums it up."

"Chivalry is not dead." She twisted the cap off a Stolichnaya and poured two glasses. "Cheers!"

As Arkady drank, he noticed romance novels stacked in orange crates; CDs, mostly opera; photos of friends, mainly female. She was at ease and definitely used to being in charge.

"See, here are my mates Olga and Jacqueline scuba diving in Greece. *Providnitsa*s, the same as me. We stick together."

He said, "I have this feeling that we met before."

"Please, that must be the oldest line in the book."

"Still, do you work at the train station?"

"As a matter of fact, I do." She drew herself up.

"As a *providnitsa*?" Arkady said. A *providnitsa* was a person of some consequence. Riding on each passenger car, *providnitsa*s collected tickets, fed the stove, tended the samovar, settled disputes, and kept third-class passengers out of first class. It took a boldness that Arkady had spied in Svetlana at the grocery store.

"People think that it's the engineer who runs the train," Svetlana said. "Nonsense. Inside the train, it's the *providnitsa* with the samovar. Vodka and tea, that's what the Siberian Express runs on. And you are . . . let me guess: A musician? I love musicians and basketball players. I won't bother you with the reason why."

They clinked glasses and downed their drinks in one go. "Now tell me, Arkady, what do you do?"

"I'm with the prosecutor's office."

"Oh." She was disappointed; she had liked this man until then.

"I'm looking for a missing person," Arkady said. "I think that anything that happens on the train or in the yard, you're the sort of person who would know about it."

That was doubly bad. She screwed the cap back on the bottle.

"I don't think so."

"Take a look at her." He showed her the photo of Tatiana. The image was gray and slightly blurred, but the face was striking, slightly tilted—coquettish, even—sharing a joke with the photographer. He remembered taking it at an outdoor fair. A carousel had played "Moscow Nights" over and over.

Svetlana shrugged. "Working at a train station, I see a thousand faces in the course of a day."

"I'm talking about passengers riding first class on the Siberian Express. The train started in Beijing, stopped in Irkutsk, and finished in Moscow. Somewhere between Irkutsk and Moscow, Tatiana disappeared."

"Not on any train I've been on."

"She was supposed to have boarded the train in Irkutsk November tenth at 15:57 and was expected back in Moscow on the fourteenth, 13:45." Arkady stood up and scribbled on a business card. "Maybe you've heard of her: Tatiana Petrovna."

"Is she a movie star?"

"No."

"Then I never heard of her."

"She's a journalist."

"Sorry, dear, my shoes are awfully wet. Some other time. I wouldn't be a *providnitsa* long if I started making waves. Ta-ta."

With that, she practically pushed him out the door.

Russians were famously dangerous drivers. They were apt to fly across three or four lanes and drive so close to each other, they were practically in each other's skin. Black limos snaked through the avenues, then tunneled under buildings and hid in darkened courtyards.

For almost a month now, Arkady had suffered a lover's deprivation. Snow did not help. He once was so sure he saw her walking in Gorky Park that he had gotten out to follow her into a maze.

Tatiana disappeared between box hedges. He thought he found her on a Zen-like pebble path, only her raincoat was shorter and her face was square, a pretty Slavic face but the wrong face. The world was full of wrong faces.

Once home, he turned on the TV without bothering to turn up the sound. He found it curiously relaxing, like Obolensky's aquarium. He couldn't stand the prospect of eating alone, just

as he couldn't stand company. He found that there was little difference between microwaved pasta and microwaved *pelmeni*.
Mainly tomato sauce.

After dinner he began going over the letters he had taken
from Obolensky. Some of them were death threats, others simply
hate mail. There were fifteen letters in all, the products of fever-
ish but unimaginative minds.

He read them in one go, preferring to swallow them whole
rather than draw the poison slowly. The obsessive nature of one
writer could result in ten pages of vitriol, the same misspellings,
the same erratic scrawl. Another wrote half in cursive, half in
childish print.

"You stupid cunt, I can't wait to stick my gun in your lying
mouth, pull the trigger, and watch your blood splatter my bedroom wall. You are the International Yid who betrayed the white
race. I will fuck you a hundred times over. I'm laughing because
I picture you hanging by your tits. Did you think I missed? I just
let you go until next time."

"Next time" suggested an appointment of sorts. Previous communication, petty cruelty or pure braggadocio. Half the words
were misspelled. Was there something in the last issue of *Russia
Now* that could have incited this kind of anger? Or was it lunacy?

6

Across the river, church domes blossomed and the beauty of Moscow was sometimes hard to believe. Driving along the river as it ran along the Kremlin, Arkady saw police divert cars away from the Moscow Bridge. He pulled his car to the side of the road and got out to ask a traffic officer who was in charge.

"You want the sergeant," the officer said. "He's a law unto himself. You'll see."

A six-lane bridge was softly lit by votive candles and strewn with flowers wrapped in cellophane. The bridge had history. A heroic political activist named Nemtsov had been assassinated two years before on the flank of the bridge. He was strolling with his girlfriend after a late dinner when he was killed with four shots from a passing car. The morning after, demonstrators marched onto the bridge by the thousands and erected a makeshift shrine of candles, red roses, personal photographs, and poems. The shrine would stay up for a while but eventually the mood always changed. Demonstrators were met by riot police wearing hard helmets and swinging long batons.

On this night, the anniversary of Nemtsov's murder, demonstrators lined up along a bus and looked a little worse for wear, not bruised but scuffed. Arkady saw a flash of purple hair. He walked up to a sergeant with the triangular build of a weightlifter. He gave the impression of a fist clenching and unclenching.

"Provocateurs," the sergeant said. "They put the shrine up, we tear it down. They put the shrine up, we tear it down."

And the cleanup began. Street cleaners jumped out of trucks and stuffed plastic garbage bags with bouquets, photos, and political placards. Votive candles rang as they rolled over cobblestones, pizza boxes soared in the air, and backpacks lay in a heap. Arkady picked up one that looked familiar and found Zhenya's chessboard and chess pieces inside. He felt the nap of its Velcro bottom.

"Why have you detained these people?"

"Our detainees? Public disturbance, I guess. Hardly worth the trouble. We'll take them back to the station and rattle their teeth, that's all."

Martyrs drove Arkady crazy. There were twenty-some protesters in parkas and fur caps. Older couples clung to each other while younger victims braced to absorb the crack of a flexible baton against the knees, elbows, head. Zhenya was trying to hide Sosi behind him. Finally he noticed Arkady.

"What are you doing here?" Zhenya demanded.

Behind Arkady the sergeant asked, "You know this fuckup?"

"I'm here to pick up him and his girlfriend," said Arkady.

"For what?" Zhenya demanded.

"Hustling." Arkady held up the backpack. "This is the evidence."

It was an absurd charge, almost comical, but the bluff might work if Zhenya would only keep his mouth shut.

Sosi raised her eyes. "We needed money to eat."

So she had caught on. Smart girl.

Arkady handed Zhenya's backpack to the sergeant. "Look in the false bottom. Of course, whether or not you report this money is your business. You were the first on the scene."

"Are you fucking me over?" the sergeant asked.

"As best I can."

Zhenya contained himself until they reached Arkady's car.

"Do you even know how much money that was?" Zhenya asked.

"That's what's important? Money? I'll lend you money. Did you think about Sosi? She could have been hurt."

Zhenya looked out the window in embarrassment, a boy's response.

"Thank you," Sosi said.

"*I* don't thank you," said Zhenya.

7

Nina Orlof's flat was a museum of taxidermy, rooms full of stuffed lemurs and green monkeys that peered with glass eyes through artificial fronds. He found stuffed animals about as interesting as feather dusters. In a slinky sheath of silk, Nina herself looked like the leader of a snake cult. Her invitation to tea had come out of the blue and he supposed that it was her way of thanking him and Victor for coming to her rescue at the zoo. The main thing was that he had slept for a solid six hours and felt close to being human.

"Do you like animals?" Nina asked Arkady.

"Renko loves animals," Victor said. "He's passionate about animals. He likes to wrap himself with a puff adder. In fact, don't you have one here in your apartment? I know he'd enjoy it. People think reptiles aren't affectionate, but there's no sight more endearing than Arkady tossing a python over his shoulder. Of course, he has to keep bobbing."

"My brother exaggerates. I do not have a puff adder in my flat," Nina said.

"But she could, she could," Victor said.

"Professor—"

"Please, call me Nina."

"Nina, did you find out who set your bears free?"

"A pair of new zookeepers, young and idealistic. They spouted some new age shamanism. It's as infectious as the common cold. Too bad, but I had to let them go. The main thing is that word of the incident did not get out, and for that I thank both of you. There might have been professional repercussions. I am grateful. Just a moment," she said, and disappeared into the kitchen, then returned with a tray. "Tea? Biscuits?"

Victor was disappointed. Vodka would have been his tea of choice.

"I was impressed by the way you stood your ground with Sasha," Nina said to Arkady. "As if you didn't care."

"That's my secret weapon," he said.

"Did you hear about the body in Gorky Park?" Nina asked.

That got Arkady's attention. "What body?"

"They were excavating in back of the art museum and they dug up some bones. A partial assortment at least. Rib cage, mainly, and ankle bones. No skull. Gave the artists a fright, though."

"When was this?"

"A month ago. The bones may have been in the ground quite a while. They interviewed me."

"Why?"

"They weren't positive it was a man," Nina said. "And they want to create an exhibit around the bones."

"It could be a bear," Victor said. "Every year a hunter drags in what he thinks is a murder victim."

"It's the similarity of men and bears," Nina said. "They are the only two animals that employ plantigrade locomotion. In other words, they walk on the soles of their feet."

"And Neanderthals," Victor said. "Have you ever seen a reconstruction of a Neanderthal man? Ugliest bastards you ever saw."

"That's prejudice," Nina said. "It's been scientifically proven by DNA that *Homo sapiens* and Neanderthals cohabited—"

"Cohabited like rabbits," Victor said.

"Well, they had to be somewhat attractive," said Nina. "Don't think of them as ugly. Think of them as redheads with sultry eyes and ruby lips."

"Redheads?" Victor asked.

"Apparently a high percentage."

"Imagine a winsome lass with heavy brows slipping through the ferns of a terrarium," said Victor.

Nina protested, "And where on the tree of evolution does *Homo sovieticus* fit in? It's a sloth-like creature that hibernates in the sofa. That has to be my brother." She added in an incidental fashion, "I looked you up, Arkady. You have a checkered career."

"I'm flattered. I was unaware of having any career at all."

"In fact, I'm quite sure I know your favorite line: 'To be or not to be.'"

"That's a little ambitious for me." Arkady looked for an escape route.

"I warned you that she might find you interesting," Victor whispered.

"Victor tells me you worked on a factory ship," Nina said. "How does a Moscow investigator fall so low?"

"I had some help on the way. I was investigating a murder."

Arkady was beginning to feel a bit like a Neanderthal himself and was relieved when his cell phone buzzed. The caller was Obolensky. Arkady listened, then closed his phone. "I'm sorry, Nina. It was good to see you again. I have to go."

"Not unless you promise to come to the gallery opening tomorrow night. It might be interesting as an exhibit of the New Russian. Promise?"

"I'll come with you." Victor stood.

"No. This is something I have to do on my own. Stay and enjoy your tea."

Victor gave Arkady the look of a friend betrayed.

Tatiana's office at *Russia Now* had been trashed: desk drawers pulled out and contents upended. Her computer lay on its side in the corner. Obolensky's office was in no better shape. Books and all the magazine's prestigious awards had been swept off the shelves, his couch and chairs stabbed and disemboweled. Writers and editors crowded around like witnesses at a car wreck. Even the suckerfish in the aquarium seemed to hold its breath.

Obolensky had called Arkady rather than the police station.

"Has this happened before?" Arkady asked.

Obolensky motioned his reporters out of the room. "About

once a year. Sometimes one of us is mugged on the street outside. We know how to take care of ourselves."

"Did you report those incidents?"

"No, and I won't report this either."

"Why not?"

Obolensky waited until the last reporter had shuffled out. He
paused to clean his glasses. "I wasn't completely honest with you
before."

"No?"

"I talked to Tatiana. She is covering an important story. You
were right about that."

"What is she covering?"

"Mikhail Kuznetsov." Obolensky paused to let that sink in.
"Mikhail Kuznetsov," he repeated, "an idealistic oligarch who
spent five years in a Siberian prison for daring to criticize Putin
and his cronies. He may run for president."

"He doesn't have a chance," Arkady said.

"Kuznetsov's not only running for president; according to
Tatiana, he's running for his life. That makes him a moving
target."

"And makes her a moving target," said Arkady.

"Anyone who challenges the Kremlin runs the risk of being
murdered."

"Kuznetsov is a complicated man. He has two sides at least.
Is Tatiana waiting to see who kills him? Is that the plan?"

"With Tatiana, the plan changes all the time. Originally she
was only going to Irkutsk to interview Kuznetsov. Three weeks in
and out. Then she gained his trust and it became a much bigger
story."

"No doubt, and in the end *Russia Now* wins more prizes, while Tatiana has risked her life. I can see why you didn't tell me before."

"Because I know you. I knew that as soon as you heard, you'd go out looking for her."

"So?"

"And you would be out of your depth in Siberia. If you want to help, stay here and find the hooligans who did this. That can be the first step to finding out who is threatening her."

Arkady smiled. "Such a lovely decoy—such a waste of time. Why haven't I been able to reach her on the phone?"

"Kuznetsov doesn't know about you and we thought it best to keep it that way."

"Who is 'we'?"

"I'm not going to get into an argument over semantics."

"For a man of letters, you should be better at this."

Obolensky clenched his fists, and for a second Arkady thought the publisher would attempt something physical. He was, after all, a big man. But Obolensky changed his tack.

"Renko, try to think beyond yourself. This story will make Tatiana famous for the rest of her life."

"She doesn't think in those terms."

"Of course, she does. Tatiana is a writer. I'm a publisher. I know how writers think."

It was as if Obolensky had swum into dark water and touched a stone. An admission without words, perhaps.

"You're left-handed," Arkady said.

"As a matter of fact, yes, I am."

"And a redhead when you had hair."

"Yes."

"Nearsighted."

"Okay."

"You have either a blond mistress or a dog that sheds hair. I will go with the dog. That's the end of my parlor tricks. For real results, you'll have to give me real information."

8

A skeleton walked in Gorky Park. Supported by rods and wires, it followed the whim of a technician manipulating a remote control.

"This is the brilliant part," Nina said. "I told you how they found ancient bones during the excavation of the Gallery? They took that as the starting point of new evolution. The contribution from the zoo was advice in how to put it all together. A transformation, I should say."

"Brilliant," Arkady said.

It was a transformation, he thought, but into what? An automaton? A hairy beast? At the flick of a toggle switch, it stepped inside the gallery hall, stopped, and moved its head from side to side.

The technician said, "It's like any kid's robot, only much bigger."

"Personally, I prefer your lemurs," Victor said.

"Remember what a derelict building this was?" Nina asked Arkady.

"I remember," said Arkady.

An old warehouse was now wrapped in a translucent polycarbonate skin and turned into a venue for exhibits of conceptual art. Models wearing little more than tails and patches of leather served vodka and caviar. They filtered in and out of rooms while, as a contemporary touch, free jazz played in the background.

Victor speared something on a tray. "I think this one tried to escape. It's either a shrimp or a finger." He grabbed a vodka. "Seriously, Oedipus would rip out his eyes by their roots rather than witness this gluttony."

"Maybe we should come back on another night," Arkady suggested.

"Nonsense. I'm sure Victor can hold it together. The Gallery has a wonderful lineup of artists and celebrities."

"I just saw a man who controls half the timber in Siberia. Boris Benz," Victor said. "That's a thrill. But don't go near him. He surrounds himself with bodyguards, his old prison mates. They cover up his dirty work. I wonder why he's here."

"Maybe he appreciates art," Arkady said.

"More society than art," Nina said. "On the social calendar, this is the place to be."

"You sound like your brother," Arkady said.

"Some of them are genuine art collectors and also happen to be supporters of the zoo. I don't make judgments beyond that."

Who did? Arkady thought, The gallery was full of the rich and beautiful, balding but well-greased men with cowboy boots and silver buckles and loud ascending laughs that said, "You can't touch me. I am too rich, I am too powerful, I am too high to fall." They hung around together like a regular boys' club. They were all success stories. Some of them had made their fortune by evicting pensioners from old buildings and constructing the tall-est buildings in Moscow. Others, like Boris Benz, had despoiled the arctic wilderness to drill for oil. Benz had broad shoulders and a slack, easy smile. Just for a moment his eyes met Arkady's.

Nina led the way to the skeleton. "I want you to meet our guest of honor. I know you saw him when he came in but I want you to take a really good look."

"Someone I might know?" asked Victor.

"Oh, I sincerely hope not."

The tech hit "pause" and the skeleton came to a stop.

It was more than a robot and less than a man. Life-size and with the long stride of human legs. The cranium was round but long in the snout, its eyes a pair of ruby-red diodes.

"It's not a human," Arkady said.

"Yes and no," said Nina.

Arkady had seen a good number of dead men; an investiga-tor did. This one walked stiffly with the aid of a nearly invisible network of electrical wires. Close up, he seemed to be a man. The jawbone was missing and, likewise, the collarbone had been car-ried away by some ancient scavenger. The arms were powerful, the hands chewed down to tarsal bones. A forearm was broken and healed, signifying a violent encounter with enemies. But a *Homo sapiens* or Neanderthal?

"Bear," Arkady guessed.

"That's right," Nina said.

"Which part?" Victor asked.

"The head, ankles, and chest are from a bear," Nina said. "The rest is human or Neanderthal, but it opens up possibilities. Evolution could have gone many different ways. It's like a time machine that goes sideways as well as forward and back. Hunters considered themselves brothers to the bear. When they hunted, it was part of a complicated ritual. There was dancing and singing and communication on a spiritual level."

"Not like today," Victor said. "Today you just open a can of beer."

That brought the spiritual level down. Victor left and browsed among quail eggs and caviar while Nina defended her skeleton.

"We said that Neanderthal man couldn't speak, but he could, or fashion tools, but he could, or create art, but he could. We said his brain was a different shape, and that's true, but it could have had its own advantages. Some of it survived for a reason. Maybe someday we'll know."

"You're sympathetic," Arkady said.

"I just want to know why. I think this creature of ours could have been a survivor. He would have had his turn."

This was a different and more interesting Nina, but before she got any further, she was accosted by Gallery guests who wanted to have their pictures taken with what they already called "Bear Man."

Arkady couldn't help but be embarrassed for the creature, and he moved on to another exhibit. He found himself standing in front of a waxwork of a naked woman sitting on nails. Beside him stood Boris Benz.

"It's pain. It's an exhibit of pain," said Benz. "Or is it an exhibit of pleasure?"

"I suppose it all depends," Arkady said.

Voices in the room were hushed simply because of Benz's presence. No introduction was offered. None was needed. Everyone on earth knew who Boris Benz was, while Arkady was resoundingly inconsequential. A handshake would be nothing but a grace note.

"Are you a devotee of modern art?" Benz asked.

"Actually, this looks more like the Spanish Inquisition."

"A good point. I hear you saved our bears."

"Masha and Sasha?" Arkady asked.

"I'm a patron of the zoo. You must be one hell of a shot to bring down a charging bear."

"I'm surprised you heard about it."

"Nina told me." Benz leaned closer to Arkady's ear. "I wish I'd been there. I would have brought an elephant gun and split that fucking bear in half."

That wasn't a sentiment that Arkady expected to hear from a zoo patron.

They moved to the next room, where a motorcycle was crushed into a cube and a mirror hung in a glittering multitude of pieces.

"By the way, I think I met a friend of yours," Benz said.

"Really? Who?"

"A highly intelligent woman named Tatiana Petrovna."

"When?"

"A few weeks ago. I'm going to take her ice boating on Lake Baikal. She's intrepid." Benz smiled. "I warned her that her nipples would freeze."

Arkady stopped. "Are you sure this was Tatiana Petrovna?"

"The famous journalist, yes. She mentioned you."

"Where was she staying?"

"Last I heard, she had taken up residence with Mikhail Kuznetsov. But who knows?"

"Where?"

"Siberia."

"Can you be more specific?"

"No."

Arkady had more questions, but he caught sight of Victor weaving toward them. He had left Victor untended for no more than ten minutes, which was time enough for him to down ten vodkas.

"Asshole," Victor said.

Benz's bodyguards began to close in. At least, Arkady thought it was Benz's bodyguards; they all looked the same in their Italian suits.

"Excuse me? What did you say?"

"I said you're a greedy asshole."

Benz looked around and laughed softly. "Do I know you?"

"No, but I know you for what you are."

Benz seemed to be considering options. He could simply walk away or beat Victor to a pulp. Boris Benz was, after all, a hyper-athlete. By comparison, Victor was a physical wreck.

Arkady took Victor by the arm. "You're drunk. We're going now."

"This is your friend?" Benz asked Arkady. "Do him a favor. Take him far away."

Arkady felt badly for Nina, whose professional relationship with Benz and the zoo might be an important one.

"You understand who I am?" Benz asked Victor.

"Go fuck yourself," Victor said.

"Why?" Benz asked.

"On general principles."

"We are definitely going," Arkady said.

• • •

Dropping Victor off at his apartment was like depositing a bag of bones. Arkady was halfway back to his car when he remembered that the feral cats behind Victor's house depended on Victor to put out milk. He was such a contradiction. He couldn't take care of himself, but he made sure the feral cats never went hungry.

And what had Arkady learned? What progress had the senior investigator made? That Tatiana seemed to be making excellent progress in her own research. That she was probably still in Siberia. That she seemed to have forgotten their rendezvous in Moscow. That it was pathetic how jealous he was.

9

A few errant snowflakes drifted into the chess club as people rushed in from the cold. Arkady felt suffocated by the smell of damp wool. This was the home of what Zhenya labeled "wood pushers," mediocre players with middle ratings. Cabinets glittered with ancient silver trophies.

Everyone knew Zhenya's reputation as a hustler, and his presence at a chess tournament was virtually a scandal. Every other player had at least a master's rating, while Zhenya had no rating at all, had no use for it, didn't need it, and let it be known that he only entered the tournament to please his girlfriend, Sosi, who sat by his side and fanned out her purple hair to a mystical length.

Zhenya expressed his disdain by choosing to play at blitz speed while his opponent considered every move at a normal pace. It was like watching someone slowly, meticulously assemble a clock. Zhenya traded a bishop for a rook, doubled a pawn, lost momentum, and was caught in a pin five moves ahead. Before Zhenya knew it, the game was over. He looked up. His opponent was wearing a Metallica hoodie. He was fifteen years old.

In his second match Zhenya lost to an ancient grandfather with a wispy beard. He had not lost two games in a row for more than a year. There were murmurs at Zhenya's back. So this was the fearsome chess bandit. Onlookers hovered by the chessboard rather than miss a second of Zhenya's agony.

"It's not looking good," Arkady said.

"No, it isn't." If a man could speak from the grave, he would sound like Zhenya.

"He's got an hour to regroup," Sosi said.

"Then why isn't he eating?"

"The last thing I feel like is eating," said Zhenya.

"You have to have something in your stomach." Arkady didn't know if it was true, but it was a change of subject.

"Tea sandwiches is all they have," Sosi said.

"Good enough." Arkady stuffed money into Sosi's hands. "Do you mind? There's a cafeteria in the basement. We'll be outside."

Once they were on the sidewalk, Arkady asked, "What happened?"

"Have you ever seen such bad lighting? It's like a cave," Zhenya said.

"It's not the lights that's hurting your game. I've seen you play in a subway tunnel."

"Well, it's pretty distracting in there." Zhenya lit up a cigarette. "As soon as I got here, they informed me that I couldn't smoke. Smoking's not a problem anywhere else, but it is here. Why do they hate me?"

"Try smiling," Arkady said. Zhenya tried and produced a rictus of a grin. "Never mind. Do you think you can beat the boy?"

Zhenya dropped his usual bravado. "He plays the whole board." It was hard to say more about a player.

"Don't worry so much. You either beat him or you don't. He's two and zero and you're zero and two, which is not good but not impossible. If you win the next two games, you'll probably come up against him in the last round. There is an underhanded ploy you can try, but you have to get to the last round. Can you do that?"

"Fuck, yes."

"That's more like it. Do you know if the boy smokes?"

"Like a locomotive."

"Okay, once you're in your respective chairs and begin to play, you tap out a cigarette."

"I can't. We're not allowed."

"I didn't say light it; it's important that you don't. Just set it on the table and make sure that it's his game clock that's running, not yours."

"It's a distraction. They'll make me put the cigarette away."

"Which you will put barely visible in your breast pocket but he won't forget it. The threat, as they say, is more effective than the execution."

"That's cold," Zhenya said.

"It is, isn't it. Of course, you may not need to use it. That's up to you."

Zhenya was full of admiration. Sosi came out of the chess club carrying a plate stacked with watercress sandwiches cut on the angle. Zhenya devoured them one by one and finally smiled. "I'm sorry about the Moscow Bridge thing. I was scared." This was a major admission for Zhenya.

Now that Zhenya had revealed his vulnerability, the chess

hall was eager for a bloodletting, but Zhenya played a spotless White and won without exertion. The fourth match, likewise, was a simple lesson in mathematics, grinding out a win.

In their first match, the boy in the Metallica hoodie had taken advantage of Zhenya's overconfidence and the fact that he was used to overwhelming opponents in a matter of minutes. Zhenya had gotten sloppy and overconfident. It only took someone capable of offering a systematic waiting game to trip Zhenya up.

The fifth and final match was a duel between Zhenya and the boy in the Metallica hoodie. Playing White, the boy opened with the Queen's Gambit and followed with a suite of moves new to Zhenya. The game was always deep enough to create a flow and counterflow, first sniping and then engaging in cut and thrust. Zhenya stayed even in pieces. Bit by bit, however, he was losing ground. His men seemed scattered. Time pressure started to be more of a problem for Zhenya. This was the point, if ever, to use Arkady's cigarette trick. Both sides were even down to a queen, a knight, a rook, and four pawns, but Metallica's men supported each other, while Zhenya's were scattered all over the board. He kept his cigarettes deep in his pocket.

It was a given that chess was the most Russian, most intellectual of all mental contests. It rarely looked like fun, Arkady thought. He had seen pictures of Lenin, Trotsky, Gorky, and Chekhov playing chess. They never looked like they were having a good time. No wonder Russians flocked to it.

Now each side was down to a rook, a knight, and two pawns. White was under time pressure. Would Black offer a gentleman's draw? Not Zhenya—not while there was more humiliation to be exacted.

After much shuttling back and forth, Metallica freed a pawn

and sent it exuberantly racing across the board on its way to a second life as a queen. As for Zhenya, he finessed White's new queen by under-promoting his pawn into a relatively lowly knight and announcing as if surprised, "Checkmate!"

"I didn't need that stupid cigarette trick," Zhenya said once they were back in the car. "Fucking checkmate. And then he quits, like he has sudden indigestion. What a pussy. Sorry," he excused himself to Sosi, "but I knew as soon as he started moving his pawn down the board to become a queen, that was all he could think of. His downfall was a pawn that kept saying, 'Move me, move me.'"

"And the way they swarmed over you when they declared you the winner!" Sosi said.

"I guess the shoe's on the other foot now."

"Maybe your next lesson should be winning with modesty." Arkady opened his door to his flat and Zhenya and Sosi happily tumbled in.

The prize was a chess king set in glass; Zhenya hadn't let go of it since they left the club.

"They've invited Zhenya to other tournaments," Sosi said.

"Suddenly I've got business cards from guys who want to be my coach. Actually, the kid wasn't a bad player for a heavy metal fan."

10

The next day at the prosecutor's office, Zurin asked Arkady to walk to his car with him. Arkady was suspicious but it was a bright, sunny day, the sort that inspired people to walk their dogs.

"Do you know anyone who has a dog?" Arkady asked.

"I own one."

"Really? What kind?"

"A miniature French poodle. We have to walk it four times a day. It's a little crap machine."

Imagine that, Arkady thought. Zurin had a poodle.

Across the river, demonstrators marched with placards. They were inflamed by new evidence that the president owned ocean-cruising yachts and not one but four estates, with swimming pools, horse stables, tennis courts, and cascading waterfalls. One of them even had a separate house for ducks. Ducks! In this manner, corruption was quantified and understood.

"You had something on your mind?" Arkady asked. "Do you still dream about a posting in Cuba?"

Zurin pressed his lips together for lack of anything to say.

"I'll give you a letter of recommendation if that helps," Arkady volunteered.

"Very funny. You would probably just fuck me over."

"Probably."

"Well, you'll get yours soon enough." The prosecutor's tone changed. "How do you think it looks when a senior investigator protects a notorious dissident like Tatiana Petrovna?"

This was the game Arkady and Zurin always played: Arkady the snake charmer and Zurin the snake.

"Has she broken the law?" Arkady asked.

"It's not what she did or did not do, it's her attitude."

"You can't simply change someone's attitude."

"Why not?" Zurin asked. "Dostoevsky spent two years in a Siberian prison camp and it has to be said that he came out with a much improved attitude."

He produced from his pocket pictures of Tatiana Petrovna and Kuznetsov.

"What about the man with her?" Zurin asked. "They look like they're good friends."

"I wouldn't know."

"You never met him?""

"No."

"But you know who he is. Mikhail Kuznetsov."

"I've seen his face in newspapers and magazines," Arkady said.

"Your Tatiana seems to be more than friends with an ex-convict and a known enemy of the people."

"And what does this have to do with me?" Arkady was running out of patience.

"It's just that it's very convenient for you and for me that you will be in Siberia picking up Aba Makhmud. I want you to also track down this Kuznetsov and report back to me. We want to know what he's up to."

Arkady shoved his hands into his pockets. "Is this official or unofficial?"

"Tell me, why are you always the troublemaker? What do you gain from that?"

Arkady broke into a smile. "As Dostoevsky said, 'Right or wrong, it's very pleasant to break something from time to time.'"

11

After a binge, Victor could count on three days of delirium tremens in the drunk tank. But he had lucid spells, and even through chattering teeth he declared Arkady the greater lunatic.

"Let me get it straight," Victor said. "You propose going into the world's largest landmass, most of it frozen, in search of someone who may not want to be found?"

"That's right."

"Would you like me to write your obituary today or tomorrow? Maybe I should just leave the date open. And I suppose you don't have any leads."

"I have a lead thanks to Boris Benz. He says Tatiana's near Lake Baikal, and apparently, she's good friends with Mikhail Kuznetsov."

"I wouldn't trust Benz as far as I could throw my grandmother."

"Zurin showed me a picture of the two together."

The tank offered spare accommodations: tile walls and floors, one lightbulb, twelve beds, a defibrillator, and a pail. On this day Victor was the only occupant. He lay on twisted dirty sheets and sounded even more hollow than usual.

"You know there are different kinds of therapy: massage, water, electric shock, group. For me they have suggested implanting a 'torpedo' of medication under the skin of my butt. It's a kind of aversion therapy."

"It sounds it. We've got to get you out of here. Let me speak to the doctor."

"We've been through this a hundred times."

"Then we will do it again."

"Not this time. Nina was here. It's hard to believe but she's never seen me like this before. Handcuffed! I'm her older brother. I am a fucking disgrace. She was crying. I didn't even know she was capable of it, but I made her cry. How low can you get? So, thank you, Arkady, my good friend, but not this time. This time I'm going to stick it out."

"At least, let me get you clean clothes."

Victor shook his head violently. "No, I'll do this on my own." He turned his face to the wall.

Those were words Arkady had often hoped to hear Victor say but that Victor always turned into a joke. Now that he was saying them in all sincerity, Arkady was unprepared. Victor had become Arkady's sounding board. They were partners in a peculiar business and he had come to count on Victor for what he felt was half his intelligence and most of his wit. Suddenly he had no one to take Victor's place.

• • •

Freed from her safari gear and with her copper hair released from its tight headband, Nina seemed relaxed. As she and Arkady walked by the habitats, he was aware that in some cases, at least, animals had it easy. Emus sat on their eggs for eight weeks without bothering to leave their nest. The Peruvian condor lived seventy majestic years. Flamingo babies were balls of gray fluff with smiles turned upside down. For sheer indolence, however, the prize went to the brown bears Masha and Sasha. It was a late Indian summer day and they stretched out languorously even to their claws.

"If there is a Bear God, he would look down and smile," Nina said. "I'm relieved nobody was actually hurt."

"Except you?"

"Yes. I've lost my position as zoo director. It seems that my brother's little performance at the museum annoyed one of our most important patrons."

"Boris Benz?"

"Yes. It will be announced next week. It's just as well. I can go back to just teaching, which I much prefer. And it will leave me time to study my apes."

"I wanted you to know that I'm going to Siberia tomorrow," Arkady said, "and Victor will need help from time to time."

"Of course. I saw him this morning and he seems determined to stop drinking. I won't let him starve. Don't worry."

A swan touched down for a heavy landing in the pool, setting off comic flapping and outrage among the ducks.

"We'll see how it goes," she said.

"But no bears?"

"Bears are thugs. Gorillas are buttercups."

12

Sergei Obolensky was cleaning the inside of his aquarium with a small squeegee. After the raid on his office he had purchased a new underwater display of brilliant neon tetras and a sunken pirate chest. He had rolled up his sleeves and pulled on rubber gloves. In short, he looked like a man who dealt with worry by keeping busy.

"You can't go wrong with tetras," he told Arkady. "They look like little roadside signs."

"Shouldn't you take your wristwatch off?"

Obolensky mumbled something obscene.

"Any news from Tatiana?"

"No."

"Have you tried to reach her?"

"Have I tried? Of course I've tried, to no avail. Damn, where is that fish net? Obviously you have never worked with Tatiana. I told you before, she works alone, on her own, at her own pace.

When the story is done, she will waltz through the door and we will all look like fools for being worried." Obolensky sounded as if that had happened to him more than once.

"What about the death threats she's received?"

"Nothing new or out of the ordinary."

"In an emergency, how would you reach her?" Arkady asked.

"She has no living relatives and she called on a single-use phone, so I'm dealt out, just like the rest of us."

"Did you ever inform the police about the raid here?"

"Of course not. Do I look like an idiot?"

"Well, you don't have to help me. I'm going there myself."

Obolensky swayed on his feet. "Being an oligarch in Irkutsk is like being God."

"I want to make sure she's alive and well. You said she met with Kuznetsov in Irkutsk. I'll start there."

Arkady planned to have Zhenya and Sosi take over his flat while he was gone. "All I ask," Arkady said, "is that you collect the mail and make sure that owls don't nest in the halls."

"Where are you going?" Sosi asked.

"Siberia."

"Like, where in Siberia?" Zhenya asked.

"Irkutsk."

"How long?"

"I'm not sure."

A little deflated, Zhenya asked, "This is about Tatiana, isn't it?"

Arkady was surprised: he didn't know Zhenya was even aware that Tatiana had been gone for a long time.

"Yes, she's been away too long."

"I can set up motion detectors," Zhenya said.

"I have no doubt. I can see myself stumbling home one night and being pinned to the floor by a cyborg," Arkady said.

"What about police?" Sosi asked.

"If you have to let them in, document them on camera. Otherwise, no guns and no resistance." Arkady went off to his bedroom to pack.

Sosi wandered in. "Do you mind?" she asked.

"No, go ahead. Sit down."

She watched him pack and unpack an athletic bag; it was his aim to carry little more than a toothbrush and a razor.

She plopped onto a chair and surveyed the room. "You have a lot of books."

"Don't be misled. I haven't read them all, but if I like them, I read them again."

She nodded and hummed. Today she was wearing purple-tinted glasses to match her purple hair. It was a little like being visited by a Martian, Arkady thought.

"I walked around," she said. "Are all the banners and medals yours?"

"No, they were my father's."

"He was a hero?"

"To give him his due, he was much loved by his men."

"You sound—"

"He killed more of the enemy than of his own men, but it was close."

"Zhenya really admires you. I don't know if you know that."

He glanced her way in case he was missing any sarcasm. "No, I didn't know that."

"He talks about you all the time. 'Arkady would do this; Arkady would do that.'"

Arkady smiled. "I'll take your word for that."

"You're going to Siberia? Have you been there before?"

"Briefly," Arkady said.

"It's cold. I mean, really cold."

"So you have family in Siberia?"

"My parents were visiting professors at the university in Irkutsk. They were good teachers."

"Are they still there?"

"No, they moved back to Armenia and tried farming, but their vineyard developed a fungus and then all their truffles were consumed by pigs. Now they're back in Ararat pumping gas. I stayed in Moscow when they moved, because I was still at the university here and had a resident's permit, but that will run out in a few more months and I'll sleep where I can. Zhenya is very kind."

Arkady had ceased packing.

"How did you meet Zhenya?"

"He saw me stealing bread at a restaurant and followed me outside. He brought me food."

Arkady was reminded of Victor feeding stray cats. What if every assumption you made throughout life was wrong? Or even ten degrees off? It would add up.

"Have you ever been married?" Sosi asked.

That was out of the blue, Arkady thought. "Years ago."

"Do you have any kids?" Sosa asked.

Hesitantly, Arkady said, "I suppose you could say Zhenya is my child."

With a sweep of her hand, she asked, "Who are you going to leave all this to? All these flags and stuff. They must be worth a lot."

"I've never thought about that."

"Don't you think you should? What if the worst people got your best things?"

"That's one way to look at it. I suppose I think that maybe it's a time for letting go, not holding on. Because you can't, you know."

"All I know is you've packed that little bag ten times since I've been sitting here."

13

Arkady slept most of the flight to Irkutsk. As soon as he stirred, his seatmate pounced.

"I hope you don't mind that I ate your omelet. You were asleep."

"That's all right." Arkady had a vague memory of declining something yellow and rubbery.

"You should have taken the train. The food is much better."

"I'll keep that in mind," Arkady said.

His new friend was a native Buryat, one of the Mongolian peoples who had survived Ivan the Terrible, Genghis Khan, and Joseph Stalin, which took some resilience, Arkady thought. His father had been posted in Siberia and liked to say that Buryat men were built for wrestling. This one seemed affable enough. He was about fifty years of age, with a wispy mustache and a muskrat coat that made him look a little like a tree stump.

"Pardon?" Arkady pulled out his earphones.

The man took out a business card that he formally presented to Arkady. "Rinchin Bolot, factotum." He vigorously shook Arkady's hand.

"Thank you, but what does that mean?" Arkady asked. "What does a factotum do?"

"Well, he does everything. That's the point. Anything and everything: driver, translator, hunting guide. A factotum can even arrange romantic liaisons. At your command." Bolot beamed.

"A man of many talents," Arkady said.

Across the aisle, teenage girls huddled over a flashlight and a scented letter. Tall, blond flight attendants floated by like Viking royalty.

"Let's tackle your first problem," Bolot said. "Let's find you a place to stay."

"I've already taken care of that, thank you."

"Okay, but remember, my advice is free of charge. You know, according to Chekhov, Irkutsk was, at one time, the Paris of Siberia."

"I never knew that. Do you own a car?"

"A percentage of a car."

"About three tires' worth?"

Bolot giggled. He dove into a briefcase and fished out glossy real estate brochures. "Would you be interested in a residential or commercial property in Irkutsk?"

"Neither."

This was where the usual salesman might have given up. Bolot persevered.

"I'll pick one for you. Residential." He sorted through splashy pages of great rooms and grand staircases, billiard and screening rooms, wine cellars and indoor pools. "You see, they have everything a man could wish for. A real fantasy land with lots of style."

"'Late Oligarch'?" More than a man could wish for in one lifetime, Arkady thought. "All the furniture is twice normal size. Are your clients real people or cartoons?"

Bolot giggled again. "You're too funny." Arkady wouldn't have been surprised if he had pulled a monkey from his sack.

The plane hit an air pocket and the girls across the aisle squealed.

"Relax, children. It's always like this around Irkutsk," Bolot said. "Pilots call it the 'Bermuda Triangle of Siberia.'"

"Why is that?" Arkady asked.

"Crashes. It's a difficult landing because the runway slopes and planes overshoot. Or they're overloaded or they use faulty parts or the plane simply explodes. It's always something. Usually I take the train," Bolot said. "Is this your first time in Siberia?"

"Once before, as a boy," he said. "My father was posted at a uranium mine. The first words in Buryat I learned were 'Does your dog bite?'"

At the next bump, Bolot's real estate brochures spilled from their folders onto the floor in front of him. As Arkady helped retrieve them, he noticed that they were all offered by Global Real Estate. Boris Benz's gold embossed signature was printed at the bottom.

He handed the pictures back. "So that's Boris Benz's company?"

"It is."

"Do you work for him?"

"No, would that I did. Do you know what the sales commission for a house like this would be? It would turn your knees to jelly."

The thought inspired Bolot to summon one of the Vikings and ask for one last vodka. "You too?" he asked Arkady.

"It's a little early in the morning for me."

"What I need is an introduction to Benz. Perhaps it's intuition, but I am a strong believer in karma and I have to ask: Do you happen to know him?"

"We've met. I can't say I know him."

"You've met him and you still have your tail feathers? Now I have to say that I am impressed. I'm very, very impressed."

The flight attendant returned. Vodka rose and fell as a liquid column in Bolot's glass. He drank it in one go and the air smelled purified—"sanctified," Victor would have said.

"You want to work for Boris Benz, yet you think he's dangerous?" Arkady asked.

"Is it dangerous to walk across a crocodile? Maybe so, but worth it if there is a pot of gold at the other end."

"Is that why you're carrying around Benz's brochures?" Arkady asked.

"Oh, he doesn't even know I'm alive. All I want is to get his attention, and if I bring him a client or a business lead, maybe he will notice me."

"What do you know about a friend of Benz named Mikhail Kuznetsov?"

"Ah, the so-called hermit billionaire. I'd be a poor capitalist if I didn't know about him. They say he's even harder to get to. Do you know him too?"

"No."

"There's the rub in a nutshell," Bolot said. "It's like a club.

You can't get in unless you are a millionaire. Worse, oligarchs are moving targets. Someone like Boris or Kuznetsov has a private jet and homes in London, Moscow, the Cayman Islands. They have armies of lawyers and accountants, and whenever they want, they simply disappear."

That was the way Tatiana had vanished, as if swallowed up by Siberia. He had handled her train schedule so much, he had almost worn it through. He tried to picture where she met her mysterious sources, but all he could imagine was a landscape of prisons.

As the plane began its descent, Arkady made out the first sketchy signs of civilization. Train tracks and semaphores. But also a frozen river that wound through forest so dark, it was black. The plane's engines began groaning, and Arkady saw the outline of a city half buried in snow.

"If you don't mind me asking, where are you staying?" Bolot asked.

"The Irkutsk International."

"Ah, the International. High-class. Boris Benz owns that hotel." Bolot approved.

The Vikings went to their perches. The airplane's wheels locked into place. The control tower bucked up and down. The sun as it rose burst the glass of the tower and then broke into a million violet lights, not totally unlike Paris.

14

Tolya was the young police officer assigned to be Arkady's driver. He met Arkady at the Irkutsk airport before driving him to a holding cell. There, they picked up Aba Makhmud, the man accused of trying to shoot Zurin.

The three men started the two-hour drive toward a transit prison outside of Irkutsk where Makhmud would be tried and sentenced. If found guilty, he would be moved to a larger prison where, without hope, he was likely to become a different creature, one tougher and more violent than the one he had started out as.

Tolya and Makhmud had little in common. They were the same age, but the policeman was Russian from his blue eyes to his flaxen hair, while Makhmud was dark and sullen as a wolverine.

"These are our pastel nights, our northern lights and cruel weather," Tolya intoned. "Where ice floes break with the sound of cannons and heroes march into exile. Where troikas fly overhead and houses turn to tar black. Or do you prefer 'ebony'?"

"It's your poem, Tolya," Arkady said.

"But, being from Moscow you may have a more sophisticated ear."

"I would no more get between a man and his poems than get between a bear and her cubs."

Aba let out a derisive snort. Tolya shot Arkady a sideways look and twisted in his car seat to include Makhmud. "What do you think of the poem?"

"Personally, I think it's shit."

"I should have expected as much from a someone who only reads the Koran," Tolya said.

"Fuck you!" said Makhmud.

"No, fuck *you*!"

"This is erudite," Arkady said.

"I am not going to say another word to him," Makhmud said, "let alone help him with his shit poetry. He wouldn't know poetry if it bit him in the ass."

They drove in silence and mutual contempt along a street deep in winter ruts.

Tolya had won a Pushkin Day poetry contest and his life had never been the same since. "I enlisted in the police academy so that I could concentrate on my poetry. I ignored the fact that my fellow officers were rascals and thieves."

"Petty thieves," Makhmud said. "They probably stole candy bars."

In the holding cell, Makhmud was charged under Article 295 of the criminal code with trying to kill Prosecutor Zurin. He had been denied his one phone call, stripped of his private attorney, and assigned a public defender who advised him to confess. So he confessed. Did it matter? It was a given that Chechens were incorrigible murderers. Pick any assassination of any political dissident or a contract murder, and Chechens were to some degree involved, according to the police.

In repose, Makhmud was a good-looking boy with dark, curly locks. He stared out the car window as if committing to memory his last free moments.

"I've heard about you," he finally said to Arkady.

"What have you heard?"

"I heard you work for Prosecutor Zurin."

"He's my boss."

"How can you work for a pig like that?"

Arkady had no answer. Which was not good, he thought. He should have a ready answer for embarrassing questions. He should wear armor.

Tolya leaned close as he drove. "I have many more poems, some of a bucolic nature, other memorials to be read at a graveside. I'm sure that, given the chance, I could find a wider audience. In the tradition of Chekhov and Dostoyevsky, I've chosen a prison theme."

"Prison poems? That would be interesting," Arkady said.

"That's the idea." Tolya got so close again. "I already have a title. 'Souls in Transit.' It evokes the suspension of time."

Prisoners in transit might wait a day or a year in suspense. A cell designed for four prisoners might hold twenty men with a single pail for slops. The heat, even in the dead of winter, was so stifling that men sometimes passed out on the floor. Misery had an epic quality.

"How far have you gotten?" Arkady asked.

"So far, not a word actually written."

"Not a word?" Makhmud sneered from the backseat. "The idiot's never going to write a single word. A poem cannot be suppressed. It erupts."

"If anyone is the idiot, it's you. I bet you think you can gain your freedom by ratting on your friends," Tolya said.

"I never ratted out anyone and never will." No accusation could sting a Chechen more.

Conversation ceased as they drew up to a chain-link fence topped by barbed wire where a closed-circuit camera looked them up and down. Everything moved in stages. They rolled by a guard tower to a windowless main building that looked more like a meat locker than a prison. Armed guards studied their identification, waved them into a courtyard, and motioned for them to wait. And wait. Finally, Arkady got out, pulled his hat over his ears, and wrapped his scarf up to his eyes.

A metal gate rolled open and a man in a fur hat stepped out.

"Kostich?" Arkady called out.

"You're early." The warden took his time, as if basking in a sunlamp.

"I'm bringing you the prisoner Aba Makhmud for interrogation," Arkady said.

"Makhmud the cop killer."

"He didn't kill a cop and hasn't been convicted of attempting to kill a cop yet," Arkady said. "In fact, the dossier is actually skimpy."

"But enough to proceed. You have the suspect and his confession. It seems to me that most of your work is done. All you have to do is fill in the blank spaces."

"I need to hear the confession."

"And my friend Prosecutor Zurin?"

"In the pink."

"And the prisoner?"

Arkady motioned for Tolya to bring Makhmud from the car.

"Take the handcuffs off him," Kostich said. "Let's get a look at this ferocious assassin." Makhmud looked up at the sky and shivered as the warden circled him. "Take your last look. He won't look like this when he comes out."

Arkady was vaguely aware of the muffled sounds of a fight emanating from the main building. What did they do for entertainment in this prison? Arkady wondered. What weapons were available? Kitchen knives? Potato mashers? Pots and pans? In some high-security prisons, men were never released from leg shackles. They fought on their backs like beetles.

"I need this suspect in undamaged condition and available for interrogation in two days," Arkady said.

The warden bent over to cough up a ball of green phlegm.

He wiped his mouth and said, "Of course, of course. Every formality will be observed."

Two guards took Makhmud in hand and almost ripped him out of his boots. Stripped of bravado, he cast a desperate look at Arkady.

On the drive back to Irkutsk, Arkady carried the image of Makhmud with him. How could he sympathize with a would-be murderer? It was a perverse game the mind played.

Tolya asked, "Can we talk?"

Arkady pulled his scarf down from his face. "That's what we're doing, shivering and talking."

"I'm having a problem with one of my partners. He's stealing from the evidence room and I can't do anything about it," Tolya said.

"Why not?" asked Arkady.

"If I make a fuss, he'll blame me, and it would only be my word against his."

"That happens a lot in police work. I would advise either say nothing or agree to share the goods. Police veterans can be bullies. Who else have you told about your situation?"

"No one. You're the first."

"And you've known me for less than two hours. That's not a strong basis for trust."

"Sometimes enemies are the best measure of a person's character."

"So true."

"I heard our Prosecutor Nikolai talking to your Prosecutor Zurin on the telephone. They're birds of a feather. I got the feeling Zurin couldn't wait to get you out of Moscow because you're such a pain in the neck."

"I like to think so," Arkady said.

Irkutsk was a city of two minds. It was a modern Soviet city and a quixotic collection of old wooden houses amid colorful onion domes. A vast public space was taken up by the park where Lenin Prospect met Karl Marx Square. Pedestrians moved with deliberation through drifts of snow, and even the ponies in the park leaned into the cold.

Arkady tried to call Tatiana, Zhenya, and Obolensky from his hotel room, but the calls failed and he'd never felt more isolated. Rather than eat alone, he settled into the hotel's Irish pub. It seemed every Russian city had one. Arkady chose a booth and ordered something called a "plowman's lunch." He didn't know what it was or what it hoped to be, but cheese and bread and pickled onions were involved.

He picked at his food and studied the meager six pages of Makhmud's preliminary investigation, the charge so neatly wrapped in advance. What did he know about Makhmud beyond the fact that his brief life was soon to be given a bad twist and that attacks on the police were handled with special fury?

Name:	Aba Makhmud
Age:	20
Height:	2 m.
Weight:	70 kg.
Hair:	Dark brown
Eyes:	Brown
Nationality:	Russian
Marriage Status:	Single
Residence:	Moscow
Ethnicity:	Chechen
Education:	Vocational
Military Service:	Dishonorable discharge
Employment:	Mechanic
Criminal Record:	Hooliganism, car theft, antisocial behavior

A preliminary investigation stated that on January third, without provocation, Aba Makhmud had fired a 9mm Beretta in an attempt on People's Prosecutor S. I. Zurin in Patriarchal Park in Moscow. He didn't offer any reason or remorse for the act.

"Naturally you're having a Guinness with that." Rinchin Bolot slid into the booth. "I hope you haven't forgotten me. We had such a good conversation on the plane."

"Yes, we did. How did you find me?" Arkady gathered his notes into his dossier cover.

"I wasn't looking for you. It's pure happenstance. Fate. Am I disturbing your work?"

"No."

"Good." Bolot turned to the bartender. "A Guinness for me too."

"Do you believe that?" Arkady asked. "That everything is fate?"

"Of course. What else? Can you imagine how confusing life would be without fate? In fact, I can produce evidence for you. Remember how on the airplane you were curious about Mikhail Kuznetsov?"

"You found him?"

"I wouldn't go that far, but progress has definitely been made." He lifted his glass. "Cheers!"

"Exactly how much progress?"

"I have every good reason to believe that Kuznetsov is nearby. Which, considering he could be in the South of France, is a lucky break."

"How do you know?"

"He was seen at an ice sculpture exhibit and his picture was in the newspaper."

"Was anyone with him?"

"In fact, he had a beautiful woman on his arm."

"This is the 'hermit billionaire' we're talking about? Do you have the newspaper?"

"Unfortunately, no. However, I'm learning the way you think. For example, I found you in this booth in this pub. Why? Because you have the mind of a detective. From this booth and only this booth, you can survey the entire clientele coming or going. I learn something new every day."

"I thought you were trying to get to Boris Benz."

"I'm rethinking that venture. The problem is, if you work for Benz, you have to snatch your dinner from the lion's mouth."

"How is Kuznetsov different?"

"Kuznetsov is not Buryat, but he is, at least a little bit, Siberian. Benz is an outsider and only cares about himself. He's a gang leader and Kuznetsov is a statesman, so I've decided to look for him instead."

"That's generous of you."

"That is just the first of many services I can provide for you as a factotum. I know the lay of the land."

"And you own three out of the four tires on your car."

"And I speak Buryat. Do you speak Buryat?"

"What does that have to do with Mikhail Kuznetsov, the wealthiest man in the world?"

"I don't know. Neither do you. Now look: See these people coming in the door? Describe them."

Arkady saw four Mongolians in quilted parkas pushing through a revolving door and said as much.

"Not bad," Bolot said. "But only two are Mongolian; the other two are Buryat. They're hunters, home from a week in the taiga tracking sable and lynx. You can see by their snowshoes and small-caliber rifles."

"How can you tell the difference between Mongolians and Buryats?"

"All Buryats are Mongolian but not all Mongolians are Buryats. See, now they're heading straight for the bar, so they had a good hunt."

"It sounds as if you have hunted."

"I've done many things," Bolot said enigmatically. "Most Russians have only scratched the surface of Siberia."

"It's an entertaining thought, but I already have a car and driver."

"You mean that bumpkin boy from the police? He couldn't find his ass from his elbow. You could be two places at once if we work together."

Oddly enough, Arkady thought, Bolot had a point. And once the investigation of Makhmud was over, Arkady would continue searching for Tatiana and still need a car and driver. Who better than a native?

"How much would you charge for this service?" Arkady asked.

"This is the best part. Nothing."

"Except the cost of a fourth tire to your car, which would make it effectively yours."

"Yes. That might be the case."

"We'll give it a trial run."

"Excellent." Bolot smiled so brightly, his gold tooth winked. "What do you have to lose?"

15

As the warden led Arkady and Makhmud to the interrogation room, the prisoners in their cells were watchful and silent, turning as a group like fish in an aquarium.

It was the sweat of bodies and the funk of stale cigarettes, the rotting smell of addicts and the fruity, ever-present bouquet of human waste and buzz of flies that made life sad. It was the triumph of hopelessness.

Warden Kostich said, "It's not the Winter Palace, but what do they deserve?"

"It is a little cold," Arkady said. His lips felt blue; maybe they didn't look it, but they felt it.

"He not going to talk," Kostich said. "He hasn't said a word since he's been here, not even to his public defender. Anyway, what do you care? You're the investigator for the prosecutor Zurin. If he never talks, you've still done your job."

When they reached the interrogation cell, they found it already occupied by two guards and a drunk in a disheveled suit.

"Who is this?" Arkady asked.

"The public defender." Kostich dragged the man by his necktie to a sitting position and attempted to perform introductions. "Marcus Federov, this is Arkady Renko."

Federov slumped back on the bench.

"Will somebody get the public defender a cup of tea?"

"I don't think he's in any condition to defend anyone," Arkady said.

"He's probably been here since yesterday," Kostich said.

"It looks that way," Arkady said.

The warden pulled Marcus Federov to his feet. It was difficult to keep him upright on unsteady legs, and the effort cost the warden a coughing jag.

"You should see a doctor," Arkady said.

Kostich spat blood into a handkerchief. "What would the doctors tell me? That I have tuberculosis and they have to retire me early at half pay? They'd love to do that. They'd get a bonus. Fuck the doctors."

Arkady almost sympathized with the warden. Tuberculosis stalked the guards as well as the prisoners. The prison was a place where bodies crawled over each other and mixed their sputum and bacilli, and it occurred to Arkady that the warden was as much a prisoner as Aba Makhmud.

"Has the public defender apprised the defendant of his rights?" Arkady asked. "Has he been allowed to make his one phone call?"

"Shit," said Kostich.

"I didn't think so," Arkady said.

The interrogation room had a Formica table with cigarette scars, two benches screwed to the floor, white walls, white bars, and a bucket to spit into.

"Okay, let's clean this shithouse up," said Kostich. "Pour some strong coffee into our friend Marcus and get him out of here."

Another guard led Aba into the interrogation room and seated him opposite Arkady.

Arkady set his tape recorder in the middle of the table and turned it on.

"Check. I am Arkady Kirilovich Renko, senior investigator for the Moscow prosecutor. Present with me are Warden Vasily Kostich and the accused, Aba Makhmud. It is January 10, 2019, and"—looking at his watch—"ten a.m."

"Name?"

Silence.

"Date of birth?"

Silence.

"Do you know what you're accused of?"

Makhmud folded his hands and looked down.

"At this rate we're going nowhere." Kostich was disgusted. "All we need is a confession and we have that. I just need it on tape. Call me when he's ready to talk." The warden got up and left.

Arkady and Aba watched the spools of the recorder grind. Arkady reached over and turned it off.

"These are our pissy nights, in prissy tights and totally fucked weather. Or do you prefer 'ebony'?" Arkady asked.

Makhmud couldn't help himself. "That Tolya, he is the source of the worst poetry I have ever heard in my life."

"It's pretty bad," Arkady agreed.

"It's pathetic," Makhmud said.

"So, can you answer some questions?"

Makhmud shrugged. "It doesn't change anything. Why should I help you? You're the prosecution, the enemy. I've already made a confession. What more do you want?"

It was progress, Arkady felt. He lit cigarettes for Makhmud and started again, but with the most innocuous biographical questions. It was a little like plumping a pillow, getting a prisoner to relax.

A half hour into the conversation, Arkady asked, "How is your family going to take this?"

"My mother will cry, my father will be proud, and my brother will laugh."

"What have you got against Prosecutor Zurin?"

"He's a sack of shit."

"I mean specifically."

"He just is."

"'Just is'? Okay, what does he have against you?"

"He has a hard-on for Chechens."

"That's it? According to the statements of eyewitnesses, you attempted to shoot Prosecutor Zurin. Did you know he was going to be there at Lovers' Bridge?"

"No."

"Was he with anyone?"

"Maybe, I couldn't tell."

"Traditionally, lovers declare their love by hanging a padlock on the bridge. It's very popular. Were you with a girl?"

"No. It's an idiotic fad. It doesn't mean anything."

"Then why were you there?"

"There's such a thing as walking by."

"Were you going someplace?"

"No."

"And you happened to recognize Prosecutor Zurin?"

"I would recognize that scumbag anywhere."

"Did you have words?"

"No, I just gave him the finger."

"That's quite an escalation, from a finger to a gun. All without a word?"

"That's the way it was."

"Zurin said nothing?"

"What does it matter? Either way, I tried."

"You don't seem to be a very good shot. What time of day was this taking place?"

"Broad daylight. Hey, maybe I should be the investigator. I think I'd win this case pretty easily. Is Zurin going to be there when I get sentenced?"

"In absentia. He's a busy man."

"I bet he is. I just bet he is. He'd love to turn the screw. So, how many years should I expect to get?"

"That's a problem. Encroachment on an officer of the law is terrorism. Even if we get them to drop the charge of aggravated assault and catch an amnesty, maybe ten years."

"Ten years." Makhmud exhaled a long plume of smoke. "That's the spring and summer of my life, isn't it?"

"Not a bad way of putting it."

On the way back to the hotel, Tolya snapped glances at Arkady. "You didn't sign off on Makhmud's confession."

"That's right."

"Why? Everyone else is satisfied. Public Defender Marcus is satisfied. Zurin is satisfied. Even Makhmud is satisfied."

"*I* wasn't satisfied," Arkady said.

"With what?"

"We'll clear it up. As the warden likes to say, nobody behind bars is going anywhere."

Tolya pondered what Arkady had done. "I don't get it. I say if a man wants to go to jail, you should let him."

"Well, I'm a killjoy."

As soon as Tolya dropped him off, Arkady went to his room and dropped flat on his bed and closed his eyes. He found himself caring more about Makhmud's case than he had anticipated. He tried calling Tatiana, but it was like playing a slot machine that never paid off. After ten rings, he hung up and tried Zhenya without success. Finally, when he started to feel that everyone he knew had moved to a different planet, he tried Victor at his house.

"Where the devil are you?" Victor asked.

"Irkutsk."

"You actually went. Are you on a case or simply out of your mind?"

"I'm out here to find Tatiana, but what you don't know is that Prosecutor Zurin has asked me to interrogate a young Chechen named Aba Makhmud."

"What's he accused of?"

"Attempted murder. He shot at Zurin and missed."

"Too bad."

"You haven't heard from Tatiana by any chance, have you?"

"No, but I wouldn't expect to."

"How are you doing?" Arkady asked.

"I'm afraid I'm in disrepute. Bad behavior since my last binge. Why I should give a damn, I don't know, but Nina is losing patience. If it weren't for you, they would have dropped me down a deep hole long ago."

"I can come back."

"Do that and I'll shoot you."

"In that case, I have some work for you. Are you sober?"

"Oddly enough, I am."

"The Aba Makhmud shooting took place January third at Lovers' Bridge in Moscow. It's a favorite sight for photographers to take wedding pictures. Find out who was working the bridge that day between the hours of two and three p.m. It should be fun."

"It sounds like hell."

"If they're professionals, they'll have digital contact sheets. Go to the bridge and chat up the photographers. They will remember because of the shooting. Get contact sheets from them."

"Won't that cost a lot of money?"

"Not if you tell them it's a police investigation. The important thing is to get all the photos you can. Different people, different angles."

"It sounds like you're getting interested in this kid Makhmud and getting carried away."

"I'm here on an investigation. I might as well act like an investigator."

Arkady looked out his hotel window. An argument was taking place in a welter of red police lights down on the street, where officers seemed to be choosing sides or going with the highest bidder. Arkady was not going to get involved.

"Arkady?" Victor asked. "Are you there?"

"I'm sorry, my mind wandered."

"I was asking how long this case is going to take. We don't want to get too far out of touch. Is it beautiful out there at Lake Baikal?"

"I haven't been there yet."

"I read about it. Deepest lake in the world. Holds more fresh water than all other lakes in the world combined. It has all kinds of fish and animals you never see anywhere else. Like the DTs."

"That's one way to describe them," Arkady said.

"And then you'll come back, right?"

"After I find Tatiana."

"I'm on my way to Lovers' Bridge. Call me back tomorrow."

Arkady hung up. Then he dialed Tatiana again and let the phone ring ten times before giving up.

16

It was late afternoon by the time Arkady left the hotel and walked down to the Angara River, as it churned its way north. He veered to Central Square, where music of the Beatles was being piped through loudspeakers.

The square had been transformed into an illuminated dreamscape of ice and music. He walked through a maze of ice sculptures and stopped to watch children scream with pleasure as they flew down an ice slide. Hannibal's elephants climbed across the Alps, Pinocchio was astonished by the size of his nose, Don Quixote raised his lance, a porpoise leapt into a crystal wave. Arkady especially liked a sculpture of three drunken reprobates sitting on a bench, looking for trouble. Even their little dog seemed to be looking for trouble.

He paused to contemplate an ice creature that was half tiger, half beaver, with a sable in its mouth.

"It's Babr, an imaginary creature," a voice said. "It's on Ir-kutsk's coat of arms."

Arkady turned to find Bolot standing behind him.

"Are you following me, or just lurking in general?"

"It's fate," Bolot said. His face was creased by a huge smile. The earflaps of his muskrat hat gave him a devil-may-care air. "Remember, I have hunted sable."

"I remember," said Arkady.

Bolot followed as Arkady moved on toward a single ballerina standing in front of a glistening corps de ballet.

"Beautiful." Bolot spread his arms as if he could take credit.

The hand of the prima ballerina suddenly snapped off. Arkady thought perhaps the wrist was too delicate to support the hand. While he stood still watching, two more holes silently pierced her heart. These were rifle shots coming from the direction of the Senate.

Arkady scanned the crowd. The festival was filled with children in spite of the late hour. Younger children rode on their parents' shoulders and more were still arriving.

"Get your head down!" Arkady shouted at Bolot.

Bolot was ahead and unaware. "Why?"

"Someone's shooting at us. Do you have a gun?"

"No. Why would I have a gun?"

"Then get the police."

People around Arkady didn't realize they were under attack. Children screamed with glee as fireworks sizzled overhead. Whistling pinwheels, sparkling fountains, and weeping willows lit up the night. A bullet snatched Arkady's fur hat off his head and he hit the ground, his face planted on the ice. He dared not move. Next to him the bullet went on spinning, nose down, until it expended all its rotational energy and came to a stop. A subsonic bullet was able to kill at five hundred meters. Paradoxically it could penetrate steel but was stopped by ice.

Arkady dodged from one ice sculpture to another as Don Quixote's head shattered and Pinocchio lost his nose. One of Hannibal's elephants lost a tusk, yet the crowd saw only fireworks.

Arkady tracked the shot to the Senate where a figure stood on the Senate roof. Dressed in black, he could have been invisible. Arkady fought his way through the crowd into the building, but by the time he climbed four flights of stairs and emerged on the roof, the shooter was gone.

Arkady went to the edge where the figure had been and looked across a square full of people swaying and dancing to "Yellow Submarine." One man moved purposely through the crowd carrying what looked like a ski bag and paused for one moment to look up at the grand finale. Chrysanthemum fireworks blossomed one by one and comets streaked across the sky.

Bolot arrived with policemen, who played the beams of their flashlights over the gutters of the building. There were no bullet shells. This had been a fastidious assassin.

"Did you see what he was wearing?" a policeman asked.

"He could have been in black or dark blue. I just saw him in silhouette."

"And?"

"He was in a parka and carrying a long bag."

"Did you shoot?" the policeman asked.

Arkady caught his poorly hidden amusement over a Moscow investigator who tried to shoot out fireworks.

"No. I wasn't carrying a gun."

"To be honest," Bolot said, "I myself didn't hear or see any shots being fired."

"I counted six silent rounds that hit close by," said Arkady, "including one I pulled out of the ice." He produced the bullet, the only proof he had that the event was not a creation of a fevered brain.

"Do you want to make a police report?" Bolot asked.

"About what? That I was surrounded by hundreds of witnesses who hadn't seen or heard a thing?"

"We'll look around just in case," the policeman said.

How had the shooter picked him out from all the men, women, and children who had filled the square? And how had he missed? Perhaps he didn't mean to kill Arkady, only scare him. In that case, the shooter had succeeded. This was when he really needed Victor.

"You know," Bolot said, "I pictured a Moscow investigator coming to Irkutsk and catching criminals with the snap of a finger."

"Me too," Arkady admitted.

As soon as he was back at the International, Arkady called Victor.

"It's about time," Victor said. "I thought you had forgotten me."

"Someone shot at me."

"That sounds like progress."

"It depends on your point of view."

Victor cackled. "The sniper who attacked you must have been a very good shot or a very bad one."

"That's insightful," Arkady said.

"If it's any comfort, your enemies, whoever they are, may just be biding their time. Maybe they just want you to leave Siberia."

"Who do you think they are?" Arkady asked.

"Maybe someone who is connected to Tatiana. Do you know people in Siberia?"

"A few."

"Then odds are at least one of them wants to kill you."

That sounded logical, Arkady thought.

"I don't know if you're ready for good news, but I went down to Lovers' Bridge as you asked. It's unbelievable. We've got all these young couples and their bridal parties crowding onto the bridge and plenty of photographers to take their pictures. Even in the freezing cold, Chechens want to have their pictures taken. Their weddings are extravagant affairs. The brides all look like swans and the grooms all look like geese and Bentleys are stuffed with dowry money. And keep in mind, relations between relations are not always happy ones, especially if they've had any vodka."

At the mention of vodka, Arkady opened up the room's minibar.

"Fights break out," Victor continued, "particularly when Chechens are involved. Not that they're always to blame, but they're not very good at waiting in line. Push comes to shove, and suddenly you have a confrontation. The bride starts to cry. Grandfather has a heart attack. It's a tinderbox. And then somebody reveals himself to be a genuine asshole. You'll never guess who."

"Who?"

"Apparently, Prosecutor Zurin has a Cuban sweetheart. She

wanted to have her picture taken on the Lovers' Bridge and he didn't see why he had to wait in line. He's a big shot, after all. Guns were drawn all around. One was fired in the air and Aba Makhmud ran away into the crowd. The next day he was picked up by the police for attempted murder. What is interesting is that my photographer friend had taken a picture, before everything got out of hand, of Makhmud in a dark suit posing with the bridal party. Five minutes later, immediately before the fight, he is in a leather jacket."

"Makhmud changed jackets?" asked Arkady. "Why would he do that? Did he anticipate a fight?"

"Who knows?"

Arkady asked, "The same photographer took both pictures?"

"Yes, and the date and time are always recorded on the film's contact sheet. Makhmud was questioned but escaped to Siberia before Zurin could identify him."

"Does your friend the photographer save rejects?"

"Generally, photographers throw away their rejects after a day, but we got lucky. He must have a million of them." Victor made the sounds of a man settling into a good book. "Tell me about your brush with death."

"It's getting late, but anyway, tonight I was at an ice sculpture festival, when someone started shooting. They were using subsonic sniper bullets. A half dozen silent rounds. I had the distinct impression that they were aimed at me at a distance of at least three hundred meters, I would say. You can't see, but I'm putting a finger through my hat."

"That doesn't sound like a welcome mat. It doesn't have anything to do with Makhmud, does it? This could be one of Tatiana's friends telling you to go home."

"Well, as you said, it's progress."

"No, it's insane. And how is your head? Obviously, you do not intend to keep it out of harm's way."

"It would be helpful if your photographer friend could scan all the contact sheets of the Chechen wedding and onlookers for that day and send them to me here. Cubans, too, while you're at it."

"Why not the moon?"

"And any of the dowry car."

"Anything else?"

"Send them here, the same as the rest." Arkady had Bolot's email address on his card. "Send them to my factotum."

"What's a factotum?"

"I'm not sure, but I seem to have one."

17

The next morning Arkady and Bolot were having coffee in the International's restaurant, when a stream of beautiful women wrapped in mink and sable passed by their table.

"You seem distracted," Arkady said.

Bolot slapped his forehead. "My brain must be numb. I had forgotten that the Global beauty pageant starts today. Mongolians love beauty pageants. Do you know why?"

"Why?"

"Mongolia has the most beautiful women in the world." Bolot sighed.

"Did you get the wedding party pictures from my friend Victor?"

"Yes, I found them on my laptop this morning."

"Would you care to share them?"

"Oh, right." Bolot reached into his briefcase, pulled out a manila envelope, and added a magnifying glass.

"You think of everything."

"A factotum must."

The camera focused on a bride whose dress was as white as the wings of a dove. A musician plucked at a balalaika. Men and women danced. "Love" padlocks were fastened to the bridge like the bells on a donkey. Zurin and his friend, the tropical Cuban flower, stood nearby. She wanted to have her picture taken, and Zurin started pushing guests in the wedding party aside. One minute everything was gaiety, the next a brawl. Mayhem. There were pictures of chairs upended and punches thrown. Zurin tried to cover the camera lens with the meaty hand of authority. Aba Makhmud stood staring at a phalanx of police in blue uniforms.

"Anyone I know?" Boris Benz appeared at the table, his head cocked with curiosity. By his side was a Buryat bodyguard as hard as a barrel, with a crew cut and a penetrating stare.

Arkady whisked the photographs back into the manila envelope. "An old friend's wedding pictures." He stood to shake hands. "Have you met my assistant?"

Bolot was awestruck. He stood and bowed. "An honor."

"Sit down, sit down," Benz said. "Am I interrupting?"

"No. What are you doing here?" asked Arkady.

"I'm a Moscow boy, you know, but I do have some interests here. It's my Xanadu, my pleasure dome, and what's a pleasure dome without a beauty contest? But what is an investigator from Moscow doing here? I like to think I know what goes on in my hotel."

"I'm interviewing a detainee here for Prosecutor Zurin."

"All the way from Moscow? Oh, I doubt it's as simple as that—I doubt that very much—but here you are. Are you a fan of Mongolian wrestling? Timur here can unscrew a man's head."

"He must be handy opening bottles."

"That's very funny. I have an idea. Why don't you come meet the girls. I guarantee it's a once-in-a-lifetime experience."

Bolot almost tipped over his chair, he got up so fast.

In the ballroom, contestants had set up their makeup kits. They went about their business in a businesslike fashion, smoked cigarettes, and paced the floor dressed in little more than hairspray and robes. Beauty was their trade. Skin tones varied from pale to dark, and shapes ranged from petite to statuesque. Arkady recognized the two "Vikings" from the plane.

"You know how beauty pageants are run?" Benz asked.

"I've never seen one," said Arkady.

"Well, this is a contest, not a survival game. Some come with managers, some with mothers. Contestants represent every part of Siberia, and if they can say something patriotic about their homeland, that's always nice. Tonight they will dress in their regional costumes, talk about their customs, and display their individual talents. Then, after intermission, we will have the traditional swimsuit competition. A million dollars goes to the winner and a week on my private South Seas island. The girls must win the judges over."

"How do they do that?" asked Arkady.

"That's up to them. We will find out. Maybe they are singers, dancers, or athletes, maybe even hunters."

"Are the girls allowed to take any good books to the island?" Arkady asked.

By now the contestants were listening and Benz turned to them. "The judges are actors, celebrities, trendsetters, and all of them are millionaires." He turned to Arkady. "It's a fantasy. For every man there's a fantasy woman, don't you think so, Renko?"

"Perhaps. And there are fantasies that are real."

"You mean Tatiana? She's a higher-class fantasy. But she has already made her choice."

"No one told me."

"I saw her just yesterday. She mentioned you."

Arkady couldn't help himself. "What did she say?"

"She said you were a very persistent guy. Now you'll have to excuse me. Many pretty women to attend to. But you know what? You should come by the pageant. It's opening night. She might be there; you never know. You, too, Bolot."

On the way to the transit prison, Arkady asked Bolot, "How rich is Benz?"

"I thought you didn't care about that sort of thing," Bolot said.

"How much?"

"Since you ask, in Siberia, Benz owns a healthy percentage of natural gas, petroleum, life insurance, rare minerals, real estate, television stations, and a pizza chain. Kuznetsov owns about the same."

"What's the difference?"

"I'd say that Benz is a little heavier in the hydrocarbons." Bolot cast an anxious look in Arkady's direction. "I'd say you shouldn't mess with either one."

"I totally agree."

Arkady thought it was fortunate that in Makhmud he had someone other than Tatiana to worry about. He played a flash-light over the photographs Victor had sent. What Arkady had seen of the photographs taken on Lovers' Bridge made less sense than ever, and somehow he knew that Prosecutor Zurin was behind it all. None of it was planned. All of it seemed inevitable.

When Makhmud was brought to the interrogation room, it appeared that the idea of spending years in prison had finally penetrated. He was pale, with dark circles under his eyes.

"How are you feeling?" Arkady asked.

"I'm fine."

"You don't look fine. Have you had anything to eat?"

"He barely touched his breakfast," Warden Kostich said.

"I'm okay," Makhmud insisted. "But I want some nice clothes. I was wearing decent threads when the police picked me up."

"Noted." Arkady wrote: "The prisoner Aba Makhmud wants nice clothes back."

"And shoes. Handmade. They stripped me of them when they took my clothes."

"All right.

"Just so we're clear . . ." Arkady put his tape recorder on the table and pressed ON. "This is Senior Investigator Arkady Renko of the Moscow prosecutor's office interviewing the prisoner Aba Makhmud, who has confessed to the attempted murder of the Moscow state prosecutor Zurin. We are here to take testimony and determine whether he should be convicted."

"Can't we just cut through all this bullshit?" Makhmud asked.

Arkady continued: "Also present are Warden Wasily Kostich, and Public Defender Marcus Federov. Citizen Makhmud, is there anything in your previous testimony that you would like to change?"

"No."

The public defender's tie was as tight as a rope. He was eager to point out that the detainee had already confessed. "All you have to do is sign off on his confession and spare us the endless questioning. It will only make things worse."

"You may be right, but I need the sequence of events explained," Arkady said. "It shouldn't take more than a minute." He pulled out three contact sheets and laid them facedown on the table along with the magnifying glass. Federov's face fell. Perhaps he would have to cancel any social engagements he had planned.

"I want you to identify some of the people in these pictures." Arkady turned over the first sheet and pointed to a picture of Aba in a black suit. "Who is that?"

"Me."

"You were with the wedding party? Where?"

"The groom is a friend," Aba said. "And we were on Lovers' Bridge."

Arkady pointed to a picture of Zurin. "And who is this?"

"The asshole who was trying to push ahead of us and have his picture taken with his girlfriend."

"Correct. Do you know who he is?"

"I know now. It's Prosecutor Zurin."

Public Defender Federov jumped to his feet and demanded that the slur on Zurin's good name be noted.

"Did you at any time take testimony from Zurin?" Arkady asked Federov.

"It was not necessary. I'm a busy man."

Arkady asked Aba, "When did you discover Prosecutor Zurin had accused you of attempted murder?"

"When I talked to the police."

"So you had no intention of attacking a public official. Did your defense attorney tell you that if the fight was spontaneous, not a premeditated act, it would make a difference in your sentence?"

"No, he didn't," said Makhmud.

Federov threw up his hands. "The boy confessed. What does it matter?"

"It's a mitigating factor," said Arkady.

Arkady turned the next contact sheet up. Pistols were drawn, an elderly Chechen swung his crutch, a pair of policemen tried to peel one man off another. And there was Aba in the foreground, punching Zurin.

"That's even better than a confession," said Federov. "Photographic proof."

The next picture showed Zurin pointing a gun into the air while his other arm encircled the waist of a lustrous, caramel-colored woman who was spilling out of her dress. Who would have thought it of Zurin? A passionate, intimate relationship.

"According to Zurin, it was only after he drew and fired his weapon into the air that everyone scattered," Arkady said.

Arkady turned again to Makhmud. "You've had run-ins with the police before?"

"No."

"Never?"

"Never. It was all started by that pig trying to push ahead of everyone else."

"Maybe," said Arkady.

Arkady turned over the next picture like a winning card. It was a wide-angle photograph of the fight and included more crowd pictures. He indicated a man wearing a leather jacket in the background, pointing a pistol. Who is this?"

"I can't see," said Aba.

"Use the magnifying glass. You should recognize him. It's you. It seems that you are in two different places, wearing two different jackets at the same time."

"It's my brother."

"What is your brother's name?"

"Bashir."

"Who's older?" Arkady asked.

"Bashir is. What does it matter?"

"Why would you allow the police to believe it was you who fired the gun in the direction of Zurin and Señora Lupa?"

"Because I did. Just because you don't have a picture of me pointing a gun doesn't mean I didn't shoot at him."

"This is where we take a break." Arkady turned off the tape recorder and turned on his laptop with a picture of Zurin with Señora Lupa on his arm.

"Where the devil did she come from?" Kostich asked.

"Havana."

Arkady then turned to the files on the two Makhmud brothers.

"Just because Aba claims to be a violent criminal doesn't make it so. Aba Makhmud's big brother, Bashir, has a long history of crime, from car thefts to smuggling arms. Everything but homicide, and maybe a touch of that too. You, on the other hand, have a clean record," Arkady said to Aba. "I bet you have a grandmother who keeps you in at night. And maybe it's not you but Bashir who carries a gun to scare the piss out of loud Russian bullies. But the next time Bashir gets arrested, he's a recidivist and he is put away for life—unless, of course, his little brother takes the blame and gets no less than ten years, while Bashir walks. Is that the deal you made with your brother?"

Aba hesitated. "He said with my clean record I would only get five months probation."

"Well, he was lying, and you're in the system now."

"For what?"

"For obstruction of justice," Arkady said.

"But I get out, right?" Aba said. "Some paperwork and then I can go home."

"It's not as simple as that," Kostich said. "You're in my custody."

"Then you can let me go," said Aba.

"It's more complicated than that," Kostich said. "You have to be convicted to be released, to keep the paperwork straight."

Federov agreed. "You will still need a public defender. That could be expensive."

"Records have to be corrected," said Kostich.

"But it was a mistake," Aba said.

"No, it was not a mistake," Kostich said. "It was a deception that you and your brother cooked up."

"You mean I'm fucked anyway?"

"It's serious business," Arkady said. "I wonder if it would expedite matters if I called Prosecutor Zurin and made a personal appeal to have the charges dropped. All the charges, the arrest, time in detention, everything dropped as a misunderstanding."

Kostich listened with his mouth agape. "Why would he do that? He was the one with a bloody nose and a flesh wound. Besides, he hates you."

"Let me give it a try." Arkady went into the hallway.

• • •

Zurin came on the line sounding quite hushed for one in the afternoon. "I told my secretary no calls, especially none from you. I'm lunching with the prosecutor general. This better be good."

"The photographs came back."

"What photographs? I don't know what you're talking about."

"Photographs taken January third on Lovers' Bridge. Did your wife ever meet Señora Lupa?"

"Wait." Arkady heard a shifting of bedsprings on the other end and then, "Don't try to blackmail me, you bastard."

"Why would I do that?"

"Is there a problem?" a feminine voice asked.

"It's nothing," Zurin said.

"I thought you had the room for the day." She had a throaty sibilance.

"Is that Señora Lupa?" Arkady asked.

"No."

"It sounds like a Cuban accent," Arkady said. "Are you in your office?"

"I'm going to string you up like a dog until your red dick sticks out."

"I hope you're talking to me and not the prosecutor general."

"What do you want?" Zurin demanded.

"I think I should be going," Señora Lupa said.

"No, wait, wait." There was misery in Zurin's appeal and the sense of bedsheets cooling.

"I want you to drop all charges against Aba Makhmud," Arkady said.

"Why would you want me to drop charges? He tried to kill me."

"You have the wrong man."

"Who is it?" Señora Lupa had a sleepy voice.

"Room service," Zurin answered.

"Drop the charges," Arkady repeated. He knew that Zurin would. He was a man in love.

Aba Makhmud was released and so disbelieving of his good fortune, he dove into Bolot's car.

Arkady hardly believed it himself and stole a look in his side mirror to make sure they weren't being followed.

"Do you have anyplace to stay back home?" Arkady asked Makhmud.

"My grandmother's. You were right about her."

"Do you have any other friends or relatives you can stay with?"

"Sure, plenty."

"How many stepped forward when you were put in jail?"

"They were afraid of Bashir."

"Sometimes friends will do that."

"Aba can stay with me tonight for a while," Bolot said.

"I don't know," said Aba.

"The television works."

Aba produced a sound that could have been "Thank you."

"But I will pay for Aba," said Arkady.

"No, he is my guest," Bolot said. "No guest pays in my house. Besides, you've introduced me to Boris Benz. I hear opportunity knocking."

18

Arkady scanned the beauty pageant crowd. Not seeing any sign of Tatiana, he worked his way from one end of the ballroom to the other with Bolot at his side.

Bolot was as excited as a child given keys to a car. "There's only one condition. All contestants have to be Siberian," he said. "In some pageants the girls walk like royalty. In others they swivel and sway their hips. If they walk in three-inch heels, they need to wear ankle straps. Tricks of the trade."

Arkady wasn't really listening. "You've been to many of these?"

"They're all heartbreakers. Contestants can starve and train for a year and end up with nothing."

Lights darkened and a tremor of anticipation went through the crowd. It was time for the show to begin.

A Sami girl from the reindeer country strode onto a spotlit stage wearing a headdress of pearls that swayed with every step. A Tuva girl took a deep breath and sang two different octaves at the same time to powerful erotic effect. At least Bolot seemed to think so. Arkady was too distracted to notice. An archer shot a single arrow through synchronized swinging bottles. A ballet dancer in a white tutu performed a death scene from *Swan Lake*.

Boris Benz stepped up to the runway with a microphone and asked, "Out of these amazing women, how do we pick a winner? We haven't even reached the swimsuit competition. We'll have an interlude so that the contestants and members of the audience can get to know one another. Relax, have a drink, dance, and enjoy yourself."

Most guests retreated to the traditional waltz. "Money on the hoof," Arkady's father, the general, liked to say. He loved to waltz and occasionally dropped one of his many medals down his partner's décolletage. A search for the missing medal was always the highlight of the evening, to hear the old man tell it.

While they wandered among the guests, a young contestant stepped forward to offer them flutes of champagne. She wore a gold silk dress embroidered in silver and, on her head, feathers sewn into silver beads.

"My name is Alika," she said.

"Where are you from, Alika?" Bolot asked.

"From the Yakutsk, in the far north."

"Stunning," Bolot said. "Would you like to dance?"

Arkady surveyed the room once again and spotted Boris Benz. Next to Benz stood Tatiana. She was beautiful in a long black velvet dress trimmed in ermine. The man next to her had to be her billionaire friend, Mikhail Kuznetsov. It was as if she were standing between a leopard and a jaguar, two variations of the same animal.

"Excuse me," Arkady said.

Tatiana stared in disbelief.

Arkady thought he might have made a mistake. He felt like a trespasser.

"You found me," she said.

"So it seems," said Arkady.

He had imagined his reunion with Tatiana a hundred different ways, but not like this.

Kuznetsov shook Arkady's hand. "I have been looking forward to meeting you," he said. He was a man not likely to be on the cover of *Cigar Aficionado*, but was the reassuring face that Siberia showed the world. Tall and slim, he was elegant in a tuxedo. Arkady, by contrast, looked definitely rumpled.

"And where is our friend Bolot, the famous factotum?" Benz asked.

"The last I saw him, he was dancing with a contestant from Yakutsk."

"You came all the way to Siberia to find me?" Tatiana was still in shock.

"It wasn't easy," said Arkady.

"I know a place where we can talk," she said.

"You're going to miss the swimsuit competition," Boris said.

"We won't be long." She led Arkady to the hotel restaurant.

Jellies and jams were already set out for breakfast. They ordered coffee and sat down in a booth.

"I told you not to follow me," she said.

"You knew I would. You left a railway schedule in my apartment and circled the dates you were going to go and return. Only you didn't return."

"I wasn't finished here."

"With what?"

"Research," Tatiana said.

"With Mikhail Kuznetsov?"

She didn't answer.

Finally, Arkady said, "You know you're a very difficult person to be in love with. Why didn't you answer my calls?"

"I thought it was too . . . dangerous."

"What's too dangerous?"

"Oligarchs." She put her hand on his. "I'm sorry. I was trying to keep you out of it, but not calling, as it turns out, was exactly the wrong way to go about it. I don't want you here. Just being here, you endanger yourself, me, and most of all an important story."

"And exactly how am I ruining your chances to write it?"

"Many of the people I'm writing about are criminals. They're already suspicious of me and I need to gain their trust. An investigator from Moscow will automatically put them on their guard. I need to be independent."

"You need a bodyguard."

"Kuznetsov says the same thing."

"He's right."

"How did you find me?" she asked.

"Obolensky."

"The keeper of secrets."

"So, who are the oligarchs you're writing about besides Kuznetsov? I hope it's not Benz."

"Among others. Oil; it's always oil. The people at the top change, but it's always about oil."

"Have you got an exclusive story on who has control of the oil fields in Siberia?"

"They're all over the map."

"That's right. I'm guessing your story also has something to do with people who actually live in these places."

"It's an ecological nightmare. They're razing the land around prospective wells and displacing the people who live within fifty miles of them."

"And Kuznetsov is helping you."

"He's an oilman and a good source of information."

"Is that all?"

"He's become a friend. I'm also helping him with a book he's writing."

"Where are you staying?"

"The paper can't continue paying for my research, so I'm staying in one of Mikhail's properties here. I know what you're thinking, but he lives elsewhere."

"So Victorian."

Bolot bounded into the restaurant. "Ah, there you are. You missed the swimsuit contest, the best part!"

"Sit down," Arkady said. "This is my friend Tatiana Petrovna. Tatiana, Rinchin Bolot, my friend and colleague."

Bolot was touched. Every time Arkady introduced him, he was promoted to another level.

"Now I understand why my friend here has been looking for you," he said.

She laughed. "And I understand that you are his factotum, whatever that is."

It was a long time since Arkady had seen her laugh.

"I should get back to Aba." Bolot stood up.

"Let me show you around Irkutsk tomorrow," Tatiana said to Arkady. "It's more interesting than you think."

"Of course," said Bolot, who was as eager as a wet dog.

19

Arkady looked out his window at the melting ice sculpture of a dove. Or of a pigeon. Or a dirty sock. Hard to say. It was pathetic how finding Tatiana had elated him. He tried to sleep after his few minutes with her, but there was no hope. Instead, he called Victor, his partner on sleepless nights.

"You landed right in the middle of Tatiana's sacred research," Victor said. "No wonder she's angry. She's always been a pain in the ass about that kind of thing. Don't you know anyone who can look out for Tatiana so you can come home?"

"I know someone who would like to look out for Tatiana."

"Another man?"

Arkady ignored the insinuation.

"I need to find out more about Boris Benz and Mikhail Kuznetsov. They're both contenders for oil east of the Urals." Benz and Kuznetsov had made their initial fortunes in the world of oil rigs, where a missing finger was a badge of honor.

"Here's the problem," Victor said. "Tatiana is fatally attracted to dangerous stories, and you are attracted to her. It makes for inevitable consequences."

"I just need a little help, thank you."

"I have the impression that Benz is capable of murder," Victor said. "From what I hear, Kuznetsov has clean hands. He'd hesitate. On the other hand, are they enemies or are they partners in crime?"

"Oddly enough, they appear to be best friends."

"One of them obviously wants you out of the way. Which one?"

"I have no idea. I just landed here."

In frustration, Victor changed the subject. "How is our friend Aba?"

"He's free, but his brother, Bashir, might kill him out of sheer bad humor."

"The ones who intrigue me are Prosecutor Zurin and the voluptuous Señora Lupa. My respect for the prosecutor has doubled."

"He's fooled us all. You haven't heard from Zhenya, have you?"

"No. I'll go check in on him. Anything else?"

"Would you see what you can find out about Mikhail Kuznetsov? I can't believe he's as clean as people say."

20

The next morning Bolot and Aba joined Arkady in the hotel dining room.

"Thank you, but do I really want to go for a walk in the world's coldest city?" Aba asked. "No, thanks."

"You'd rather wait in the lobby?" asked Arkady.

"I'll take my chances with all these fellows." Aba nodded to a group of Chinese uranium miners.

"So you just came for the breakfast," Bolot said.

"Don't worry, I can entertain myself. I bet there's a bookstore in this hotel. I can buy something to read."

The miners became animated with sideways looks when Tatiana glided by. She could turn heads when she wanted to.

"And who is this young man?" she asked.

"My young protégé. His name is Aba," Bolot said.

"I hope you're going to take a walk with us," she said to Aba.

There was something about a beautiful woman that made a young man reckless.

"Sure." Aba stuffed a roll into his jacket pocket.

"Better wrap up," Tatiana warned him.

"Chechens don't get cold," Aba said.

They walked along the Angara River under a low ceiling of clouds. Any other river would have been subdued by the cold; the Angara heaved itself along its banks.

Irkutsk was a university town full of students circulating from coffee shops to their first classes of the day. Walls were plastered with notices for chamber music, karaoke, flamenco. What impressed Arkady was the number of Buryat students. Many of them had made the leap from herding reindeer to an urban lifestyle in one generation.

Aba pointed to a blue mansion with white wooden lacework that made it look as light as a cloud.

"It was a rich man's city built by exiles and serfs," Tatiana said. "To begin with, Siberia was a land of Mongolians before most of them were slaughtered by the Cossacks. So mix together Mongolians, Slavs, and now Chinese, and the population changes. It's always changing."

Tatiana walked ahead and Arkady caught up to her.

"What does Tatiana have against Arkady?" Aba asked Bolot. "She doesn't act like a girlfriend."

"She has her reasons, I suppose."

"I wouldn't take it if I were him. On the other hand, she's pretty hot."

"Don't talk that way if you prize your head."

"Any other advice?" Aba asked, loud enough for all to hear.

"Warn anyone you see with a blue nose to head for shelter." Bolot wiped his own nose. "It's the first sign of frostbite."

Tatiana was cold, as if covered by a fine frost. Arkady had the sense that she was as trapped as he was. Their hands almost touched as they walked, but she remained distant.

"You know, don't you, that Benz is a killer and Kuznetsov is his best friend?" said Arkady.

In a low voice she said, "I know that. You may be right about Benz, but that doesn't mean that Kuznetsov is the same. A lot of people think he's just what the country needs. I told you he's writing a book, didn't I?"

"A fairy tale?"

"The truth."

"Where do Serge Obolensky and *Russia Now* fit in?"

"When the time comes, I'll give him an exclusive article."

"About Mikhail?"

"Among other things. I'll also write about Putin's Siberian watch dogs who arrested him."

"Can you be objective about him?"

"I think so."

"What else will you write about?"

"Bears."

"Bears?" It wasn't as if he didn't believe her, but he had to laugh. "There's a bear problem in Siberia? You came out here from Moscow to write an exposé about oligarchs. Now you're writing about bears?"

"That's right. Bears are causing problems at the Global oil mines."

"That could be climate change," Arkady said. "Bears are showing up in places where they haven't been seen for years. Is Kuznetsov helping you?"

"He grew up here."

"I see. Then he would naturally have an advantage in tracking the local wildlife."

"I don't expect you to believe me."

"I'm trying to, but you're asking me to start from a crazy premise. Money laundering, smuggling, even murder. These things I understand. I'm going to give you the benefit of the doubt, because sometimes I see things that other people don't. So you see bears? I do too."

"But I'm writing about real bears," she said. "They're not hallucinations."

Arkady shrugged. "My hallucinations are real to me."

Aba and Bolot caught up to them.

Aba let his teeth chatter as a demonstration of his misery. "It is really fucking cold," he said. "The snot in my nose is running like pearls."

"That's the poet in him speaking," Bolot explained.

Something about Aba reminded Arkady of Zhenya.

"How is Zhenya?" Tatiana asked, as if reading his mind.

"Staying out of trouble, I hope."

"I hope so too."

"I'm having Victor look in on him every so often."

They stopped in at an art gallery with a bear theme: paintings of bears, stuffed bears, and wooden bears that played tug of war. The next stop was a bar.

"No bears," Arkady said.

They ordered beef dumplings in hot broth. When Arkady leaned forward to steam his face, a bear amulet swung forward.

"Where did you get that?" Tatiana asked.

"Bolot gave it to me."

"It's a tooth from a bear, an amulet. It invokes the strength of the bear," Bolot said. "Very important for an investigator for the prosecution."

"Sometimes he acts more like a defender," Aba said. "He saved me from prison."

Tatiana turned toward Arkady. "You mean you're here because of Aba?"

"Zurin wanted me to interrogate Aba for the prosecution, but Aba was innocent. Aba didn't shoot anyone, but Zurin wanted to send him away for years. They would have, but Zurin got greedy and was caught in a honeypot."

"'Honeypot'?"

"It's called a honeypot when you set a young woman on a middle-aged man. It's also called entrapment."

"Zurin will have your head on a pike when you get back to Moscow," Tatiana said.

"Well, that's nothing new," said Arkady.

When they returned to the International, Aba let out a whoop of relief and headed for the bar with Bolot. Arkady had the sense of a conversation unfinished, half-frozen, as if his time with Tatiana were full of suspended words. They settled in the lobby.

"Is your story a little like a honeypot?" Arkady asked.

"In a general way it is," she said. "Oil is the honey that lures men in."

"Who's in it?"

"For a start, Boris Benz and his friends in the oil transport police. There are a hundred cars per train, and each car carries one hundred thousand dollars' worth of oil. Sometimes they allow Benz to send tanks that are only half-full so the buyers pay full price for half the oil."

"It's more than I expected."

"It's fatal if Boris is caught," she said.

"Mikhail must know all this, right? He's helped you with the research. What else is Benz into?"

"Everything. Nobody dares touch him. Developing new oil fields, transporting the oil, gas stations, and, on a local level, he's building hotels and running beauty pageants."

"So you carry out your investigations while Mikhail watches over your shoulder, and when he decides you know too much, he'll, what, cut off your head?"

"I trust him."

"Because Mikhail and Boris Benz are old friends and in business together?"

"I'll know when Benz is getting greedy and Mikhail wants to be an honest *biznessman*."

"Now that he's made his first billion."

"You're so suspicious."

"Maybe I think the two are brothers under the skin."

"How can I convince you?" she asked.

"Take me to Chita."

"Oh, no, that's a bit too much. Mikhail won't like that."

"If he's running an honest operation, he won't care."

21

In December of 1825, three thousand troops rose up in St. Petersburg to abolish serfdom and overthrow the tsar. Nine thousand loyalists fought back and won the battle in Peter's Square. Over 120 of the rebels, many of them aristocrats and intellectuals, were exiled to Chita and forced to work in the silver and salt mines from six in the morning to eleven at night. Ever since, Chita had been known as a prison city, a uniformly ugly city of factories and shabby wooden houses built, in good part, by prisoners and the children of prisoners.

Like all Siberians, the people of Chita half foundered on their expectations. Some opened their chains and irons and lived the bitter lives of exiles. They felled the taiga to build their ships and mined the hills for gold, uranium, and precious stones. Finally, oligarchs arrived to drill for oil.

It took Arkady and Tatiana a little more than an hour to fly south over the Angara River and Lake Baikal to arrive at

Chita in the early evening. One of Kuznetsov's drivers picked them up.

"First time in Chita?" he asked.

"First time in a long time," Arkady said.

"Don't go by first impressions," the driver laughed. "It gets worse. A few days ago an oil tanker on a train headed to Moscow exploded about two kilometers from the station. It went up in flames for no good reason. They say you could have seen the blast from the moon."

"Does that happen often?"

"It's Chita. Anything can happen. 'Not yet ready for tourists,' the guidebooks say."

The driver plowed through drifts of snow to avoid hitting cars out on the road.

"Was anyone killed?" Tatiana asked.

"A couple of railway workers. The Russian Transport Agency put some money together for the widows. Quite generous, in fact. But they can afford it, can't they? They're all billionaires. So, I'm taking you to the Montblanc?"

"Yes," Tatiana said. "My friend is going on to the Admiral Kolchak."

"You're not together?" he asked.

"Apparently not," Arkady said.

The Montblanc was a stylish hotel sheathed in black marble. It suggested business conducted on the run and no downtime. Perhaps a massage. A doorman huddled inside the lobby, away from the cold. When Tatiana got out of the taxi, she pointed toward dark oblivion.

"Your hotel is a couple of blocks in that direction."

The Montblanc seemed to be an establishment familiar to her.

A bellman took her bags and in long strides she walked through its automatic doors. There were no other cars.

"I'll walk the rest of the way," Arkady said.

He didn't need any more humiliation from Tatiana. It was no use trying to rekindle a fire that was damp. He was tired. Instead of just turning around and leaving immediately, he would sleep and then take the first plane back to Moscow. Whatever story she had dug up was all hers.

As he walked, blocks stretched to infinity, breath crystallized, and daylight faded. The neighborhood deteriorated from stores and restaurants to bars and dives. Graffiti in Russian and Chinese was scrawled across empty buildings. Footsteps moved in and out of the dark and finally a sign for the Admiral Kolchak appeared. It had to be a joke, Arkady thought. Kolchak had been the White Russian commander and a bitter enemy of the Red Army. At the end of the war he was shot and pushed under the river that ran by the hotel.

A circle of elderly women hunched over a mahjong table in the lobby. Signs were written in Mandarin and Russian, and the young clerk behind the desk wore a plastic tag with her name, Saran.

"I'm staying one night and this is my only luggage." Arkady displayed his bag and ID.

The clerk lifted her eyes. *Sea Serpents of the Deep* lay in front of her on the desk. Devil sharks and giant squid had all her attention.

She hardly acknowledged Arkady, picked up the key card, and led him to a room on the second floor with just enough space for a bed and a sink. He resisted the miniature bottle of vodka that was offered, although he thought that with very little effort he could feel abysmally sorry for himself.

• • •

The phone rang. "Can you come down?" Tatiana asked.

They found an empty mahjong table at the far end of the lobby.

"I'm sorry I had to put you through hoops like that. I had to be convincing to them."

"Who is 'them'?"

"I think maybe Kuznetsov's enemies."

"But you're not sure? And they're following you?"

"I don't know, but it's Kuznetsov's hotel, and I have the feeling that whoever it is expects me to check into the Montblanc alone."

"It sounds like it's Kuznetsov himself who wants to be sure you've checked in alone. You're trapped in the bear's den. Is it worth it?"

"It is if I want to write my story."

"Is this a story about how a pair of oligarchs made their first million dollars?"

"Billion dollars."

"Billion. Thank you. And what about Boris? Isn't he pals with Putin? Don't they go out in the taiga and shoot bears together?"

"Mikhail has Boris under control."

Arkady wasn't sure about that. Benz put Arkady in mind of the proverbial snake that bit according to its nature.

"Well, I'll tell you where Kuznetsov fits in: he's fallen in love with you," he said.

"You think so?"

"I recognize the signs." Arkady made an intuitive leap. "Or is it more complicated than that?"

"I admire Mikhail. Benz can steal a fortune; Mikhail can change Russia."

That was not a direct answer but Arkady was not sure he could stand total honesty.

"Change Russia? That's a bold statement."

"You don't know him," she said.

"I feel like a mere mortal."

"You're being cynical."

"I hope so. I hope I've learned something from my years in Moscow."

"This is Siberia."

"Siberia, the home of the gulag."

"Speaking of the gulag, I brought you something." She pulled a folder from her purse and passed it to Arkady. "It's the first half of Mikhail's book."

Arkady weighed the pages in his hand. "What the devil am I supposed to do with this?"

"He just wants your opinion."

"Kuznetsov wants the opinion of an investigator? About what? Politics, high finance, the arts?"

"It's a memoir of sorts. You should be flattered. He doesn't show this much interest in just anyone's opinion."

"Including the police?"

"Anyone. It's up to you. I have to go back. It's almost eleven, and they'll wonder where I am," Tatiana whispered. "Take a look at it at least."

"Will I see you again? Or do we have to continue with this game of hide-and-seek?"

"Of course not," she said. "I'll meet you at the Montblanc for breakfast."

22

The next morning Arkady watched everyday traffic from his hotel window. Chinese construction workers pushed barrows up and down ramps. Girls in uniform walked hand in hand on their way to school. A sandwich wrapper skipped on the breeze in a tug-of-war, and life seemed alive simply because he had finally made contact with Tatiana.

"I'm just awaiting orders," Bolot said when Arkady called.

"How is Aba?"

"The boy is no problem. He writes most of the day, no trouble at all. Did you know there was such a thing as a rhyming dictionary?"

"No."

"Neither did I, but Aba consults one all the time."

"He's writing poetry? That's a good sign," Arkady said.

"It's cheating. Do you think Pushkin used a rhyming dictionary? I doubt that very much."

"Well, you're a purist."

"I don't mind having him around."

"You've seen no sign of his brother, Bashir?"

"No, thank God."

"Did you know that Chita is the murder capital of Russia?"

"No."

"No? I thought you knew everyplace in Siberia like the back of your hand."

"There are a few places not worth knowing," Bolot conceded.

"I need my factotum down here as fast as possible."

"I'll take the next plane out. Aba can watch my place."

Arkady went to the front desk and found the clerk Saran still immersed in *Sea Serpents of the Deep*. She had a black braid as long and glossy as a bellpull.

"If there aren't any monsters here, I'd like to extend my stay," he said.

She didn't crack a smile. "Do you believe in sea serpents?" she asked.

"And dragon eggs. There used to be maps of them."

Her eyes lit up. "How did you know that?"

"I saw a map of them at a museum in Moscow. They stopped making maps of them when Chita was declared a 'secret' city."

"You mean when they were making weapons and bombs here. Not now."

"Well, they don't advertise it. Do you have any modern maps of Chita?" Arkady asked.

"Why do you need a modern map?"

"Because I want one. Is that an unusual request? I want to be able to walk around the city."

"I don't have that kind of map," she said.

"Why not?" he asked.

She gave him a look.

"Then can you point me to a clothing store?" Arkady asked.

She released a slow smile. "Better than that, I will take you there."

Clutching her *Sea Serpents* and grabbing a scarf and quilted coat, Saran led the way. He guessed her age was around twenty-five, but a young twenty-five.

"Okay. Saran is short for what?" he asked.

"Sarangerel. It means moonlight."

"Are you from here, Sarangerel?"

"Yes, always. I live with my mother."

"And husband?"

"No husband anymore." As if it was a bad idea she once had. "It's my family's hotel."

"And the mahjong players?"

"They're here all the time, all the time, like cows. My mother is Chinese."

"And your father?"

"He's Buryat, but he's dead. What use is that?"

At the open-air market, merchants took great pleasure in haggling, moving as stiffly as chess pieces in the cold. Arkady and Saran wandered through a colorful maze of fish stalls selling omul, sturgeon, and salmon, all from Lake Baikal. Goat heads, plastic shoes, *Star Wars* rugs, and DVDs were spread across the floor in wooden trays. When they got to clothing, Saran held out her hand like a traffic cop.

"Everything you want is here. Shirts, blue jeans, even suits, all at good prices. I'll make sure."

Arkady knew that she was getting a percentage of everything he bought, which was only fair. He selected shirts, black pants, underwear, and socks, the minimum attire for an investigator on the prowl.

"That's all? You need another sweater. It's not even cold yet."

This was news to Arkady.

On the way back, Saran relaxed and became more talkative. "You know about shape-shifters?"

"What are they?"

"Shamans. They have the power to become any bird or animal they want to be. And do you know about cosmonauts who went into outer space and never returned?"

"No. What happened to them?"

"They landed in a forbidden zone and had to fight the yeti. You should see the size of their feet."

"Have you seen the size of their feet?" he asked.

"Pictures of them. And what do you know about the Kraken that lives at the bottom of the sea and scares away all the fishermen? And what about mermaids who rescue fishermen who have fallen into freezing water? That's what you should really be investigating."

"I think so too," he said.

• • •

Boris Benz was standing outside the Admiral Kolchak looking somewhat like a convivial bear.

"Has Saran been bending your ear with her monster stories?" he asked.

"You mean about the sea serpents that live in Lake Baikal?"

"Those are the ones," Benz said. "By the way, why are you staying in this third-rate hotel? It's clean—Saran sees to that—but hardly up to the Montblanc's standards. I can't believe Tatiana didn't put you up in a better hotel."

Saran stalked off to the lobby with Arkady's purchases. "This is not a third-rate hotel. I'll put your clothes in your room, Investigator Renko."

"I apologize, Saran," Benz called out.

"Her husband, Dorzho, is a good fighter," he said in an aside. "I used to sponsor him at the boxing club." He shook his head. "She's so sensitive."

"And informative," Arkady said.

"She believes in the supernatural, but she's cute, isn't she? Have you had anything to eat? Let's have lunch at the Montblanc and talk."

"Don't you have an empire to run?"

"I always have time for a friend."

Arkady leaned back as coffee was poured. Benz offered a silent toast with vodka.

"Let me ask a question first, if I may," Benz said. "Has Tatiana Petrovna found what she's been looking for?"

"I can't say. I don't know what she's after."

"Why did she come to Chita?"

"Again, I don't know. She keeps me pretty much in the dark."

"But you're an investigator. You should know these things."

"I know less and less about Tatiana."

"I think you're being too modest. She didn't know you were coming to Chita. You surprised her. I think it's possible you have your own agenda, in which case, maybe we can work together."

"I thought you worked with Mikhail Kuznetsov."

"To a degree. I would file you under insurance. I can always use more of that in Chita."

"I'm an outsider. What do you imagine I could do for you? Apart from telling you what Tatiana's up to."

"Many pots are boiling. Take your pick. Maybe you would like to investigate the corrupt public defender system that makes it possible for a prisoner to never see a real lawyer. Of course, it doesn't matter, since there are not enough real lawyers to go around and the good ones are driven to drink. Or maybe you would like to investigate the assaults on Chinese entrepreneurs. Mainly restaurants. My God, if we didn't have Chinese restaurants in Chita, we wouldn't have any decent food at all."

"Is that it?" Arkady asked. "Is that the list of criminal activities for a Moscow investigator? Can I then retire to a tropical island like a toothless crocodile?"

Benz sat back and crossed his arms. "I have to say, for prickliness, you're a match for Tatiana."

"Probably."

"How long have you known Tatiana?"

"Over a year," said Arkady.

"She's like a monkey that falls into a fruit bowl," Benz said. "I'm afraid that one day she'll go after a grape and never come back up."

"Not the analogy I would have picked."

"So I hear you actually shot a bear," Benz said. "That's something you can tell your grandchildren."

"I tagged a bear at the zoo would be more accurate."

"Still, you stood up to the charge of an eight-hundred-pound brown bear. Not many men can say that. You know, while you're in Chita, we should go bear hunting. The company has its own cabin."

"Won't they be hibernating?"

"We can always stir one up. It will be great fun. We can helicopter in and out."

"You've done it before?"

"For friends. Americans love it."

"Can you track in the snow?"

"More fun that way."

"Don't you need a license for this sort of thing?"

"Where we're going, no one will even know we're there."

"Sounds enticing. I'll have to think about that."

"A once-in-a-lifetime event, I guarantee." Benz opened the menu of the Montblanc and studied what was offered. "Anyway, let's order. I'm famished. I recommend the liver."

23

Kuznetsov was the last person Arkady expected to admire. However, he had a certain perspective on life—the long view, some would call it. His book, *Prisoners*, was not a self-aggrandizing account of his own time in prison but portraits of other men who were serving sentences of five or ten or fifteen years.

For example, Arkady was intrigued by the story of a violent prisoner called the Butcher. He had a reputation that lived up to his name, and the only creature that dared approach him was his beloved pit bull. However, the dog was accidentally shot with a bow and arrow, and someone had to relay the news to the Butcher. Instead of reacting with violence as expected, the Butcher turned into a meek shadow of himself. Easy prey. Now, that was a storyline, Arkady thought.

The book was a compilation of stories like that, each one no more than a few pages. He told tales about murderers and thieves who understood how important it was to defend even a shred of honor. Some were heroic, others pathetic, all full of rue. One man had amassed a fortune in cigarettes. The moment he stepped out of the prison gate and was a free man, his treasure was worthless. The stories tended to be obsessed with perceived insults, letters from home, days left to serve. Reading was taken seriously, and learning was respected. One man beat his cellmate to death for tearing out the last fifty pages of *A Tale of Two Cities*.

Kuznetsov learned that there were more than two ways to flip a coin. He played the honest broker for cigarettes and circulated books like a lending library. By the time he came out of prison, he had developed the skills of a negotiator and politician. He stayed on the good side of both the Russian penal system and the "black camps" of career criminals. He was a shrewd criminal lawyer.

Lenin Square was Mikhail Kuznetsov's choice for a rendezvous. In the middle of a vast open space, mothers walked around fountains with their children, wrapped in voluminous scarves. Old couples held hands to steady themselves, while others walked quickly, with determination. In Chita, walking had its dangers, however. Some cars were right-hand drive, some cars were left-, and all were driven like racecars.

Arkady and Kuznetsov made their way to the giant statue of Lenin. One bodyguard followed their progress from a Jeep Cherokee; another walked behind them.

"I liked your stories," Arkady said. "They're honest and well written, but you could get professional opinions from real editors to tell you what they think. You could even ask Serge Obolensky."

"Publishers will say anything to land this book. With you, I get an honest reading."

"You mean, everyone wants to know what you're up to, and I don't give a damn?"

"That's what appeals to me. You don't care."

"But I do care about Tatiana's safety," Arkady said.

"She's been my good-luck charm and she's a great journalist who never reveals her sources. I'd hate to lose her."

"Is she in any danger?"

"Probably, but, as you know, she loves a good cause."

What Tatiana loved even more, Arkady thought, was a *desperate* cause.

"And what is today's good cause?" Arkady asked.

Kuznetsov broke into a grin. "That's the interesting part. All I ask is that people follow their conscience, not their fears. No political party, nothing they can pin down."

"Who is 'they'?"

"You know. The Kremlin."

Kuznetsov's cause was exactly the kind of political groundswell that the Kremlin feared most.

"Is Boris Benz involved?" Arkady asked.

"No, not Boris."

"How can you still be friends?"

"We've been friends for years. We met in prison: I was in for my politics; he was in for forgery. By the I time I got there, he had already surrounded himself with thugs who protected him in exchange for future jobs in the oil business. He had one or two supposedly dry wells that were actually pumping oil without the Kremlin's knowledge. He called it a 'resurrection.' It has a nice, biblical ring to it, don't you think?" Kuznetsov allowed himself a smile. "I understood I needed his protection in prison and told him I had a plan to accumulate oil mines over time. He liked my plan and we joined forces. Once out of prison, we dug new wells on land north of Lake Baikal. You know what I did when I made my first hundred thousand? Set up a charity. I was thinking ahead. And you know what surprised me? It made me feel like a better person."

"And Boris Benz—is he a better person, or is he still working with his old prison mates?" Arkady asked.

"I'm afraid he's still in touch with them, and I don't like it. I've tried to get him to stop taking stupid risks, but I'm not going to bring the law in. You don't betray a friend. That's the lesson we learn in prison."

"And you can keep your political life separate from your business interests?"

"Our business relationship has nothing to do with my politics."

"How do your followers get together? How do you know where to meet?"

"Word gets out."

Arkady shivered, just enough to adjust the internal thermostat of his body.

"Boris has invited me to go bear hunting with him," Arkady said.

There was a pause, no more than a ripple on water, before Kuznetsov asked, "What did you tell him?"

"I didn't say yes or no."

"We've had a problem with bears up there. Once they get into the garbage, they think they're entitled; and once they're entitled, they become possessive. It can really be a problem. In general, the less human contact, the better."

"I heard there are some oil rigs that are virtually under siege by bears."

"That's an exaggeration. In the fall we have streams that run red with salmon, and that's what bears prefer. We have to keep in mind that we're in the oil business, not the fish business, and not in the hunting business either. My problem is not bears; my problem is finding out why my oil tank on the train blew up."

"The explosion that happened a few days ago?"

"That's the one. I suggest you stay away from Boris Benz for the time being."

"I'll keep that in mind," Arkady said.

"Well, I've enjoyed our conversation. I'll have more pages for you soon," he promised. He waved, and the Grand Cherokee rolled forward.

Arkady was virtually alone in the square, trudging and freezing and trying to get a signal on his phone. He had planned to meet Bolot in front of the government buildings in Lenin Square once he landed, but Bolot was late.

Bolot finally arrived in a white van, the kind used for delivering flowers or meat. "It took forever to get this van. No cars available at the airport. I think there's a gold rush or something. I'm sorry, it's a little beat-up. It was just in an accident."

"Don't worry. I'm not superstitious."

"That's easy for you to say: you have an amulet."

"Do you want to take it back?" Arkady asked.

"No, that's really bad luck. I'm starving," Bolot announced.

"We'll stop for something." Arkady remembered that Bolot

was ruled by his stomach. "But first we're going to the train station. That's close, isn't it?"

Five minutes later Bolot pulled up in front of a pink train station adorned by white Doric columns. They walked through the station and out the other side, where they hopped across the tracks.

Arkady asked a worker in coveralls directions to where the explosion had taken place.

The man walked backwards and pointed west. "Well, there's not much left to see, but it's that way."

"Did they say what caused it?"

"They say human error. But they always say that, don't they? Blame the workmen. There was an explosion, but only a couple of them were killed. You just don't see that very often."

"See what?"

"A fireball. Burned the oil tanker right down to the wheels, lost thirty thousand gallons of crude oil."

The man turned back and shouted something while Arkady and Bolot walked in the opposite direction.

"What did he say?" Arkady asked.

"Train's coming."

"I don't see it."

"I can feel it," Bolot said.

"There's plenty of clearance between trains, right?"

"I'm sure there is." A horn blasted and suddenly the train turned a curve and was barreling toward them. They jumped over several tracks to get out of the way of a red behemoth surrounded by purple haze. The train rolled on and on; perhaps a hundred oil tankers, containers, and freight cars passed by at a low rumble.

Arkady and Bolot trudged on until they finally reached a

semaphore that stood between the tracks like a solitary witness. The smell of oil still hung in the air, and a shadow of black extended in all directions except where new tracks were laid.

"Well, was it a blast or just a fire?" Bolot asked.

"It was an explosion that started the fire. Those fires are nasty and black."

Bolot started writing in his notepad to show his worth.

"How long did it take to burn out?" Arkady asked.

"Good question."

"Was it contained and analyzed?"

"Another good question." Bolot kept writing.

Arkady looked at the husk of the oil tanker and came to a decision. "Let's go back," he said.

"Isn't it time for dinner? Distances are longer when you haven't eaten," said Bolot as they got back to the car. "You never eat, do you? I've noticed that when you do, you just rearrange your food. You know, you need calories to stay warm."

Arkady took the wheel and drove toward the hills, stopping once to pick up burgers.

"Where are you going? This looks like rugged territory."

"I have an idea," Arkady said.

"You never let on that you spent so much time in Chita."

Ever since Arkady had arrived in Chita, the city had been filtering back to him. His favorite picture as a boy was of Cossacks overwhelming the Mongols. The Cossacks were little more than pirates, but they had muskets and won Siberia for the tsar.

The faster he drove, the more the van bucked, until he was forced to slow down. As they crept along, he had the feeling he had been at this same geographical point before, perhaps even with the same vortex of snow spinning overhead.

"Where are we?" Bolot asked.

"At an army tank graveyard." Arkady stopped the van and got out. Headlights from the van picked out a pair of signs, one so pocked by bullet holes it was illegible, and another that said, PROPERTY OF THE STATE. Target practice. Wind whistled through the bullet holes.

Arkady and Bolot walked between rows of tanks, nothing less than a thousand T-26s and T-34s, decapitated monsters with treads extravagantly wrapped around their bodies and with armored skirts and cannons pointed in all directions.

"You remember this?" Bolot asked.

"My father was stationed here for several months, and some places you never forget. This was my playground," Arkady said. He remembered how he and his friends used to play war, dropping through open hatches, hurling stones and clots of mud instead of Molotov cocktails.

Bolot pulled off a glove and held out his hand to catch flakes and watch them melt. "A storm is coming. I can taste it," he said. "If we want to get back to the hotel, we should start moving."

24

They entered the lobby of the Admiral Kolchak and Arkady introduced Bolot to Saran.

"My friend needs a room and a sauna. Maybe a vodka too."

Factotums had to rest now and then, and Bolot hadn't had a chance to relax since he arrived in Chita. Saran produced towels for Arkady and Bolot. She was all business.

"The *banya* is out back. Temperatures should range between 150 and 175 degrees, no higher and no longer than six minutes. You will have to share with the miners."

Steam exploded as water was ladled onto hot stones. Barely visible, Chinese laborers sat knee to knee along pine benches. Someone slapped Arkady's back with a small branch of pine. There were certain rituals a man needed to alleviate the rigors of life, and this was one of them. For many, this was as close to heaven as they would come.

"Is good?" A young miner laughed with delight.

"Is good." Bolot leaned back with his glass of vodka.

Arkady's eyes were closing, he was so tired. He needed to rouse himself, dress, and make contact with Tatiana.

When he reached the lobby of the Montblanc, he heard the voices of Tatiana and Kuznetsov. They were sitting at a banquette, drinking champagne, when Tatiana raised her eyes and saw him.

"Arkady, come join us."

"What are you celebrating?"

"The book," she said.

"After I met with you this morning, I called a publisher in Moscow and he seems interested in publishing the book. He will want to see the chapters I've written before he decides."

"That's reason to celebrate. And you are still writing your article for Obolensky?" Arkady asked Tatiana.

"Of course."

More champagne arrived at the table. Arkady had not eaten and felt lightheaded from the sauna. He threw back his champagne. Then another.

"Whose comes out first?" Arkady asked.

"First my book about political prisoners comes out," Kuznetsov said. "Then Tatiana's article will appear in *Russia Now*, making a connection with me and other prisoners, exposing the political nature of arrests and Siberia's prison system."

"Why are you always the one taking chances?" Arkady asked Tatiana.

"What do you mean?" asked Kuznetsov.

"By writing a book about prisoners, you humanize them and the reader sympathizes with them. Rightly so. Then Tatiana comes out with an article that, among other things, describes how the government puts oligarchs who dare question Putin in prison. She becomes the target and lands in jail."

"I don't see it that way," Kuznetsov said.

"Then why not let her article come out before the book?"

"It can only cause trouble," Kuznetsov said.

"Tatiana's not a revolutionary," Arkady said. "She's a journalist."

"I love listening to men talk about me in the third person. If publishing my article second helps his book, I'm happy to do it."

"I'll change the subject," Arkady said. "Today I visited the scene of your oil tanker explosion. Maybe I should say 'snow wreck,' because it could have been caused by a blizzard."

"It was disastrous," Kuznetsov said.

"Have you looked at the rails? Yesterday I took a walk along the track. They were never switched for the approach to the station," Arkady said. "Do you think they were unable to switch the tracks because of the snow, or were they intentionally not switched?"

"That is to be determined," Kuznetsov said. "If I were paranoid, I'd think someone was trying to ruin me." He offered to pour more champagne.

"No more for me," Tatiana said.

Arkady pushed his glass forward. "Are we still celebrating?" he asked.

"No," Tatiana said. "I don't think so."

• • •

At two in the morning Arkady walked back to the Admiral Kolchak under the mistaken assumption that brisk exercise would revive him. He flopped down on a chair in the dark of the lobby, unaware that Saran was watching him from her perch behind the desk.

"Can I get you something?" she asked. "Vodka? Tea? The samovar is hot."

"Hot tea would be nice."

She brought him a cup and returned to her desk, sitting and crossing her feet.

"Sarangerel, it seems to me that you're here day and night," Arkady said.

"I start around six in the morning. In the afternoon my mother takes over until I come on again for the evening guests."

"That sounds tedious."

"No, no. It gives me a chance to read and it gives my mother a chance to play mahjong with her club. She wins, but not too much. She wants them to come back."

"How are the sea serpents?" he asked.

"Well-behaved."

"Except for the fire-breathing ones. You have such an imagination. Have you ever thought about writing?"

She smiled. "I like making up stories."

She had red ribbons entwined in her long braid and flashing eyes as round as silver coins. He pictured her on a troika, her single braid flying, chased by wolves.

"You went to see your friend from the other night? She's pretty."

"Tatiana? Yes, and brave and intelligent. She's all those things, but she's foolhardy too."

Arkady wondered if Saran had been waiting up for him. "You have a new ribbon in your hair. Was there a party?"

"No." She blushed.

"Shouldn't you go to sleep? You only have few hours till you have to be back here," he said.

"Oh, no. I never get tired," she said. "I can stay up all night."

"By any chance, do you remember a train accident that happened about a week ago?"

"There was a huge explosion about this time of night. We all woke up and ran to the windows."

"Did you see anything?"

"A blizzard was coming down, but you could see there was an orange-and-black fireball in the direction of the station. Everyone helps when there's a fire that big. We ran and tried to help put it out with water and snow, but there was no putting it out. It burned itself out the next day. I remember Boris Benz walking around what was left of the train car with his friend, Mikhail Kuznetsov. Around and around."

"How did they seem with each other?"

"I thought they were arguing. I couldn't hear what they were saying. It's probably lucky they didn't have knives."

"You're an observant woman, Saran."

"Why are you interested in them?" she asked.

"It's complicated, but I'd like to explain it to you when I'm thinking straight."

"Tomorrow?"

"Good."

25

"We tested the bombs from station to station," Arkady said. "My parents were sent here. At that time Chita was a testing ground for all sorts of weapons."

It was morning, and Saran was showing Arkady the city.

"How long ago was that?"

"I was a boy."

"What do you remember?"

"I remember my father's aide-de-camp. I called him 'Uncle' Seva. He was a political thermometer, an absolute hard-liner when it came to the party line, but he would have cut anyone in half who touched a hair on my head."

"It must have been hard."

"No, it was the norm. I even had a pet. A pet lizard."

"What was your mother like?"

"I thought she was beautiful. My father thought so too. He died thinking so."

"How old were you when she died?"

"Ten."

"Too young."

"Everyone is too young when their mother dies."

Saran nodded as if listening to the pages of a book. "Might I ask how she died?"

"The doctors said she was high-strung. Probably today they would have given her a more precise diagnosis. Anyway, she took her own life."

What he didn't say was that his father had left him alone with his mother while he went hunting with his friends. He blamed Arkady for his mother's suicide. Before stepping into a pool, his mother had weighted herself down with stones that he had helped gather for her. Too late, he understood why she had wanted so many stones.

"Oh," Saran said. "That's the saddest story I've ever heard."

Arkady realized he had tipped the mood in the wrong direction.

They walked up to a small, dark wooden house with warped shutters painted a cerulean blue. Saran leaned back looking at it, a dreamy expression on her face.

"I'd like to live in a house like this," she said.

"Maybe not *this* house," Arkady said. Actually, it was a reconstruction of a Decembrist house and put him in mind of paintings he had seen of Moscow in the eighteen hundreds.

"Why not?"

"Too dark and cold inside."

"It would only take a little fire in the fireplace to brighten things up."

"Maybe you're right."

The Decembrist wives who followed their husbands to Chita

had made homes for themselves and grew friendships. They introduced music and education to the region. One wife even smuggled in her spinet.

Snow began to fall as they walked on. "Is that why you admire Decembrist wives?" Arkady asked. "Because they chose to leave everything behind for love?"

"And because they made something good from a terrible curse. What I don't understand is why some of them left their children behind. Can you imagine?"

"Maybe those mothers knew their children would be loved and cared for in St. Petersburg, but their husbands would have nothing."

They walked on alongside a huge plastic coil that snaked through the city carrying steam to heat buildings. White clouds spewed from cracks in the coil.

They stopped in front of the Siberian Boxing Club with a life-size neon tiger above the doorway. Boxing was all the rage, and this was a serious training facility.

"Boris Benz owns this place," she said.

"Have you ever been inside?" Arkady asked.

"Yes. My husband, Dorzho, used to train here. He wanted to be a boxer."

They entered a large hall containing two boxing rings, speed bags, and heavy punching bags. One corner of the room sold energy drinks and snacks.

On the wall a poster promoted a boxing tournament at the end of the month. Fighters competing from all over Siberia held up their fists. On one side of the poster was a large photo of a Siberian tiger; on the other was an equally large photo of "Rocky."

The gym was open from six in the morning to midnight. A

janitor perpetually swept the floor. Through a door in the back they passed rows of metal lockers to a small restaurant and bar.

"They have Chinese, Mexican, and Ukrainian," Saran said, "but I can promise you, they'll all taste Chinese."

They ordered Gatorade and pot stickers and returned to the hall, where they watched boxers skip rope to work up a sweat. In another ring, young men sparred. They seemed to prize drawing blood as much as slipping punches. A bald man walked around the ring barking, "Anton, duck! Left. Right. Left again. Christ, it's like you want to get hit. Fuck it, take a break."

The trainer got down from the ring and stood next to Arkady.

"See, I'm trying to teach them how to box and survive, and they want to get all scarred up because it makes them look tough. Scars are the new tatoo."

Two traffic police approached. "Hey, look who's here, Dorzho's porcelain doll. I forget: What's your name?"

"Saran."

"That's right. Whatever happened to Dorzho? I haven't seen him here for a while."

"He fell off a cliff," she said.

"Accident?"

"No, he just disappeared. A year ago."

Arkady had never heard bad news delivered with such equanimity.

"Back to work." The trainer groaned as he climbed through the ropes.

The bell was struck and the traffic policemen started trading odds on their favorite. But they didn't stop there. They began speculating about which of their screen idols was tougher, "Rocky" or Steven Seagal.

"Let me ask you this," said one. "Could either of them beat a bear?"

This took some thought. "Neither. But I could if I was drunk enough."

"Now you're getting ridiculous." They slapped each other on the back.

"So, Saran, does that mean you're free?" one of them asked.

"No, I'm not free."

"Oh, you mean you're with this man standing next to you?"

"No, this is my friend, Investigator Renko from Moscow."

"Oh. A big-city investigator. I guess that means our girl is off-limits."

"Right." Arkady already felt his bones ache because he knew where the conversation was headed. He was too old for this kind of drama.

"Let's go," Arkady said to Saran.

"Not leaving already, I hope?" It was Boris Benz. "These boys giving you trouble?" The very sight of him prompted a deferential step back.

"Do you know them?" Arkady asked.

"Of course. I'm a sponsor. But it looks like these guys are antagonizing the customers, am I right?"

"Just joking around, boss."

Benz turned to Arkady. "Have you thought more about hunting with me up north? You can even bring along your friend, Bolot. I bet he's a good shot."

"You're serious about this," Arkady said.

"We'll helicopter in. I'll start you off with three clips and all the time in the world. First man to kill a bear is the winner."

"You mean this is a contest?"

"No, but this year we have to cull some of the bears around the rigs. They can be a real problem for the workers up there. This just makes it more interesting."

"I have to get back to the hotel," Saran told Arkady.

"Let me know what you decide," Benz said.

"I will," said Arkady.

They found Tatiana waiting in the lobby along with Saran's mother and other mahjong players. Tatiana looked curiously from Arkady to Saran.

Saran's mother got up from her table. Other players rose to redistribute themselves at other tables.

"We had no idea you were going to be gone so long," Saran's mother said. It was a mild rebuke.

"We ran into Boris Benz at Dorzho's old haunt, the boxing club," Saran said.

"Why would you want to go there? Bad enough you're married to that lowlife."

"I was showing Arkady a little of Chita and he wanted to go in."

"He would," laughed Tatiana.

"He just wanted to see it. He didn't want to box."

The old lady looked at Arkady. "I should hope not."

Saran took up her post behind the reception desk and opened her book to where she had left off. Her mother rejoined the game.

"I was wondering when I would see you again." Arkady steered Tatiana to a sofa in the corner.

"It doesn't look like you've been suffering."

"No, I've been quite entertained, but that's not why I'm here."

"Remind me: Why are you here?"

"To get you back to Moscow."

"Well, I'll come back eventually. Let me do my work."

"That's what I'm afraid of. You do your work so well, you will get yourself killed. Isn't Kuznetsov afraid he might be putting you in danger?"

"I haven't asked him."

"How is his book progressing?"

"At the moment, it's come to a stop."

"Why?"

"Trouble with the rigs up north. Someone is tampering with them. Probably the same people behind the train explosion."

"Benz has invited me to go hunting with him up by the rigs," said Arkady. "Maybe I'll take him up on it and see what I can see."

"Don't go with Benz. I don't trust him and he will have complete advantage. It's his territory."

"I'll take Bolot with me. He understands survival in the snow. At least, he should."

"How long do you think you will be there?"

"No more than one night."

"Maybe I'll come with you. It will be perfect for my article. When do you go?"

"Tomorrow," Arkady said.

26

Arkady could see that Boris Benz enjoyed flying his helicopter.

"For versatility and power, there's nothing like it," Boris shouted over the sound of the rotors. "We're talking four blades, full speed to dead hover, backwards, straight up, dive-bomb. It's a hummingbird! I suppose you think I'm crazy."

"Not necessarily," Arkady said.

It was six in the morning. Arkady and Tatiana filled the seats behind Boris, while Rinchin Bolot slept in the back.

The helicopter cruised at eighty kilometers per hour, smoothing out clouds that pressed against Chita's eastern peaks.

"You look a little green," Tatiana said.

"I'm fine," Arkady said.

As they descended through the clouds, a long blue lake came into view. A ship moved ponderously through icy water. What looked like an abandoned village of fishing shacks lay along its banks.

"Lake Baikal," Benz called back. "Largest body of fresh water in the world." The helicopter climbed again into the hills on the western side of the lake.

"Tell me," Tatiana asked Benz, "are you really going to be able to figure out what's going on with the oil rigs? Are you an engineer?"

"I'm an investor. Whether it's a shirt factory in Italy or a bank in Germany, I can understand a business problem better after a visit on the ground. Then we can get down to the serious business of hunting bear. The real question is: What does this have to do with your article?"

"Well, I'm writing about oligarchs and how they make their money. And here I have two prime examples of oligarchs who make their money from oil."

Arkady noticed the change in the tempo of the rotors. They were slowing. He leaned back and shook Bolot. "We're almost there."

"I just fell asleep." Bolot was peeved.

"Red lights ahead!" Benz yelled back. "Someone will be waiting for us down below."

The helicopter descended and stepped into its own shadow on a landing pad. From the window Arkady saw a man push blocks in front of the wheels.

"Here we are," said Boris. "Everybody out."

Their breath crystallized in the freezing morning air as they exited.

Boris and the other man secured the rotor blades and helicopter body with tie-downs.

"Georgy, meet my friends Tatiana Petrovna, Rinchin Bolot,

and Arkady Renko. Arkady is an investigator, so we had better watch our step," said Boris.

The joke was getting tired, Arkady thought.

A teardrop had been tattooed beneath Georgy's right eye. Arkady wondered if he was one of the ex-prisoners that Benz was known to hire.

Everyone carried rifles, backpacks, and food from the helicopter to an old snowcat. They climbed in and Georgy drove into what looked like an impenetrable forest.

Their first stop was Kuznetsov's disabled Oil Rig G2. Like an animal with a dead brain, a small red light on an electric panel indicated the system was alive but shut down.

"This was the most productive of all the rigs up here, so of course it's the one that was sabotaged," Georgy said. "Someone poured concrete into the hole."

"Any idea who?" Arkady asked.

"Obviously, somebody who's out to get Kuznetsov. Some of his other mines were tampered with, too, but we were able to get them going again."

Arkady could only imagine how lonely the work would be up here in the taiga. What else was there to do but mind the wells and hunt for food?

"Have you seen any bears?" Tatiana asked Georgy.

"Now and then. They're supposed to be in hibernation, but you never know. Brown bears sleep lightly and will come out if there's any disturbance. The main thing is we keep an eye on them."

"How many have you seen since, say, a month ago?" Boris asked.

"One bear keeps cycling back through, searching for food; at least, I think it's the same one. It's big, and as you know, a hungry bear is a dangerous bear. If it's a good food year, he will have enough fat on him to last the winter in hibernation, until at least mid-April. We're in January, so it means the bear I sighted is hungry."

"Right: this has been a bad food year for bears," Bolot said.

"Are you going to hunt?" Georgy asked Tatiana.

"No," said Tatiana, "but I'll get some work done."

"The base camp up ahead is comfortable and well heated. You can work there."

"Good," she said.

Georgy slowed down.

"The snowcat can't climb this last hill, so we have to get out and walk."

They started climbing toward the main cabin in snowshoes.

"I'll have to get used to these things." Tatiana struggled to walk.

"Just lift your knees and feet when you walk, making sure the front of the shoe doesn't pick up too much snow," said Bolot. "They'll sink down a few inches but no more." He moved energetically. This was his area of expertise.

Tatiana took three large steps, turned to say something to Arkady, and fell.

Arkady pulled her up.

"Let me show you how to turn," Bolot said. "If you're turning left, first put your weight on your right foot, move your left foot left, then bring your right foot around. Okay?"

"Not okay, but I'll try."

An arctic fox tiptoed across their path ahead. They crested

the hill and a million kilometers of thick taiga covered with snow spread before them.

The cabin was simple and efficient. A wood-burning stove provided a minimum of heat, and next to it there was a metal tub for melting snow. A large round table surrounded by chairs sat in the middle of the room. A bedroom slept six, with a crude bathroom attached to it.

They sat around the table, devoured the sandwiches they had brought for themselves, swiped the table clean with snow, and threw the remaining crumbs and food wrappings into the large bear box outside.

The bear box stored food in a can on one side and garbage in a can on the other. The box was locked, and handles to open the two sides were constructed in such a way that the bears couldn't fit their paws in.

"So, in case I meet a bear, what should I know?" Arkady asked.

"It's best to shoot from a distance of one or two hundred yards," Bolot said. "If you can, aim at the hump on his back so the bullet will pierce the lungs. That's a quick kill. If the bear charges you, shoot at the two lungs and keep shooting until you're sure it's dead."

"And forget all that bullshit about shining a flashlight into a bear's eyes to scare it away," Georgy said. "It doesn't work."

"And if any one of us scores a kill," said Benz, "fire two shots into the air to let the others know. Our goal is to fly out of here by nightfall. With five pairs of hands, that should give us plenty of time to dress a bear."

"Four pairs of hands. I'm having nothing to do with it," Tatiana said.

"What if we don't find one by then?" Arkady asked.

"That's simple. If you're willing, we can stay overnight. But first things first. An extra outhouse is over there by the blue beacon. Carry a flashlight and rifle at all times, even if you don't think you need one. It will make us all feel better. You, too, Tatiana," Benz said. "Remember, a bear can run faster than you can, and where there's one, there may be two or, more dangerous, there may be cubs. Either way, if you wound it, you kill it."

"You could set a trap for it," Georgy said.

Benz laughed. "We're not here to fucking trap bears; we're here to hunt them."

"Somebody will be up to replace me, right?" Georgy asked Benz. "My ass has been sitting on that stove for the last six months. And it's just getting colder and darker."

As they started out, Arkady and Bolot headed in one direction, while Benz and Georgy headed in another.

"I want to take a look at that rig we passed. Any objections?" Arkady asked.

"As long as we get to the bear before they do."

It took half an hour to make their way through the snow before they reached the broken rig. Snowshoe prints packed the snow around it. A drill pipe lay on the floor. Arkady and Bolot dug around the hole to reveal a cap of cement.

"This had to be a group effort," Arkady said.

"Why can't they just drill the cement out and replace the oil pipe?" Bolot asked.

"I think it would be impossible to drill out twenty feet of cement."

"Okay, shall we go? According to my compass, north is that way." Bolot pointed to the darkness of deep woods. "Look for scratches on trees. They love stretching and clawing; they're like cats that way." Bolot spoke with authority. "In lean years bears hibernate in haystacks or fallen trees. When hungry, they're alert to anything passing by. Then there are 'rovers': bears that keep searching for a place to hibernate. And the female bears have their cubs in these caves. They let them out for periods of time in the spring before herding them back into the cave."

"Good mothers."

They had been snowshoeing for an hour and Arkady was out of breath.

They trudged on until they heard a rifle shot. Then two more in quick succession.

"There's our signal. Benz must have found something," Arkady said.

They moved in the direction of the sound and saw Benz and Georgy standing over the body of a deer.

"I thought we were bear hunting," Bolot said.

"My instincts took over," Georgy said. "Hard to pass up fresh meat."

"How much time do you want to spend dressing it and hauling it back?" Bolot asked.

"It won't take long," Georgy said.

"Why don't we leave it for a hungry bear to find?" Benz asked.

"I have a better idea," Georgy said. "Let's cut it up, take some of it back to the cabin, and leave some here. That way we'll be able to find tracks in the morning if it doesn't snow in the meantime."

"What's to prevent another animal from eating it?" Arkady asked.

"I brought along bags that are supposed to keep animals from smelling food," Georgy said.

"It might work for other animals but not for bears," said Bolot. "Their sense of smell is unbelievable, at least a thousand times better than ours. They can smell a carcass from twenty kilometers away."

The four men skinned and cut up the deer, leaving a major part of the carcass in two of the food bags. They stuffed the other two with meat to take back.

"Well, we won't have to worry about food for a while," Benz said. "We have to take this back to the food bin. Otherwise we'll have more than one bear following us."

"I already have the sense that someone or something has been following us," Georgy said.

"I didn't see any other footprints on the way," Benz said. "Let's go."

They turned to walk back.

"You've shot a bear, haven't you?" Arkady asked Bolot. He touched the bear's tooth that hung on a leather thong around his neck. "Is this the real thing?"

"Yes, it's the real thing," said Bolot.

"How did you come by it?" asked Benz.

"When we were kids, about fifteen or sixteen, my brother and I went to hunt a bear that had been stealing food from our village. We told our parents we were going, and of course they told us not to. They thought if they hid the rifles, we wouldn't dare go. We took wooden spears with sharpened tips to hunt the bear and drank a little vodka for courage. We approached the bear's cave. One bear came out, then two. We thought we were dead. Nobody believed it when we dragged two dead bears into the village. Your amulet comes from one of those bears."

"I'm honored."

"In the Buryat culture there's a whole ceremony with a shaman and much fanfare in praise of the bear and the hunter. It's serious business," said Benz.

"We feasted for days and smeared ourselves with the fat from the bear," said Bolot. "We felt like bears. Strong and fearless."

The sun was straight overhead, and as they neared the cabin, they saw large paw prints overlap the prints left by Georgy and Benz.

"I think you were right, Georgy," Arkady said. "You were followed by a bear. I wonder where it went."

They all stopped and searched for more prints.

"The cabin," Arkady said. He lurched ahead, running as fast as snowshoes would permit.

The lean-to over the bear box had been torn apart and thrown aside. The food box itself was overturned, which was almost impossible, since it weighed at least a hundred kilos and was bolted to the ground. So far, no blood.

"Tatiana!" Arkady yelled. He opened the door of the cabin to what appeared to be an empty room. From the corner he heard a sound. He pulled the couch out, pried an iron skillet from Tatiana's hand, and lifted her up. She clung to him, her face buried in his neck.

"She okay?" Bolot asked.

"She's okay," Arkady said. Anger and relief overwhelmed him. Why had he allowed her to come up here?

"It was huge, bigger than any bear in the zoo," Tatiana said as Arkady helped her onto the couch.

"You saw him?" Arkady asked.

"When the crashing began, I peeked out the window. He was furious. I was sure he would break into the house, because he wasn't getting anywhere with the bear bin. He must have stopped because he heard you."

"You didn't want to use your rifle?" Benz asked.

"I wasn't thinking. I grabbed what was there." She laughed.

Benz sat on the couch next to Tatiana. "I know we planned to stay just one day, but we've laid a trap for the bear. Do you feel you can stand being here one night? We should be able to follow his trail in the morning."

"Yes, of course I can."

"I'll stay with you," Arkady said.

"Or I'll come with you," Tatiana said.

"Is it too early for dinner?" Georgy asked. "Or maybe we should try to pull up the bear box and bolt it more firmly to the ground."

"How about pouring cement over the bolts?" Bolot asked.

"Not a bad idea," Benz said. "If we can find cement."

The three men left and Arkady moved next to Tatiana. She leaned against him and closed her eyes.

27

The next morning Benz and Georgy pushed through the snow as Tatiana followed at a slower pace with Bolot ahead of her and Arkady behind her.

"What have you got in that second backpack?" she asked Bolot.

"In one I have food and extra clothes for the expedition, and in the second I have emergency gear."

"Like what?"

"I have one knife and a whetstone for cutting up a bear. Then there's a handsaw, leather thongs, and game bags."

"What are you expecting to happen?" Tatiana asked.

"Remember," said Arkady, "Napoleon lost Russia because he didn't bring along enough supplies."

"I notice you brought a pencil and pad. Your supplies?" Bolot asked Tatiana.

"And a pencil sharpener."

"You expect to do some writing?" Bolot asked.

"I hope to," she said.

Conversation came to a halt as they approached what was left of the deer. The bear had, as Georgy predicted, ripped open the food bag and dragged the carcass into the woods. Benz, Georgy, and Bolot followed the bloody trail. Arkady and Tatiana trekked one behind the other through dense woods, sometimes losing sight of the men ahead.

They had just caught up to Benz and Georgy when nine hundred pounds of ferocity came barreling through the trees. The men raised their rifles, took aim, and shot. A regular firing squad, Arkady thought. Though badly wounded, the bear continued to hurl himself at them through the snow. Benz moved fifty feet around him for a better angle and aimed at the ruff of his neck. The bear finally dropped.

They stood in awe around the immensity of the bear's body sprawled in front of them.

"My God," said Arkady.

"You mean, 'My Bear,' " said Benz. "Tatiana, do you think this is the same bear you saw at the cabin?"

"Has to be," she said.

Benz was obviously elated that he had fired the winning shot, maybe a record shot. He took a tape measure from his backpack and, giving Georgy one end at the bear's short tail, paced the distance from head to toe.

"This bear is nine meters long. That's a hell of a big bear," Benz said. "Too big to carry back."

"Let's just take the head as a trophy," Georgy said. "We already have enough venison in the bin to feed a family for the rest of the winter."

"Isn't that contrary to the hunter's code?" Tatiana asked.

Georgy gave her a disdainful look.

"You might not want to carry back the meat," Bolot said, "but there are others who live around here who will be happy for it."

"Who lives around here?" Tatiana asked.

"You may not see them, but they're here," Bolot said.

"I'm going back to the cabin with Georgy," Benz said. "If you want to look out for the natives here, that's your business. But don't take too long."

"I don't think we should split up," Arkady said.

"Why? What are you afraid of?" Georgy asked.

"Not afraid; just too many nasty surprises happen up here."

"Forget that," Georgy said. He borrowed Bolot's handsaw and set to work quickly separating the bear's head from its body and bagging it.

"We'll have a fire going for you when you return," said Benz. "Remember, we want to fly out tonight. It's one o'clock now. Do you think you can make it back by three?"

"At least by then," Bolot said.

The two men disappeared into the woods.

Meanwhile, Bolot knelt next to the bear. "There's a quick and easy way to do this. By just cutting out the muscle from outside the ribs, we don't have to deal with intestines and all the organs."

Tatiana pitched in with Arkady and Bolot in rolling the bear onto its side. With a broad razor-sharp blade, Bolot made a slit from the sternum to the groin and cut through the hide from the inside of the right front leg and from the inside of the right back leg. Together they pulled the hide back to the spine, exposing the flesh from one whole side of the bear's body. Bolot cut off the muscle meat. He handed the pieces to Arkady and Tatiana, who swiped them with snow before putting them into one of Bolot's bags. They rolled the bear to its other side and Bolot again cut the hide from inside the left front and back legs, and together they pulled it back to expose the muscle from the other side. The meat filled another large bag.

"Do we want to keep the hide?" Bolot asked.

"I don't see how," Arkady said. "We have too much to carry as it is."

"We can make a sled with branches," Bolot said, "like a troika, but we're the horses. Then we can cover the branches with the hide."

Arkady appreciated the way Bolot was able to turn obstacles into solutions.

"You're a very handy man to have around."

Bolot grinned. "People tell me so."

They found three strong branches thick with smaller branches and pine needles, cut off smaller branches from the ends, and lashed the branch ends together with the leather straps that Bolot carried in his backpack. They laid the hide on top so nothing could fall through. Now they had a sled, Russian-style.

Arkady grabbed one of the three branches and together with Bolot they heaved it over rough terrain. Tatiana followed.

Finally, enough snow began to fall to smooth the passage of the sled through the woods.

Bolot's relief was obvious. "See, this is what they should have had for the talent portion of the beauty pageant: a Buryat woman making a sled and pulling it across a snow-covered stage."

"No," said Arkady. "It should have been a beautiful Venus in a bearskin pulling a two-hundred-pound man on a sled."

Tatiana couldn't help but laugh, then stopped.

Two bodies lay in puddles of blood and snow, their faces covered with white ice crystals. The bear head had rolled five feet away.

Horror descended on them. Tatiana and Bolot stepped back in disbelief.

Arkady pressed his fingers against Benz's carotid artery. "No pulse. There won't be any fingerprints, but we know it wasn't an animal that killed them. They were shot from a distance."

"Who?" Tatiana asked.

"Good question," said Arkady. He looked at the snowshoe prints surrounding the body. He walked in a circle around them.

"I see a number of tracks, but I don't think there was any struggle. Benz and Georgy had rifles they could have used, so it must have happened all at once. Their backpacks and their guns have been taken. Bolot, will you take Tatiana back to the cabin? I want to follow these snowshoe tracks before they disappear under more snow."

"How do we know the killers aren't back at the cabin?" Tatiana asked.

"There's a logic to what she says," Bolot said.

"Leave the sled," Arkady said. "We'll stay together and follow the tracks, but we have to move quickly."

They began following the snowshoe prints, which became fainter as snow continued to fall. Bolot ran ahead and out of sight. Within minutes he reappeared at the top of a ridge pointing to smoke billowing into dark clouds.

"The cabin," said Tatiana.

Arkady waved Bolot back. "Could you tell if the snowcat was still up there?"

"I didn't see it."

"Okay, let's head for the helipad."

This time Bolot handed Arkady one of his two backpacks and ran in the direction of the helipad.

Arkady held on to Tatiana's arm as they followed. They had been trekking since dawn and she could no longer lift her snow-shoes without catching snow on them and falling.

The first thing they saw as they came out of the woods was that the helicopter was gone but the snowcat was there. Bolot was poking around in its engine.

"Someone must have driven it down from the cabin and taken the keys with them. The carburetor is gone too," he said.

Arkady looked at his watch. "It's going to get dark soon. We have to find shelter before nightfall or we'll freeze to death. I don't think Tatiana can walk another step."

"Bear meat. I'm going back for the sled," said Bolot. "Then I'll check to see if anything's left of the cabin."

"Do you happen to have any extra clothing in that second backpack?" Arkady asked.

"Of course."

"Do you mind giving it to Tatiana?"

"Not at all." Bolot pulled out a fluorescent orange hoodie. "And you have matches?"

"I have a lighter. Any extra sandwiches?"

"In here." Bolot tossed him his other backpack and left.

Arkady led Tatiana to the cab of the snowcat and bundled her up in Bolot's orange sweatshirt.

They sat in silence. The immensity of Boris Benz's death was only now sinking in. It was impossible to believe he was dead because, despite his faults, he was a man who was bright and damnably charming.

"Would a bear attack us here?" she asked.

"He would have a hard time getting inside the snowcat, and generally bears go out of their way to avoid humans."

"Why did he attack today, then?"

"He must have been surprised and threatened."

"Would a bear attack for a sandwich?"

"He might try, but we won't let him get it." Arkady wrapped his arms around Tatiana and held her close. "Right now I should get out and start building a fire."

"You think just being inside together won't keep us warm?"

"Not once the sun goes. And we'll want to cook some of the bear meat when Bolot gets back." He looked around the snowcat's interior for anything that might be useful in building a fire and found official-looking papers in the glove compartment.

"I have notebooks." Tatiana dug into her backpack.

He had to laugh. "Great, and the pencils will make good kindling. I'll bring you back twigs to whittle down with your sharpener. Shavings will help start the fire."

Arkady emptied his backpack, hooked that and his rifle over his shoulder, and stepped out of the truck to a blast of cold air. He looked for dead trees and bushes that had not fallen into the snow and, using Bolot's knife and handsaw, cut branches and twigs from them and placed them in his pack. From fir trees he cut pinecones and low, small dead branches that were shielded by the bigger ones above and had not yet touched snow on the ground. He rushed to the snowcat, where Tatiana set to work with her pencil sharpener.

"I love it," Tatiana said. "Sharpening pencils is now my greatest survival skill."

Arkady wiped a portion of the helipad clear of snow and laid the small branches in a grill pattern on the concrete. Around the grill, he placed larger pieces of wood, log cabin–style, in hopes that they would protect a small fire and dry out enough to burn.

"Ingenious." Tatiana crouched down beside him and presented him with a bag full of shavings, paper, pencils, cones, and twigs. Using the grill as a base, they piled first a layer of twigs, then paper and shavings. Arkady reached into his pocket for his lighter and aimed into his well of kindling. As it ignited and burned, he placed bigger branches on the fire.

From a corner of the helipad, Arkady pulled two large rubber chocks within feet of the fire. He and Tatiana collapsed against them and basked in its warmth.

28

Bolot emerged soundlessly from the half-light. By the time Arkady heard the crunch of footsteps, he was already close enough to kick aside Arkady's rifle.

"I'd have missed you anyway," Arkady said.

Bolot had brought back not just the sled but also extra clothing, piled on top of the skins. Arkady recognized the topmost item as the jacket that Benz had been wearing.

"Took me ages to strip them," Bolot said. "They're blue and stiff as boards."

"What did you do with the bodies?" Tatiana asked.

"Left them where they were." Bolot handed them the clothes. "I had to come back the long way round, just to check that whoever murdered them is gone."

"And?" Arkady asked

"And I think they have."

"You *think* they have?" asked Tatiana.

It was the first time in their acquaintance that Bolot sounded worried. "I can't be sure, obviously, but I'm still here, and you're still here, right? The helicopter's gone, and the cabin's nothing but hot cinders. I couldn't even get close to it, let alone retrieve anything, so my guess is that the killers have retreated to civilization."

"Or to Chita," Arkady said. "Any clue as to who they are?"

"None at all. The only thing I found is this, but it may be nothing."

He held up a key ring. Half a dozen keys of varying shapes and sizes hung from the snout of a silver fish. "I found it under the snow next to Benz's body."

Arkady was holding Benz's jacket, which was encrusted with frozen blood. He checked the pockets. They were all zipped up. The key ring, therefore, couldn't have fallen out.

He examined Georgy's jacket too. Same result.

Bolot nodded. "The key ring must have come from the killer."

Arkady held his hand out. Bolot gave him the keys.

"Evidence," Arkady said.

He unzipped the pocket in his parka, put the key ring in, and zipped it shut.

"Why didn't they come after us?" Tatiana said.

Bolot shrugged. "Maybe they didn't know we were here."

"Or maybe killing us wasn't part of the plan." Arkady shivered. He was getting cold already. "I suggest we cook the bear meat on the fire because we need to keep the fire burning and we need to eat. Bolot, you and I will take turns watching out for bears. Two hours on, two hours off. And tomorrow morning, assuming no one's come to get us, we leave."

"Where do we go?" Tatiana asked.

"We flew over a railway line on the way here," Bolot said. "That's the BAM. It runs east to west, so if we head due south, we'll come to it sooner or later."

"What's the BAM?" Tatiana asked.

"It's the old Baikal–Amur main line, an old construction project. Stalin ordered it to run several hundred kilometers north of the Siberian Express, which he thought was too close to the Chinese border."

"Any idea how far away it is?" asked Arkady.

"I don't know," Bolot said. "Five kilometers? Twenty?" On a flat tarmac road in the summer, they could have knocked off twenty kilometers in a few hours. In the winter, crossing the snowbound taiga could take days.

"Wouldn't it be better to stay here?"

"Maybe. If we knew for sure that rescue was coming, then yes. But we don't. Better to do something than nothing."

"The Siberian dilemma," Arkady said.

The ice crystals round Bolot's mouth cracked when he smiled. "Indeed. Yes indeed. Exactly that." He clapped Arkady on the shoulder.

"Siberian dilemma?" Tatiana asked.

Bolot gestured in Arkady's direction.

"A fisherman is on a frozen lake. He moves around, listening all the time for the ice cracking beneath his feet, ready to jump back to thicker ice if necessary, but sometimes he's not quick enough. The ice breaks. He falls in."

"So, what's the dilemma?"

"I heard it from my wife, Irina. If he pulls himself out of the water onto the ice, he'll freeze to death in seconds, a minute at most. If he stays in the water, he'll die of hypothermia in five."

"Then he must stay in the water," Tatiana said.

"Why?"

"He lives longer. Only a few minutes, but longer is longer."

"No. You're thinking like a Muscovite," Arkady said.

"I am from Moscow," she said.

"Think like a Siberian."

Her brow furrowed as she tried to remember what Bolot had said. Better to do something than nothing. She smiled, knowing she had the answer.

"I was wrong," she said. "He gets out of the water."

"Why?" Arkady asked.

"Because that way he's doing something. He gets out; that's the crucial thing. He doesn't just wait to die. He moves; he might run; his circulation starts up again. He might warm up the whole lake. You never know."

"The lesson is it's better to take action than be passive," said Arkady. "Better to fight than to surrender, even if you know you're going to die."

Tatiana's words, her rationale in working out the dilemma, were almost word for word what Irina had said when she first told Arkady about the Siberian dilemma, and Arkady didn't know whether this made him happy or sad.

"Tell me about Irina," Tatiana said. "I know how she died from a medical error. Tell me what she was like when she was alive."

"She was a remarkable woman, a lot like you."

"In what way?"

"She was brave to a fault. She didn't mind putting herself in danger, and that frightened me. And she was beautiful."

29

Bolot was insistent that they cook the bear meat for several hours, way longer than Arkady and Tatiana thought necessary.

"Bears often carry parasites," Bolot explained. "You don't want to catch trichinosis, trust me. Happened to two friends of mine. One of them got severely ill, the other, severely dead."

Beyond the leaping flames of the campfire and the sizzle of the fat was darkness and silence. The three of them sat at points of a triangle so that between them they could see anything or anyone coming out of the forest.

It was a matter of percentages. Without the fire they'd be dead by morning, so they needed the fire. Without the meat they wouldn't have the energy to make it to the railway line, so they needed the food. If a bear smelled the cooking and came searching, they could shoot it. The only situation in which this all worked against them was if the man or men who'd killed Benz and Georgy were still around. In that case, Bolot, Arkady, and

Tatiana silhouetted against the fire would be sure targets for anyone with decent aim.

"Is it ready yet?" Arkady asked.

"You'll thank me in the long run," Bolot replied.

Eventually he decided that even the hardiest parasite would be, by now, little more than carbon and ash. He cut the meat into long strips and served it off his knife. It was tastier than Arkady had expected, like beef, but with a distinctly gamey flavor.

"Bears are omnivores, so they taste like their last meal," Bolot said. "Berries are good. But if they've been eating salmon, they smell like low tide on a hot day." He made a face.

"Can you taste a hint of berry?" Arkady pictured Bolot as a sommelier in a Moscow restaurant, giving newly minted oligarchs a crash course in vino culture. "What do you think?" he asked Tatiana.

"It could do with some vegetables."

"The chef regrets that vegetables are not in season," Bolot said with gravity.

They could still laugh at small jokes.

"Eat until you're full, and then some more," Bolot said. "We'll need all the energy we can get for tomorrow."

Only when Arkady felt himself eating with joyless repetition did he stop.

"I can do my turn too," Tatiana said.

"Absolutely not," Arkady said.

She lay on her side and pulled her knees up to her chest to stay warm.

Bolot nodded in Tatiana's direction. "You better go first."

"What about you?"

"It's nine p.m. I'll wake you at midnight."

Arkady lay down next to Tatiana. She took his hands and pressed them to her chest. Arkady molded his shape to fit hers. He was sure he couldn't fall asleep, but he went out like a light.

Bolot woke him at twelve o'clock and took his place next to the fire. Tatiana didn't stir. Arkady stood up, rifle in hand. He put more wood on the fire and watched the flames rise and settle. His world extended to the edge of the fire. The taiga extended for thousands of kilometers in pretty much every direction, but now it seemed as remote and otherworldly as the moon.

30

Once there was light enough to see by, they were on their way. With no more than a nod, Bolot took the lead, and Arkady brought up the rear.

"Bears are still the threat," Bolot said. "If a bear doesn't see you, don't disturb it. If the bear does see you and stands up, he may just be curious. Back away slowly if you can. If the bear follows you, stop and stand your ground."

Bolot's pace was metronomic. Tatiana, more at ease with the snowshoes than the day before, followed in his footsteps. Arkady followed in hers, as if the three of them were marking a safe path through a minefield.

The world was white. When there were no trees to break the horizon line, it was impossible to see where land ended and sky began. The effect was unnerving. Arkady found it easier to look down at the snowshoe prints in the snow. They seemed proof that they were making headway. Otherwise, everything stayed the same: his speed, his breathing, the ache in his legs, the glare of the snow. No one spoke. Speaking was a visible waste of breath. Sooner or later they were bound to reach the railway. They stopped for five minutes every hour to drink some snow-melt and catch their breath.

"We can't stop for any longer," Bolot said. "If we do, our muscles will seize up and we will never get going again."

It was past two. They'd been going for eight hours. Despite the freezing weather, Arkady felt himself sweat. He was wearing one layer too many. He should have taken off one of his sweaters earlier. He thought about asking Tatiana and Bolot to stop, but didn't want to break their rhythm. He would catch up with them soon enough.

He stopped, placed his rifle on the snow by his feet, shrugged the backpack off his shoulders, unzipped the parka, and took off his sweater. Tatiana and Bolot were a hundred feet ahead, disappearing over the crest of a low hill. He fixed his sight line on that.

As he reached down for his backpack, he sensed the bear. He turned to see a slab of brown standing upright no more than twenty feet away. It was an old bear, a veteran with beady brown eyes, not a specimen you would find at the Moscow Zoo. His head swayed from side to side and when he roared, it came from his gut. The bear charged, and in the moment before it reached him, Arkady saw old scars and wounds that crisscrossed his scalp and the ebb and flow of muscles as he reared up. The Russians had a word for that kind of sight, *grozny*, which meant in equal parts awesome and terrible. *Grozny*, as in Ivan the Terrible, and *grozny*, as in the bear that was about to kill him.

Arkady grabbed his rifle and fired. Blood sprayed the snow. Not even Arkady could miss a target that big from that distance, but it wasn't enough to stop the bear, let alone bring it down, and now it was on top of him, swiping left and right, all claws and gaping mouth. Arkady heard a roar, but he couldn't be sure if it was him or the bear.

He fired again. The trigger clicked on an empty chamber. He jabbed at the bear with the rifle, trying to slam the barrel into its mouth. Another swipe sent the gun spinning into the air, taking Arkady with it. For a brief, peaceful moment there was nothing but white, and then Arkady landed and the air rushed from his lungs. He felt as if he'd been hit by a car.

Arkady remembered General Renko barking out instructions in the voice he had always used when talking to Arkady, the same voice he had used on his lowliest, most inept, most slovenly conscripted soldiers.

"Play dead or be dead. Lie flat on your stomach to protect your vital organs. Lace your hands over the back of your neck to cover the arteries there."

It was a long time since Arkady had felt any reason to be thankful to his father. He rolled onto his stomach and covered his neck as instructed. The bear turned Arkady over. It mauled him and shook him like a rag doll. Play dead or be dead. Pain dug deep within him as if he was being torn from the inside out. Yellow teeth took his parka and flesh down to the bone of his arm, and he felt his right hand go numb and limp. The bear redoubled his attack, picking Arkady up, swinging him left and right, and dropping him. He tore the skin off part of Arkady's forehead. Arkady heard the huffing and snuffling and smelled the rot of his breath. The bear wouldn't quit. Arkady played dead. There was nothing else he could do. Eventually the beast would give up and leave him alone.

A shot was fired, then another. The bear staggered, paused as if he heard a distant call, then pitched face forward. He was dead before he hit the ground. Blood spewed from his mouth and ears. Arkady heard Tatiana's and Bolot's voices. He couldn't make out what they were saying, but it didn't matter: he heard the terror and knew it wasn't good.

31

Bolot and Tatiana patched Arkady up as best they could. They removed his shredded parka and Bolot took out his knife to cut what was left of it into strips, which he used as tourniquets. Over these went Arkady's sweater, which they found lying in the snow. Tatiana put her fur hat on Arkady's head to help preserve the heat there and to keep torn strips of cloth in place. Finally, they helped Arkady stand.

"Put your arms over our shoulders," Bolot said. "It will hurt like the devil, but it's the only way to support you. Besides, we need to keep your arms high. That right arm in particular."

He raised his arms. Bolot had said it would hurt, and he was right. The muscles in Arkady's back and shoulders felt as though they were being torn apart all over again. He gritted his teeth.

"Your legs are fine, so you can walk," Bolot said. Arkady noted how measured his voice was. This was Bolot taking care of him, his factotum who found solutions where others saw only problems; a man whose calm under pressure had helped keep both Tatiana and Arkady from panicking. Arkady was suddenly grateful to whoever had placed them next to each other on the plane to Irkutsk. Maybe Bolot was right after all: maybe it was fate.

"Slow and steady," Bolot said. "We don't want to get your heart rate up too much . . ." "And bleed you out quicker" went the second half of that sentence.

They set off, Arkady draped between them and trying not to sag too much. It was a condition every Russian knew, a man with too much vodka inside him being half carried, half dragged by his friends. Bolot soon had them in a rhythm: short steps so Arkady and Tatiana could keep pace. A human troika without a sleigh.

Arkady dripped blood as they walked. He wondered if bears could sense blood in the snow the way sharks could sense it in the water. One foot in front of the other, each foot nearer the railway line. He didn't ask Bolot how far they had to go. His world was pain. It would be so easy just to stop, but he knew they wouldn't let him. He could tell them to go on and leave him there, but they'd refuse.

Arkady didn't know how long they walked, only that it was still light when they struggled up a short hill and found themselves on a berm that ran along a railroad track.

"This is it," Bolot said. "Can you stand on your own for a moment?"

Arkady struggled to stand straight with Tatiana's arms supporting his upper body.

"Good."

Bolot gently removed Arkady's arm from across his own

shoulders and motioned for Tatiana to do the same. He shrugged off his rucksack, took Tatiana's off her as well, and jabbed both packs into the snow a few feet apart.

"Okay. Tatiana and I are going to lower you down to the ground. Keep your arms on top of the packs."

They gently lowered him. Arkady adjusted his position slightly.

"Comfortable?" Bolot asked.

Arkady allowed himself a groan.

"What now?" Tatiana asked.

"Now we wait. Stay with him. Talk to him. We can't let him sleep."

Arkady wasn't sure how long he could wait. He was equally aware that he had no choice. A train would come in time or it would not. Life versus fate.

"Arkady?" Tatiana sat and held his head in her lap. "Tell me where you'd like to go when we get out of here. Anywhere in the world."

Arkady tried to focus. A foreign city, perhaps, like Prague, with cobblestone streets where he could wander all day and sleep with Tatiana all night. He was, after all, an urban animal.

She rested her head against his, trying not to touch anyplace where the bear had mauled him.

Bolot wore his bright orange sweatshirt to be more visible. He marched along the track as if motion alone could make the train come sooner.

"Half an hour until it's dark," he said. "Don't worry, he won't die."

"How do you know that?" Tatiana asked.

"I know."

He pulled a flashlight from his sleeve like a conjuror producing a rabbit from a hat.

"I'll wave this around like a madman."

"Do you know how many trains pass here every day?" Tatiana asked.

"I forgot my timetable." He smiled. Besides, every Russian knew that timetables weren't worth the paper they were printed on. Trains could be days late, not just hours. They came when they came and they went when they went.

Bolot continued to pace. Tatiana murmured in Arkady's good ear, not so much words as vibrations through his bones. He didn't care what she said, only that she was there. Darkness and cold came together. Arkady felt he was dying like mercury in a thermometer, slowly and by degrees.

32

The warmth of the train carriage was stuffy and drowsy after the cold. Eyes wide with curiosity watched as they brought Arkady in. Passengers pressed up against each other to give him space, making an exclusion zone around him in case his misfortune was infectious.

A *providnitsa* commandeered a sleeping compartment for him, chased out the drinkers, and bustled around Arkady with her samovar and tea.

"Ust-Kut," said the *providnitsa*. "There's a hospital in Ust-Kut." Ust-Kut, a chant which the train's wheels took up as they moved along the tracks. Ust-Kut, Ust-Kut, Ust-Kut.

Arkady's life came in snatches, as if consciousness was a series of puddles he could jump through like a child. In and out.

Now he was on a hospital bed. A strip light glared at him from the ceiling. Paint peeled off the walls exactly the way he imagined the bear had ripped the skin from his body. Tubes snaked from him up to clear bags held on poles. He was an octopus, sprouting tentacles from unlikely places.

A nurse the size of a shipping hazard peered over him and smiled. Some of her teeth were missing, some were gold, and the sight was so unnerving that Arkady hoped he wouldn't give her cause to smile again.

A man with rimless glasses came into view. He was carrying a clipboard. Arkady watched the doctor's hands, marveling at how hairy they were. The backs of his fingers looked like fur had been pasted onto them.

"Investigator Renko? I'm Dr. Poloz." Sounded like Bolot. This, too, pleased Arkady. Poloz and Bolot. Maybe they could be friends. "What can I tell you? You're a lucky man."

Arkady didn't feel particularly lucky, but he conceded that everything was relative.

"Let's see." Poloz consulted his clipboard. "You've broken your right arm, so we reset it. That's the only break, rather surprisingly, though we had to reattach a couple of tendons, and the nerve damage means you will need physical therapy and exercise to regain full use of that hand. Your vital organs are unharmed, which is good news. But lacerations are a whole different matter. Your back's a disaster zone, there's damage to your windpipe severe enough to stop you speaking for a few weeks, and your face, well, you'll have a romantic scar on your forehead for the rest of your days. The biggest issue right now is infection. Bears are walking bacteria carriers from all those dead animals and carrion they feed on and the roots they dig up, so the wounds they inflict tend to be pretty filthy. Teeth or claws, it makes no difference. We've cleaned the wounds up as best we can, and we have given you antibiotics. Only time will tell.

"He's developed sepsis," Arkady heard Dr. Poloz tell Tatiana and Bolot. "Probably inevitable even with the antibiotics. At the very least, the inflammation of the brain means he'll be suffering hallucinations. Beyond that, I don't know."

The nurse with golden teeth made a point of refilling Arkady's IV bags with something different each time: vodka, of course, but also honey, and diesel fuel from a jerry can. Arkady was a shell and about as mobile as an upturned beetle. The nurses turned him when they had the time and inclination. He didn't want Tatiana to see him like this, but he had no way of telling her.

Arkady designed escape plans of staggering complexity; fire alarms, medical trolleys, air vents, and ambulances all were involved, but each time he attempted one, the nurses caught him and strapped him back into bed. The straps were real, he thought in a moment of clarity, so maybe his attempts had been too.

Would they send a priest to give him last rites? Arkady hadn't been to church in a long time, and he wasn't sure how much of the liturgy he remembered. Did it matter? He couldn't speak. He wouldn't be expected to join in.

The prospect of death focused the mind. Arkady had never wondered or worried too much about his legacy, such as it was. He had never felt the need to leave his mark on the world, either through achievement or progeny.

There were those who'd be sorry to see him gone and those who'd be delighted. Given the identity of those in both camps, the latter was, in its own way, as much a compliment as the former.

Two weeks passed before the antibiotics finally did their work. Arkady's infections and sepsis began to disappear.

Bolot was sitting by his bed.

"Raise your good hand if you can hear me. Good. Now listen. This place is a death trap. You don't need me to tell you that. And I won't lie, Arkady. You're not in a good way. Our best hope—maybe our only hope—is to get you out of here. They'll kill you here; you know they will. They won't mean to, of course, but they will. Raise your hand if you agree."

Once more the hand went up.

"I won't tell you where we're going, because you might think I've lost my mind. Tatiana did when I first mentioned it to her. But I convinced her. So here's the question: Do you trust me?"

"I have to," Arkady said. "You're my factotum."

33

Slowly, painfully, Tatiana and Bolot prepared Arkady for the journey that lay ahead. Bandages stuck where wounds wept and cried for mercy. He had lost so much weight that new clothes hung off him like flags. Neither Dr. Poloz nor the nurse with the gold teeth tried to stop him. They clearly wanted his bed for the next patient.

A digital clock with the day and date hung above the main door. It took Arkady forever to do the simplest calculation. It had been in fact two weeks since they'd set out with Boris Benz on his helicopter.

The cold was a shock after being inside so long. Bolot and Tatiana laid him down in the back of an old panel truck on blankets and pillows and covered him up. There was something to be said for this, Arkady thought, this outsourcing of literally every decision to someone else, this total lack of personal responsibility.

"I've checked it over thoroughly," Bolot said. "Snow tires,

new spark plugs, oil, extra vodka for antifreeze. The good news is it hasn't snowed for a week, the weather's clear for the next few days, and we're sticking to the main roads. The bad news is we've got a long way to go."

A black ribbon of road rolled out endlessly in the glare of their headlights. Kilometer after kilometer, hour after hour. For Arkady it was like watching the phases of the moon pass by.

He slept most of the way, waking only to find Tatiana dabbing his mouth with a sponge. His stomach was so shrunken from two weeks without food that even a glass of water would come straight back up again. The hallucinations were now coming mainly in the form of nightmares, which made them slightly more manageable; but he shivered hot and cold, at one point throwing off the blankets and asking for an open window when it was fifteen degrees below zero.

Tall poles wrapped in sails of blue, yellow, red, and green snapped in the wind. Beyond them, a sheet of ice stretched to the horizon. Bolot gestured expansively toward it as though he were its first discoverer: "Lake Baikal . . . and this is Olkhon Island."

Arkady had heard of Olkhon Island. It was in the middle of Lake Baikal. But he didn't remember them having taken any kind of ferry to get there, or even a smaller boat, and in any case the lake was a sheet of ice.

"We drove across," Tatiana said. "The ice is more than a meter thick in places. Perfectly safe." Safer than most roads, Arkady thought. So safe that even a drunk driver would find it hard to crash in several thousand square kilometers of frozen lake.

They found a cabin where a wall of postcards spoke of summers full of tourists and backpackers. This time of year it was empty. There were three rooms: two bedrooms with bunks and one room with a table, benches, and a small woodstove. Bolot laid out hard-boiled eggs, cheese, curd, biscuits, and of course vodka. Arkady was allowed a hard-boiled egg and water.

Bolot cleared his throat. "As to why we're here," he began, and then stopped suddenly, worried that Arkady would think this trek across Siberia had been a fool's errand.

"We're here because Bolot's a shaman," Tatiana said decisively, "and he's going to perform a healing ceremony on you to draw out any remaining infection."

It was the sincerity in her voice that struck Arkady. Tatiana was the most rational person he had ever met. Life for her was facts and evidence, right and wrong, power and resistance. The Tatiana whom Arkady knew would no more have given credence to shamanic healing than to magic carpets. She would have dismissed shamans as charlatans, conjurors, neurotics, psychopaths, showmen.

"For us," Bolot said, "for the Buryat, the bear is lord of the forest. When the bear attacked you, it took your soul. Well, one of your souls. You've got three. The first is in your skeleton and vanishes when you die. At the same time, the second one transforms into someone or something else: a person, an animal, another living being. You're not dead, though." Not yet, Arkady thought. "So you've still got those two. It's your third soul I need to find. It travels the world, sometimes in dreams, sometimes not. That's the one you're missing, and without it your body can't function normally or heal itself."

It was this place, Arkady thought. Not just this island or this lake; this place. Siberia. He had felt it up in the snow around the oil wells. This was where strange things happened and stranger things were just around the corner. Bolot and his bear amulet, Saran and her monsters of the deep. It was a zone on the edge where planes of existence overlapped. Nothing was inexplicable. It was just that Arkady had not yet found a way to decipher it. How could he? He was a city boy, at home among buildings and people, among the endless scurrying, among everything man did to suppress what lay beyond. Tatiana was his friend; Bolot was his friend. That much he knew.

That Bolot was a shaman was perhaps the least surprising part of it all. Of course he was a shaman. At some level Arkady had always suspected something like this. Bolot was too much a force of nature to be merely a factotum or even an entrepreneur. Bolot was an iceberg, all bright surfaces and hidden depths, and like an iceberg he rotated now and then to show a new face.

Arkady smiled and nodded, and the relief on Bolot's face was obvious.

"How did you know you were born to be a shaman?" Tatiana asked.

"I first fell into a trance when I was nine," Bolot said, "but only as an adult was I initiated into the practice. The powers were too great for even the hardiest and most resourceful child to bear. Being a shaman is a curse as much as a blessing. I resisted it in the beginning, and the pressure drove me half-insane. I stayed in a tree for weeks and ran naked across the ice for two days, but I couldn't flee the calling. So I journeyed into the underworld, where the Smallpox People cut out my heart and boiled it, and the Master of Madness stripped me of skin, the Master of Confusion stripped me of muscle, and the Master of Stupidity stripped me of organs. I was a skeleton wandering in the dark, not sure what I was seeking but somehow aware that I'd know when I found it. Then the Masters rebuilt me, and a silversmith made me eyes that could see new worlds, and a blacksmith pierced my ears with iron fingers to allow me to hear the plants talking. Now, if I wanted to, I could twist my head off."

Bolot hung a metallic circular mirror around his neck so it rested on his chest to absorb energy and deflect attacks from malevolent spirits.

"Think of me as a spiritual doctor," Bolot said, "and sometimes as a fishing guide." He took a copper mask of a bear's head and placed it over his face.

The place Bolot had chosen for the ceremony was on the edge of the lake. It was called *Shamanka*, Shaman's Rock. The story was that an eagle had traveled between the spirit world and the human one. There it lay with a Buryat woman, who conceived the first human shaman, from whom all other shamans were descended.

An eagle flew overhead, tipping on a wing.

"Excellent," Bolot said. "This is a good sign."

"If you say so," Arkady said.

Bolot led the way to a stone shelf between twin peaks. He beat his drum upside down and Arkady felt it as much as he heard it. Bolot began to chant, a sound that seemed to come from a great distance. The wind picked up to announce the bear spirit's arrival. Bolot moved in circles, treading the same loop over and again, jerking as though touching a live wire. His drumming grew louder. Bolot, with the copper bear's face in the half-light, was now grunting and snuffling, and Arkady had the strange feeling that he was watching a man change his shape.

Bolot slumped to the ground and lay still. His chest rose and fell as he sank into a deep sleep.

How long did they stay like this? Arkady couldn't tell. Time was an abstract concept to him. It was day or it was night; that was all he knew.

Bolot got to his feet and leaned over Arkady, so close that he was resting his head on Arkady's chest, and then he shook his head so suddenly and violently that Arkady wondered if he was having a seizure. He shook his head and tilted it one way and then the other. He straightened up and pressed both his hands to the place on Arkady's chest where his head had been.

"I've put your soul back," he said from behind the bear mask. "I can see you are skeptical."

Arkady apologized. "I can't help it. I have a skeptical soul."

34

Arkady knew when he woke up the next morning that he was on the mend. He was still weak, of course, as much from lack of food as anything else, but he knew that the worst was over. His hallucinations were gone, and the air was so crisp and clear that he could practically drink it. He even managed to say a few words, although his voice was rusty from lack of use.

It was coincidence, of course. He must have been shaking off the infection even before he left the hospital, and Bolot's elaborate ceremony had been nothing more than good timing and the power of suggestion.

Tatiana tended to Arkady's dressings and during the day, when he needed to sleep, rolled against him and read old travel magazines and brochures the trekkers had left behind. At night Bolot slept in the second bedroom, and in the bedroom closest to the fire Tatiana climbed up to the bunk above Arkady.

"Why don't you stay down here with me?"

"You're not ready."

"Who's to say I'm not ready?"

"Me."

He found it impossible to sleep, sensing her just three feet above.

Each day he ate a little more: some soup, dry toast, and local fish. When he was stronger, Bolot and Tatiana took him on excursions through towering pines that reached down to the shoreline, where they watched the lake shimmer.

One day Bolot and Arkady walked into the woods and glimpsed reindeer as they brushed their furry antlers against low branches.

"They say that a hunter can chase a reindeer all day long only to find, once he has killed it, that the reindeer is a beautiful woman. It happens all the time."

"Really?" Arkady asked.

"It's what some people say."

Arkady didn't want to contradict him.

"I don't know if Tatiana is a reindeer," Arkady said. "I do know that she thinks she can escape hunters, and that's a dangerous assumption."

After the first week Arkady felt well enough to get back to Chita. Why he would feel duty-bound to investigate Benz's and Georgy's murders, he did not know.

"A week," Arkady said. "A week here and then I have to go."

"Now I know you're on the mend," Tatiana said. "You're being unreasonable. Ten days."

The day came when she finished bandaging his wounds. She kissed his hand and began climbing up to her bunk.

Physically he might be a wreck, but he found it easy to lift her off the ladder and onto his bed. He tasted her mouth and breasts. Her skin was salty and her eyes bright even in the dark. They stripped down to the heat of their bodies and clung to each other until the ache of anticipation was too much and she raised her body to meet him.

This was why he had traveled so far. This was what he had suffered for. The heat that spread like a blush across her breasts. The way her fingers curled. His name on her lips. And then the languor.

Bolot drove them back across the ice road ten days later. Arkady gasped the moment they left the road and drove onto the ice, but once he felt the smoothness beneath the wheels, he relaxed.

They were driving over a strange, hazardous, beautiful world. There were places he could see forty or fifty meters straight down through the ice, and he couldn't look for more than a few seconds without feeling the vertigo rise from the pit of his stomach.

"I can stay if you want me to, but I'm supposed to accompany Kuznetsov on the campaign trail when we get back," Tatiana said.

"Then you must do it. Once I find out who killed Benz, and I feel you will be safe in Chita, I'll go back to Moscow and let you do your work."

"But then I'll miss you."

"Just answer my calls."

35

Bolot helped Arkady walk through the door of the Hotel Admiral Kolchak.

Saran's astonishment gave way to flustered embarrassment.

"Thank God," she said.

"Yes. I hope you've kept my room."

"Of course." Her indignation was high until it caught on his smile. "It's just as you left it. I mean, I've cleaned it. The police came round when you hadn't returned, but other than that, yes, just as you left it. Let me help you."

"Bolot, I think I will be well taken care of from here on. Don't worry."

"Okay. I'll get your rucksack out of the car and leave it at the desk. I'll call tomorrow to see how you're doing."

Saran helped Arkady up the stairs.

"What happened to you?"

"I'll tell you when we get to the room. I can't walk and talk at the same time."

His room was indeed exactly as he'd left it. It was an unsettling feeling. He had gone one morning fully expecting to be back by evening, and it had taken him the best part of a month to return.

Now that she had a chance to study him, Saran saw a different Arkady, someone haggard, perhaps someone who had barely endured. He sat heavily on the bed.

"I lost a bear fight."

"You look it."

Arkady laughed.

"Boris Benz is dead."

"I know. It's big news here. How did he die?"

"Somebody killed him with a sniper's rifle. They also killed Georgy, the man who was looking after the oil rigs."

She leaned forward. "And Tatiana?"

"She's okay."

"Who killed them?"

"That's the question."

"Are you going to stay?" Saran asked.

"Not for long. I plan to cause some trouble and then go."

He could tell that she was saddened by this news.

"You know, I have to wonder why you still live here. You're so smart and inquisitive, not to mention pretty. Why haven't you set out to conquer the world yet?"

Saran blushed.

Arkady rose to take off his coat, and the fingers of his good hand felt something hard in one of the pockets. He brought out the key ring Bolot had found in the snow by Benz's body.

It was a moment or two before he realized that Saran was staring at him. More precisely, she was staring at the key ring.

"That's Dorzho's," she said. "I gave that to him, and one of those keys is mine."

"You gave this fish to Dorzho?"

"Investigator Renko, that isn't a fish; it's Lusud Khan, the dragon monster of Lake Baikal, if you believe in that kind of thing."

"Do you?"

"Kind of. May I take my key off the key ring?"

"Of course." He handed it to her. "Are you afraid he will come to visit you one night?"

"Yes."

"Do you know if Dorzho worked for Benz?" Arkady asked.

"Yes, in the boxing club."

"You're sure?"

"A blowhard like Dorzho shouted it all over town when he got that job. Later he worked with Mikhail Kuznetsov."

Arkady turned the key ring over and over in his hand as though it would offer up its secrets if he caught just the right light.

"Do you know where Dorzho is?" Arkady asked.

"No, but I can help you find him."

No, that wasn't quite what he had in mind. He didn't want her anywhere near Dorzho.

In the following week Saran delighted in taking care of Arkady while he regained his strength. She brought him food and walked beside him whenever he ventured out.

"You don't have to do this, you know," Arkady said on one of these walks.

"You should probably be in a hospital." She had a habit of sneaking worried glances in his direction. "Why isn't Tatiana here with you?"

"She's busy campaigning with Kuznetsov in Irkutsk and Novosibirsk."

"When does she get back?"

"Maybe tomorrow."

36

Tatiana called the next morning. "How are you feeling?" she asked.

"Better; in fact, much better."

"Are you still having trouble walking?"

"No, I'm walking farther every day."

"I wonder if you want to come over to the Montblanc this afternoon. We are filming a video for the campaign."

"'We'?" Arkady asked.

"Don't start. Yes, we."

How was it, Arkady wondered, that while Tatiana had demonstrated her love for him these past few weeks, he could still let the doubts flood in?

Kuznetsov had taken over a large suite at the Montblanc. Unsmiling bodyguards with cropped hair and suits stood outside the elevators and at the entrances to staircases. They refused to let Arkady pass, Moscow investigator or no, until Tatiana came to vouch for him, and even then it was only because they knew she was Kuznetsov's friend.

Tatiana walked over and kissed him on the cheek. "You look good."

"Saran took good care of me."

"Oh?"

In the suite, activity was everywhere. Arkady stepped over a line of cables duct-taped to the floor and dodged young interns hurrying along with clipboards.

"I need to talk to Kuznetsov," Arkady said.

"What about?"

"What happened up at the wells. There have been developments."

"What kind of developments?"

"I'll tell you when I tell him."

"Okay," she said, "but it will have to be after we're done with this."

"How long will that be?"

"An hour. Maybe two."

"Nobody will watch a campaign video that long."

She gave him a look of exasperation. "The video is only going to be 108 seconds long." She indicated a young man with black-framed glasses and blue jeans. "Fedor is the social media expert, and he says that's the optimum length. But 108 seconds isn't long, so we have to make every one of them count."

She led him into another room with curtains tightly drawn. Kuznetsov sat on the far side, hemmed in by video cameras and studio lights. He was wearing a black polo neck shirt beneath a dark gray sports jacket. Billionaire chic, Arkady thought, pitched at just the right level; not the bland suit and tie of workaday politicians, but smart enough to show that he was taking this seriously.

"Stay here," Tatiana said. "I'll tell him, but like I said, you will have to wait."

Arkady nodded. There wasn't much else he could do.

She went over to Kuznetsov and talked softly in his ear. Kuznetsov glanced across at Arkady and nodded.

There was a seat next to Kuznetsov. Tatiana took it. A man standing next to Arkady, clearly the director, clapped his hands.

"Okay, everybody. Quiet, please. Mikhail, let's do the bit about 'Another Russia.' Look at Tatiana, imagine you're talking to her and not the camera, okay?"

Kuznetsov leaned forward in his chair and looked at Tatiana as instructed.

"This election will not be an honest one. I know it won't, and so do you. But one day it will be, and that's the day we're working toward: the day when the people who come to power represent the interests of all segments of our society. Not the Russia we have now but another Russia, a better Russia, a Russia committed to human rights, the rule of law, and a strong civil society. Today I launch 'Another Russia' but I do not lead it. The last thing we need is yet another party with one man in charge. I see 'Another Russia' as a horizontal alliance of those many, many small groups who form the underlying fabric of that civil society that the regime suppresses but cannot eliminate."

Arkady wondered how many of these words were Tatiana's and how many were Kuznetsov's.

Kuznetsov sat back. The director clapped his hands again. "Excellent!"

He was good, Arkady thought. Passionate without being hysterical, sincere without being smarmy. The campaign crew approached Kuznetsov in turn like supplicants seeking approval from a medieval potentate. Arkady could hear enough of their conversations to know who was who: the strategist whispering about likely reaction from Moscow, the accountant with his spreadsheet, the pollster with her numbers, the logistics manager with a pin-studded map, and the data miner, whatever that was.

Kuznetsov spoke to each of them briefly, turning the full incandescence of his charm and attention on them with the politician's trick of making the interlocutor feel as if he were the only other person in the room. A touch of the arm here, a smile at a shared joke there. Kuznetsov was always on. Every interaction was weighted with a demand, an order, a calculation, well hidden behind his undeniable charisma. Arkady wondered if Kuznetsov ever just *was*, at work or at home. Probably not, which helped explain why Kuznetsov was a billionaire running for president and Arkady was a Moscow investigator chasing his tail five thousand kilometers from home.

Tatiana had said an hour, maybe two. It turned out to be three and a half, by which time Kuznetsov had done so many takes of so many different sections that Arkady felt he could deliver a pretty decent campaign speech himself.

"I'm sorry, Arkady," Kuznetsov said. "You know how these things are. Ten takes when one will do." He fixed Arkady with his gaze and Arkady, despite being aware of exactly what Kuznetsov was doing, still found himself charmed by the focus of such attention.

"You're a hero. Tatiana called from Ust-Kut to tell me everything that happened. You seem to be lucky," Kuznetsov said.

"Luck is important if you're going to be a hero," Arkady said.

"If I'd known that you had all gone up there, I'd have sent out a rescue party."

"You didn't know we'd gone?"

"No."

"What did you think when Tatiana vanished for a few weeks?"

"That she'd finally realized how tedious my life is." He smiled to show that he neither thought nor meant this. "Or that Obolensky had called her away to another story."

"You didn't think it strange that you hadn't heard from Boris Benz for so long?"

"Not at all. He does—did—his thing, I do mine. Quite often we'd go weeks without speaking. Nothing sinister. That's how it is when you have interests all over the country."

"You assumed he was traveling?" Arkady asked.

"I would have if I'd given it enough thought. Is this an official interrogation?"

"This isn't my jurisdiction, but two people have been killed and I would like to know why. If you went up to a remote area and didn't come back, how long do you think it would be before people noticed that you were missing?"

"Not too long, I hope." Kuznetsov gestured round the room, where a handful of people were putting equipment away or poring over laptops. "I have plenty of people who rely on me, especially now."

"So, why should it be different for Boris Benz?"

"It shouldn't. But that's not what you asked me. You asked me if I felt it strange that I hadn't heard from him. Would it have been strange for him not to have heard from me if the situation had been reversed? No, not especially."

"So you had no idea that someone took the helicopter, disabled the truck up there, and left the three of us to fend for ourselves, knowing that in those conditions we could easily have died. Did you even know that Benz and Georgy were killed?"

"Tatiana called me from Ust-Kut and told me."

Arkady wanted to believe him—he really did. The look on Tatiana's face showed she did believe Kuznetsov. She flashed Arkady warning looks.

Then again, Arkady knew something that she didn't.

"Where's Dorzho?" he asked.

Kuznetsov, who had opened his mouth in preparation for the inevitable denial, closed it again and curled his lips into a thin smile.

"I suppose there's no point asking how you know him," Kuznetsov said.

"None at all."

Tatiana looked genuinely puzzled by this turn in the conversation.

"He's in Irkutsk," Kuznetsov said.

"I'll need more than that."

"I'll give you his address. Phone number, too, if you'd like."

"I would," Arkady said. "Would you refrain from warning him in advance?"

"Why would I do that?"

"Because I want to keep what element of surprise I have. And remember, it wouldn't do your campaign any good if it emerged that you employ a suspected killer."

"Come, Investigator. There's scarcely a candidate for high office in this country who hasn't been accused of something. One might even say that a candidate is not taken seriously until then."

"Possibly. But there's a big difference between being accused of fraud and being accused of murder." Arkady wondered whether he was making himself a target and found to his surprise that he didn't care.

Tatiana was now looking at Kuznetsov. Kuznetsov returned her gaze, unflinching, before turning back to Arkady.

"Okay, if that's what you want, I won't tell him you're coming. I never gave him a direct order—not in this case. I told him to use his discretion when dealing with Benz and the oil rigs. Second, I had no idea you, Tatiana, and your friend Bolot had gone with Benz. None at all. As I said before, I would certainly have sent a rescue party for you had I known."

Here was a man, Arkady realized, who had strong emotions but who could turn them off completely when it came to making decisions. Kuznetsov's thinking ran contrary to his feelings.

Kuznetsov scribbled an address and a phone number on a piece of paper and handed it to Arkady. "Dorzho's details."

"You know them by heart?"

"Of course."

"For all your employees?"

"The ones who work directly for me, yes."

Impressive, Arkady thought, to have a memory like that. It was all he could do to remember his own telephone number.

• • •

"No way. Absolutely not. You're insane," Saran said.

Arkady wondered whether she was going to cry. He tried to make a joke of it. "It's funny: Tatiana said the same thing." He realized even as he said it that mentioning Tatiana in this context wasn't particularly sensitive.

Saran composed herself. "You really have a death wish, don't you?"

"Not at all."

"You're no match for him, do you understand? That boxing club he used to go to—you saw them. They're not messing around there. Even at your best, he will pound you like Muhammad Ali. And you're very far from your best right now. Look at yourself."

Arkady was amused but knew she had a point.

"Do you have a picture of him?" he asked.

Saran sighed in exasperation at his stubbornness. Nonetheless, she delved into one of the drawers of her desk, rummaging through old phone chargers, tubes of paper glue, and gently rolling phalanxes of loose batteries. Finally she pulled out an old photograph of herself with Dorzho on the banks of Lake Baikal, arms around each other.

"Clearly taken in happier times," Arkady ventured.

"If by that you mean that I could stand to be in the same hemisphere as him, then yes."

Dorzho was no Romeo, that was for sure. He looked more mean than stupid. He was dangerous, and it seemed incongruous that a woman as pretty and intelligent as Saran should have chosen someone as lumpen as Dorzho, but couples like that could be found all over Russia. In any other country, a Dorzho could never have dreamt of marrying a Saran. Here he was practically a catch.

"He's everything you're not," Saran continued. "And I mean that as a compliment to you." She dabbed at the corner of her eye with a tissue. "You're going to go no matter what I say, aren't you?"

"Yes."

"Then that's one way you are just like Dorzho. You are pig-headed. Take someone with you. Take Bolot. Take Aba too. You'll need them."

37

They flew to Irkutsk the next morning. Bolot and Aba were as excited as schoolchildren on an outing, which made Arkady feel like a sensible teacher trying to herd delinquents.

Bolot had found Kuznetsov's campaign speech on his cell phone. It clocked in at one minute forty-eight seconds, just as Tatiana had promised.

"I like what he says," Aba said.

Five kilometers below them, Lake Baikal stretched out, long and thin, bringing to mind a woman in repose. Bolot leaned across him and pointed to a spot about two-thirds of the way up on the western shore.

"Follow my finger," Bolot said. "That's Cape Ryty. That's where we're not going."

"Why not? Because it's not on the way?" Arkady said.

"Well, yes." Bolot's deflation was only momentary. "But even if it were, the pilot would give it a wide berth. His instruments would stop working, for a start. You know the Bermuda Triangle? Cape Ryty's the Baikal Triangle." Aba scoffed. Bolot wagged his finger.

"Supposedly, evil spirits live there. Locals won't go near it. Even if their cattle wander off, they won't go after them. Boats go missing. Just the other day, one called the *Yamaha*. Clear day, good cell phone coverage, experienced sailors . . ." He clicked his fingers. "Gone! Vanished. They never found a thing. Not a single piece of wreckage. As if it had been swallowed up by the lake itself. There was another one when the crew came back with thick beards and said they'd been gone for weeks, but they'd only been out for the afternoon. Can you imagine?"

Yes, Arkady thought, that he could easily imagine.

"There's always a reason for that kind of thing," Aba said.

"Like what?"

"Storms, hurricanes, typhoons. Enough of these things happen, and people panic and make it a myth."

Arkady looked at Bolot's phone. Little bits of slickly edited Kuznetsov should anchor him to the here and now, to the rational, to the secular, to the world he understood. He listened.

"I believe in government by parliament, by the representatives of the people. So the first thing I would do as president is reinstate term limits. Yes, I'm campaigning to do myself out of a job."

Gogol would have gotten a novel out of that, Arkady thought: the man who wanted to abolish himself. More likely a novella. A short story, definitely.

They touched down in Irkutsk ahead of time, which had everything to do with the ludicrously flexible timetable and nothing to do with the plane or the pilot. Outside the terminal building, they bargained a taxi driver down to a third of his asking price.

• • •

Dorzho lived in a district of tower blocks that came in every shade of gray.

Dorzho lived on the fourth floor of one of the identikit tower blocks. The elevator, predictably, stank of urine. Equally predictable, it didn't work. Arkady wondered when it had last worked. About the same time as it hadn't reeked of piss, he figured, the day it had been installed.

They climbed the outside stairs. Arkady took them steadily and they discussed what to do next. Arkady let them talk while he caught his breath.

"Let's kick the door down," said Aba. "It would give us the element of surprise."

"Or just annoy them," said Bolot.

"Where's a bear when you need one?" Aba said. He looked anxiously at Arkady the moment he said this, but Arkady just laughed.

"We knock," Arkady said. "No point starting things off on the wrong foot."

They knocked. There was no answer.

"Now can we kick the door down?" asked Aba.

Arkady gave him the smile of an indulgent uncle. "No need."

Bolot looked around anxiously as though expecting Dorzho to come around the corner with a posse of fellow boxers.

Aba said nothing. If he'd been a dog, Arkady thought, he'd have had his tongue hanging out in anticipation. Arkady reached into his pocket and brought out a small leather kit, which he opened to reveal a series of small tools.

"Lock picks?" Aba asked.

"Investigator issue."

The picks were small and fiddly, hard enough to use under normal circumstances, let alone with a broken arm. He handed them to Aba like a graduation gift and told Aba which one to take out and how to insert it in the lock. Only then, with his good hand, did Arkady manipulate it the way he'd been taught so long ago that Brezhnev and his eyebrows were still running the place.

He felt rather than heard the click of the tumblers disengaging. He withdrew the pick from the lock.

"Ah," said Aba.

He insisted on going in first. He was the largest, the strongest, the youngest, which made him the most qualified to deal with Dorzho. Arkady followed, with Bolot bringing up the rear.

The apartment was small and just the right side of squalid. Dirty dishes were piled high in the kitchen sink. Boxing magazines were spread across the floor. Sheets, duvet, and pillows were all russet brown, a shade that could hide any number of stains.

"Right," Arkady said. "Let's see what we can find."

What he found was ten thousand dollars in a variety of denominations under the mattress, a hiding place so unoriginal that he had almost not bothered to look there. In the bedroom closet were a pair of outdoor boots crusted with cement. On the kitchen table Aba picked up three maps that, between them, covered most of Kuznetsov's and Benz's oil fields. Kuznetsov's wells were rings in red marker.

"Look at this," Bolot said. He handed Arkady a bull sniper rifle.

"This is promising," Arkady said. "It's chambered for subsonic rounds. It could be the rifle that shot at me at the ice festival." He thought at the time that the shooter had been either the best shot in the world or the worst. Obviously, he was a real marksman if this was the gun that had killed Benz and Georgy.

He sensed rather than saw Dorzho emerge through the door and lunge toward him. He raised his arm in defense knowing that it was the one that had been broken and that it was going to hurt.

Aba came from seemingly nowhere to knock Dorzho off-balance. Down they went, Dorzho flailing with punches, but he couldn't quite get enough weight behind them. Aba sensibly chose to fight dirty. Bolot hopped around them, trying to get close enough to help Aba.

Aba jabbed with hard fingers, going for the eyes. Dorzho clutched his hands to his face.

Aba took advantage of the momentary lull to sit on Dorzho's chest, allowing Bolot to pin Dorzho's legs to the floor.

"We just want to talk," Arkady said.

"Fuck you. I can't see."

"Take your hands away from your eyes."

Dorzho did, slowly and reluctantly. His left eye was red.

"If they get off you, will you talk to us?" Arkady asked.

"Who the fuck are you?"

"Investigator Arkady Renko. This is Aba, a friend, and this is Bolot, my factotum."

"Your what?"

"My associate," Arkady said. Bolot looked pleased at the promotion.

"How did you know where to find me?" Dorzho asked.

"Kuznetsov told me."

Even prone, Dorzho seemed to slump slightly. "Okay."

This in itself told Arkady that Kuznetsov hadn't warned Dorzho in advance.

Arkady motioned for Bolot and Aba to let Dorzho go. They climbed off warily. "There's vodka in the kitchen," Dorzho said.

Fair bet there was also botulism, listeria, and the basic materials for a biological weapon, Arkady thought.

"We're fine," he said. "Mind if we go outside and talk?" He needed to get some air.

"Maybe you would like to see my beehives."

"You have hives?" Aba asked.

"Yes. Come see. They're wintering now."

They walked to the backyard, where hives stood under a thin layer of snow. Two or three bees flew in and out of the hives.

"Those are drones, on constant patrol," Dorzho said. "So, what did Kuznetsov tell you?"

Arkady bluffed. "That you killed Boris Benz and Georgy and left us for dead."

"Do you think that's true?"

"I don't know."

"I didn't know you were going to be there," Dorzho said after what could only have been half a minute. "I swear to you, that's the truth. I thought Benz was coming up alone."

Oddly enough, Arkady believed him.

Dorzho brought out a tray from his beehive to show Aba. Most of the bees slept in a wax comb, while a few stirred. They were honeybees, glossy creatures with bands of black and yellow.

"You need to move slowly around bees. The queen is always protected by worker bees, who will sting you if you move quickly. Otherwise, they're cool."

"Does she need protecting if no one's around?" Aba asked.

"Of course. There are always fucking wasps."

"Where did you learn about bees?" Aba asked.

"Young Pioneers."

Arkady needed to change the conversation from bees. "You knew Benz, obviously."

"Everyone knows Benz. I worked for him for almost a year." Dorzho's eyes narrowed. "How much did Kuznetsov tell you?"

"He's a busy man. Besides, I'd rather get it from the horse's mouth, so to speak."

Dorzho shrugged. "Benz came to me in Chita last year and asked if I wanted to work for him."

"Why you?"

Arkady watched the honeybees climb over each other.

"Why does a man like that ever need a man like me? Muscle. Protection. Doing the jobs others turn their noses up at. I did my time in the army, you know." He curled his lip slightly as he looked at Aba. "Never got to go to Chechnya."

Arkady shot Aba a look, but Aba simply smirked.

"What kind of jobs?" Arkady asked.

"You know the kind. When people need a little persuasion."

"What about Saran?"

"What about her?"

"You left her the moment Benz came calling?"

"I'm surprised she noticed."

Arkady waited for Dorzho to blame Saran or to insult her in some way, but he did neither.

"You didn't tell her you were going?" Arkady asked.

"No."

"Just walked out and never came back?"

"Yes."

Here in Irkutsk, Arkady thought, there was little chance of Dorzho bumping into Saran by chance. "So, what happened with Benz?"

"First few months, no problem. I did my job; he seemed happy with it."

"Had you ever met Kuznetsov?"

"A few times, when they did business together. Then, in the summer, Benz started to change."

"Change how?"

"He and Kuznetsov had been close. But then Benz put it out that Kuznetsov was ripping him off, and going back on agreements they'd made, and all that."

In other words, Arkady thought, standard criminal behavior. The surprise wasn't that Kuznetsov and Benz had fallen out. The surprise was that they'd worked harmoniously as long as they had.

"Do you have any evidence for this?"

"Like what?"

"I don't know. Documents?"

"Do I look like an accountant? A lawyer?"

Arkady silently conceded the point. "And then?"

"This went on for a while. And it got worse. Benz said he wanted to get back at Kuznetsov, and the best way to do that was to hit him where it hurt. He told me to go to the oil fields and meet Georgy, who was stationed there. He wanted me to mix up some concrete, pour it into the pipes, and cap them."

"And you did?"

"Of course. That's what he told me to do, so that's what I did. Took a long time, I can tell you. Those wells are deep. Georgy said they had drilled down so far that they reached hell."

"What did Kuznetsov do when he found out?"

"He wasn't happy, put it that way. Benz said that he'd heard it was the work of some eco-protesters."

Arkady remembered the story Tatiana had been looking at: the disruption of the razing of the land around prospective wells and displacing people who lived there.

"But the Buryat had nothing to do with it?"

"No. It was just me and Georgy."

"And Kuznetsov never suspected you?"

"He called me in when I was still working for Benz, and I thought he'd found out. I was ready to stonewall. But all he asked me was what Benz was paying me. I told him. He doubled it on the spot and told me I was now working for him. And then he told me to lay low for a while."

"And Benz?"

"When he rang, I told him I'd been called to a family emergency in Kaliningrad. It was the farthest place I could think of."

"Have you ever been there?"

"Never."

One bee climbed onto Arkady's coat sleeve. Another circled his collar. He realized they were Dorzho's weapon. It was almost comical.

"They won't sting," Dorzho said.

"What did Benz say when you told him?"

"He wasn't happy, put it that way."

Dorzho had used exactly the same phrase about Kuznetsov when he'd discovered the damage to the oil wells. Arkady wondered how elastic Dorzho's definition of "not happy" was. It probably covered everything from mild irritation to volcanic eruptions.

"Did he worry that you would tell Kuznetsov the truth about the wells?"

"I don't know. I couldn't tell him. Shit, I was the one who poured the concrete."

"And when I came to Irkutsk?"

"What do you mean?"

"You shot at me."

"I shot to miss. It was a rooftop shot. If I'd wanted to hit you, we wouldn't be having this conversation."

"Why did Kuznetsov order you to shoot at me?"

"He didn't. It was Benz."

"It was Benz?"

"It was the last job I did for him."

One by one the bees flew back to the tray Dorzho was holding.

"Benz ordered you to shoot at me?" Arkady found it hard to believe.

"For the second time, yes. And to miss."

"To persuade me to go back home, you mean?"

"I guess so."

"Why?"

Dorzho shrugged and gently slid the bees like a tray of jewels back into the hive. "That I don't know, but I guess he thought that you might find out something you shouldn't."

"Don't you worry that Kuznetsov will finger you for the murder of Benz and Georgy?"

"If he does that, people will know that he was behind it."

That wouldn't stop Kuznetsov. He could stand in Red Square with a megaphone and admit it all and he still wouldn't go to jail.

Perhaps it was just sensible planning. Murders between oligarchs had been commonplace in the nineties, when the Wild East was well named and the economy rapacious.

Why hadn't Benz reported that Kuznetsov was cheating him and why hadn't Kuznetsov revealed his suspicion that Benz was responsible for blocking his well and blowing up his tankers? Was it because they had once been friends?

Finally, Arkady understood. Kuznetsov's book. That was the lesson of prison, hard gained and never forgotten. You don't betray a friend.

38

Lisikhinskoe Cemetery was the largest in Irkutsk, a vast necropolis rich with gangsters, artists, and poets. The city had been home to dozens of cemeteries before the Revolution but now this was the only one that survived.

Pallbearers struggled under the weight of the coffin. Arkady knew there wasn't a body in there, so either the pallbearers were more accomplished actors than he would have given them credit for, or the undertakers had miscalculated the number of sandbags it would take to simulate the weight of Boris Benz. Russian coffins were usually left open, but not in this case. Meanwhile, bears would sooner or later find Benz where they had left him in the snow.

Arkady studied Benz's headstones. There was not one stone but three, a triptych of black marble with gold detailing. Each panel pictured Benz in a different aspect. Here he was standing in a double-breasted suit; there, sitting at a table with a cell phone; and, on another, dressed as a Cossack. It was a master-piece of vulgarity.

The smell of flowers was overwhelming. They were all imported, some presumably from vast distances. Arkady saw orchids, chrysanthemums, hydrangeas, roses, and tuberoses, splashes of color against winter's gray.

Pallbearers lowered the coffin into the grave. Kuznetsov stood motionless in dark glasses. Tatiana was next to him. To the casual observer, they looked like a couple.

Arkady didn't let his gaze linger on them too long. Instead he scanned the mourners, trying to work out who they were. Many were businessmen who had come to pay their respects; others were patrons of various social clubs and friends Benz had made in prison. Was the woman weeping silently beneath a black veil his widow? His mistress? His sister?

Arkady almost missed him. Zurin was standing at the end of a row, which was in itself unusual, as he always liked to be at the center of things. Because Arkady wasn't expecting the prosecutor to be there, it was a moment or two before his brain processed what his eyes told him. Even then, he might have dismissed him if Zurin hadn't tipped his hat.

They did not speak until the reception at the Marriott. The walls were edged with tables of blini, fish pie, and piroshki. Arkady could have ducked out, but whatever he did, wherever he went, Zurin would find him, so he might as well get it over with.

Zurin worked the room with the charm of an emissary sent

to patronize the natives: a hand on a shoulder here, a whispered aside there. He lingered long enough with each person so they would not feel cheated.

Zurin held a plate of *kulich*, a cake frosted and dotted with candies.

"You look surprised to see me here," Zurin said.

"Nothing you could do would surprise me," Arkady said.

Arkady could see Zurin parsing that sentence word by word for any sign of insolence.

"Let's see how true that is, shall we?" A serpentine playfulness vanished from Zurin's voice, and it was that change of tone that gave Arkady the sensation of standing on a precipice. He didn't know exactly what was coming, but he was sure that it wasn't going to be good.

"Walk with me," Zurin said. It was a command, not a request. He led Arkady out of the reception room and along a beige corridor. It was standard international hotel décor, all neutral colors and corporate minimalism. A matryoshka doll sat in an alcove, the sole concession to the locale. Hotels like this abounded around the world, all identical save for a single clichéd national identifier: a Maasai shield in Nairobi, a red bus in London, a bonsai tree in Tokyo.

Zurin pulled Arkady close in a bear hug. Arkady was disconcerted. It was a second, no more, before he realized what Zurin was doing. His hands were efficiently working down Arkady's back.

"I had to check."

"I didn't even know you'd be here. Why on earth would I be wearing a wire?"

"Nothing you could do would surprise me." Zurin tapped a quick text on his phone, sent it, and took a quick appraisal of Arkady's cuts and bruises. "I came to check on your progress."

"My progress?"

"Both personal and professional, of course."

"Well, I'm still here, on both counts."

"How are you recovering? Bear attacks can be very nasty."

Arkady doubted Zurin knew the first thing about bear attacks. Zurin's idea of a hike in the wilderness was walking his dog.

"But now you're up and about," Zurin continued, "and if I know you at all, you've been trying to find out who killed Boris Benz."

"I'm out of my jurisdiction here, as you know."

"Which doesn't stop you from asking around—unofficially, shall we say?"

Arkady had not survived either office politics or life in general by being free and easy with information that had come his way. He doubted that telling Zurin of his visit with Dorzho would be sensible. He didn't have any particular reason for this doubt, other than the obvious one; it was Zurin.

Arkady shrugged. "A little. But nothing as yet."

"I see."

Silence hung heavy between them.

"But I haven't come all this way just to check on the health of my number one investigator," Zurin said. "And, let's be honest, I haven't come just to pay my respects to Benz."

"You knew him, though."

Zurin waved a hand. "I know lots of people. So, if not Benz, then Kuznetsov. What do you know about him? You were supposed to report back to me on what he was up to."

246

"I only know what I see on the news."

"Your girlfriend has the inside track, right?" Arkady was silent. "Or is she no longer your girlfriend?" Zurin mimicked a weighing motion with his hands. "An investigator, washed up and burnt out, or a billionaire who fancies himself the next president."

Zurin clapped his hands together, a child suddenly bored with his game.

"Right. You know who I work for: Louis the Sixteenth, *'L'état, c'est moi.'*"

"The Fourteenth."

"Whatever. I'm just the prosecutor. The state is the president."

"Who will be returned to office in March."

"Of course. But Kuznetsov . . . Kuznetsov is a problem."

"Kuznetsov has no chance of victory. You know that. I know that. He knows that," Arkady said.

"Of course. He won't win. But he will gain support. Not just here but in the West too."

"The West can't vote for him."

"Don't be so literal, Renko. No, they can't vote for him, but they can put him on the front page of the *New York Times*; they can make him a poster boy for the movement against Putin. They can help him. Pressure through diplomatic channels. Propaganda pieces on the internet. Dark arts."

"The same dark arts they accuse us of," Arkady said.

"Of course. But whichever way you cut it, we're back at the same place. Kuznetsov is a problem."

"A problem for whom?"

"A problem for the president, of course. How would you do it, if you were me?" Zurin continued.

"Well, you can't buy him off."

"Why not?"

"First, he's too rich. Second, this isn't about money."

"Correct on both counts." Zurin wasn't asking him for advice, Arkady realized. He was leading Arkady down a path that he'd already mapped out. And where did that path end? Arkady wondered. Zurin, Kuznetsov, and Benz. How were they connected? He finally understood.

"You put Benz up to destroying Kuznetsov's oil rigs."

"Right."

"You backed Benz against Kuznetsov."

"Very good."

"You hoped that would be enough to dissuade Kuznetsov from running, while to the outside world it looked like another dispute between oligarchs."

"Ever since he's come out of prison, he's had this idea that he's a reformer, the new Tolstoy," Zurin said.

"There are worse ideas."

"Not where oil and politics are involved."

Zurin developed a smile.

"You want to kill Kuznetsov?" Arkady asked.

"Not exactly."

"What, then?"

"I want *you* to kill Kuznetsov."

39

When Arkady tried to grasp the insanity of Zurin's proposition, he had to laugh.

"What makes you think I would do that?"

Zurin stepped aside to let a busboy with a room service cart rattle by. "I know that Zhenya and his girlfriend are staying in your apartment, and my men know when they leave and where they go. I can make them disappear at any time."

"You're serious. You would have them killed?"

Zurin shrugged and made a phone call.

"Put Zhenya on the phone," he said.

Zurin turned the phone over to Arkady.

"Arkady?" said Zhenya. "Are you there?"

Arkady tried very hard to keep his voice from wavering. "Yes, Zhenya, I'm here. Where are you?"

"I'm playing chess in Gorky Park with two thugs hanging

over me. They took away our phones and they follow me wherever I go. Sosi too."

"How long have they been following you?"

"For the last two days. Can you tell these apes not to be such pussies and play me at chess? I've kicked their asses, like, a hundred times, and now they're refusing to play again even when I give them odds of a queen."

Arkady heard the fear behind the bravado. It was pure Zhenya.

Before Arkady had left Moscow for Siberia, Zhenya asked him what to do if the police came around. No guns, Arkady said, no guns and no resistance.

"Try to stay calm, they are just trying to scare you and me," he said.

Zurin was watching Arkady. He grabbed the phone and turned it off.

"A simple quid pro quo," Zurin said. "You kill Kuznetsov, the lovebirds go free."

There was no point in Arkady asking what would happen if he refused.

"Why me?" Arkady asked.

"Because you're the perfect candidate," Zurin said. He bounced on the balls of his feet, pleased with his own cleverness. "First, you can get close to him. Tatiana trusts you; therefore Kuznetsov trusts you. Second, you have a motive."

"I do?"

"Of course. Jealousy. You're crazed by love and unable to bear the thought of your woman going off with someone else."

There were times when that might have been true, Arkady conceded.

"Not to mention the fact that your struggle with the bear has left you mentally unbalanced."

"And then?"

"You'll be arrested and charged. A state psychiatrist will declare that you were temporarily insane at the time of the offense. You'll be sentenced and rehabilitated in a treatment center."

"An asylum, you mean."

"Always so blunt, aren't you? Yes, if you insist, an asylum. Then, after a year or two, you'll be released."

"And Tatiana?"

"Nothing happens to her. I doubt she'd ever speak to you again, of course, but you know: omelets and eggs and all that."

Shoot a man in cold blood, even knowing that Zhenya and Sosi's lives depended on it? He wasn't sure he could do it. In fact, he was sure he couldn't do it. Raising a gun, taking aim, pulling the trigger—all that required conscious volition. And it wasn't as if Kuznetsov's bodyguards would just be hanging around. They'd be on him in a second, probably less, even assuming he could get a weapon past them.

Zurin put his hand on Arkady's shoulder. "I know what you're thinking, Renko."

"You do? I don't."

"You're thinking one of two things."

"Go on."

"First, you're wondering whether you could arrange to have Kuznetsov arrested for something so that he would be out of reach. He could be arrested for Benz's murder, for a start. He was involved, I'm sure of it. I'm equally sure you know more than you're telling. But it doesn't matter. Arresting him just makes him a martyr. He will say it's a trumped-up charge, politically motivated. He has been in prison once, and he knows how well that plays to his supporters. So that's not going to happen."

"What's the other thing?"

"You're wondering how you could fake it. Make me think that Kuznetsov's dead, at least long enough to let Zhenya and the girl with purple hair go unharmed."

"I doubt you'd fall for that."

"You're right. No fuzzy photographs, no tomato sauce splashed around the place. This isn't amateur dramatics. When I'm satisfied that Kuznetsov's dead, I'll take away my men. Not before. You don't go through with it, then you know what happens. Same if you tell anyone about this." He smiled. "Come. Assassination is the natural order of things in politics. It's what people expect. Let's go back to the reception. They'll be wondering where we are."

It was neatly conceived, Arkady had to admit. Kuznetsov out of Putin's way, Arkady out of Zurin's. Was there a way out of it? He had no idea. Perhaps one would come to him in time, but right now he couldn't see how.

He remembered the Siberian dilemma he had discussed with Tatiana and Bolot around the fire that night in the snow. To stay underwater or to leap out? Well, this was another dilemma, and Zhenya had the word for it: "Zugzwang," a chess term meaning that any possible move would be fatal.

It could be the title of his memoirs written in the asylum, he thought.

40

The day after Benz's funeral, Tatiana, Arkady, and Bolot returned to Chita. Bolot and Aba drove his car from the airport,
dropping Tatiana off at the Montblanc and Arkady at the Admiral Kolchak.

Saran hurried across the hotel lobby to greet Arkady.

"Dorzho called. He wanted to know if I had led you to him."

"It doesn't sound like it was a friendly call."

"For him it was."

"That's good. Has he always liked bees?"

"He *only* likes bees, but the interesting thing is he hates
wasps, and it's very difficult to tell them apart. The greatest ex-
perts in the field can't tell bees and wasps apart, but Dorzho can
and he hates them."

"You can tell the difference, right?"

"Don't worry, he also told me to keep my mouth shut and stay
out of his life."

• • •

Back in his hotel room, Arkady continued to worry about Kuznetsov. He remembered a funeral he'd attended in Moscow in his early years: a gang lord who'd been killed by his main rival, not on his orders but by him personally, by his own hands, strangled in a *banya* where the two of them had been trying to parcel out their businesses. Tradition dictated that gang leaders had to kiss the corpse of a fallen peer, and failure to do so equaled an admission of culpability. It was a charade that was followed even when everyone knew who the guilty party was.

This particular funeral had been attended by pretty much every oligarch, most of them with colorful noms de guerre, like Ivan the Hand, Cyclops, the Scar, and Zhivago. They all kissed the corpse—everyone but the man responsible—and a shootout followed.

Arkady wondered whether Kuznetsov would have kissed Benz's corpse had it been there. Maybe customs seemed different now, but, deep down, Russia was still the same.

The schemes that ran through Arkady's mind were so convoluted that he felt the onset of vertigo. Every plan he considered meant that too many things had to happen at just the right time.

He wanted to talk to someone—anyone—but he knew that telling another person about Zurin's threat would merely implicate him without alleviating any of his own angst. In other words, a problem shared was a problem doubled rather than halved.

Victor, however, was someone he could talk to, someone who would understand and had a talent for scheming.

Arkady called him.

"That bastard Zurin," Victor said. "I guess he's closer to Putin than we thought. I wish we could send him back to Cuba. Let me take care of the thugs following Zhenya."

"That will get you killed. These men have automatic weapons," Arkady said.

"Can you fake Kuznetsov's assassination?"

"Zurin won't buy it. And part of the problem is that people around here are so in love with Kuznetsov, they won't let it go; they'll demand answers."

"Tatiana faked her own murder in Moscow."

"Yes, but that was a long time ago, and the two cases are totally different. A journalist can skip town and lay low, but a presidential candidate is another matter. I don't think it can be done."

"Well, with that attitude, you're fucked."

He knew that he could assassinate Kuznetsov. He'd been in his presence often enough to be accepted as part of the furniture. Kuznetsov's bodyguards no longer stopped him, let alone patted him down. Perhaps the solution was to kill Zurin, but that wouldn't solve anything, because it wasn't Zurin who wanted Kuznetsov dead. The order to kill him had come from the Kremlin.

The next morning Bolot joined Arkady for a stroll around Chita, stopping for a coffee here and a bracing glass of brandy there.

"How is the investigation going?" Bolot asked.

"Not very well," Arkady said. He didn't feel like lying to Bolot.

Generally, when people asked, he told them he was digging into Benz's affairs and hoped that no one realized that he was going through the motions.

He changed the subject. "Do you think Aba would like to go back to Moscow with me? Or is his brother, Bashir, still a threat?"

"According to Aba's mother, he's fled Moscow, so I think Aba might want to go back. I know his mother wants him back."

They stopped for lunch in the lobby of the Montblanc, where Tatiana invited them to watch the opinion polls come in. A wave of support was apparently building. The whole thing seemed like some form of performance art. Arkady wondered whether any of it was true or, perhaps more precisely, whether any of it mattered.

Did a woman in Kazan feel positively about a Kuznetsov video? Did either candidate really impact her life? Would she vote for Kuznetsov on polling day? Would she encourage others to vote? Would any of those votes be counted, or would they just be ignored? "Seventy-seventy" was what Kuznetsov had told him and Tatiana. The authorities wanted a seventy percent turnout and a seventy percent vote for Putin.

"Would you like to come with me to Olkhon Island tomorrow?" Tatiana asked. "We're taping another commercial. In front of a crowd this time."

Arkady had no interest in watching Kuznetsov play to another crowd.

"If that's the only way I can see you, then yes."

41

A train shimmered on the horizon.

"Don't worry," Bolot said. "I see it too."

Arkady wondered how many of his thoughts Bolot could read. "You do?"

"Sure. It's a mirage."

"I thought mirages were only found in deserts."

"A meteorologist explained it to me. Something to do with layers of air that distort the light off ice."

"Or they could just be glimpses of another world."

Bolot smiled. "Maybe I can make a shaman out of you after all."

Arkady, Tatiana, and Bolot were going back to Olkhon Island, this time to watch photographers take photos and videos of Kuznetsov.

. . .

"Today I pledge a billion rubles to the people of Siberia, to do for you what Decembrists did for your ancestors. Where you need schools, I will build them. Where you need hospitals, I will build them. Where you need houses, and sports facilities, and theaters, I will build them."

They stood five meters from Kuznetsov. The bodyguards were farther away, making sure they weren't in the video.

Tatiana took notes. "He's going to repeat the same campaign speech three more times today."

Kuznetsov continued, "The Decembrists were not idle in exile. They established schools, a foundling hospital, and a theater for the local population. They saw what I have seen, what every true Russian can see: that here, in Siberia, lies the soul and the future of Russia."

Meaning oil, thought Arkady. The depth of Kuznetsov's ambition was far greater than Arkady had given him credit for. Then came the masterstroke.

"Today I also renounce my interests in all Siberian oil fields. Oil, the source of our wealth, is being drained by vultures. We must change that.

"Our country needs energy in the future, but we also need to preserve our ecology. In particular we need to preserve this, the largest and purest lake in the world."

Arkady looked at Tatiana, a half smile on her face.

Kuznetsov's part was done. His next stop was at the north end of the lake. It was one of the places he'd earmarked for building a school, and there was no time like the present for getting on with that.

The film crew would stay to take some footage of the island and add special effects that would give Kuznetsov a heroic cast. Really, a billion rubles ought to make anyone look heroic, Arkady thought.

"Will I see you later?" Tatiana asked Arkady as she followed Kuznetsov toward the helicopter.

"What time will you be back?" he asked.

She laughed. "Who knows? All this time following Mikhail around, and you still ask me that? How long is a piece of string? I'll be back when I'm back. Wait for me."

Arkady luxuriated in a cigarette and watched as Tatiana and Kuznetsov climbed up into the helicopter. Then he joined Bolot for the long ride back to Chita.

Bolot drove off the island and was steering the car carefully onto the ice, when Arkady's cell phone rang.

"Tatiana?" he said.

"Arkady." She had to shout to be heard over the noise of the engine.

"The helicopter. Something's wrong."

"What's the pilot doing?"

"I don't know. Arkady, I'm . . ." Her voice faded in a hiss of static, but he knew what she'd been about to say: that she was scared. Her voice was bouncing in and out of range and suddenly she was back, so clear that she could have been right there in the car with them. ". . . says the tail rudder is stuck."

There was shouting in the background, voices urgent with fear.

"Where are they?" asked Bolot. "Ask her where they are."

"Where are you?" Arkady asked.

Silence for long seconds. Bolot was still driving, but at a crawl. "I know where they are," he said.

Arkady thought back. On the plane to Irkutsk, with Bolot leaning across him to point at the lake below. "See that place? The pilot will give it a wide berth."

"Tatiana? Are you still there?"

"Yes. We're going down!"

"Are you over Cape Ryty?"

"Where?"

"Ask the pilot."

"He's trying to . . ."

"Ask him!"

He heard her yell, once, twice, and another voice shout back at her.

"Yes," she said. "Cape Ryty. Oh, Arkady, please . . ."

"Brace," he said. "Head, legs, and arms in the brace position. You hear me?"

"Yes."

"And close your eyes when you hit. You don't want fuel in them."

As the line went dead, Bolot was already pulling at the wheel. The car drifted in a long, wide skid. The ice boomed beneath them as Bolot drove. He had a compass on the dashboard, but he didn't look at it, not once. Arkady saw that it was spinning this way and that, even though, as far as he could make out, they were heading straight ahead.

Bolot's knuckles were white on the wheel.

"Only for you would I do this," said Bolot. He scanned the

ice ahead, reading it, knowing instinctively where it was safe and where it was not. The ice beneath them was solid. "Hold on," he said.

Arkady watched a crack spread across their path as far as he could see in both directions.

"That's about a meter wide," Bolot said.

"How do you know?" Arkady couldn't possibly have judged it from this far away.

"I know those cracks. And this one, by the look of it, extends probably forty meters."

"So how do we get around it?"

"We don't."

"You're going to jump it?"

"You have a better idea?"

Arkady conceded that he didn't.

"Put your hand on the door handle," Bolot said.

"Why?"

"So you can get out fast if I don't make the jump."

The handle was on Arkady's right, so he had to twist his body to use his left hand.

Bolot pressed the accelerator to the floor, not all in one go but gradually so as not to spin the wheels and lose traction. Arkady had the curious sensation of floating.

As the crack neared, Arkady checked that his seat belt was undone and braced his feet against the floor.

There was a slight ridge on the near side of the crack. Arkady felt the car lift as it crested the ridge and then they were flying, not far but far enough. The thump as they landed jolted him abruptly from his seat and he smacked his head on the roof. The steering wheel bucked in Bolot's hands. Rather than fight it, he held it lightly, steering into the skid until he had the car under control. He gently corrected back to the course they had been on before.

"There," Bolot said.

"Where?"

Bolot pointed toward the horizon. "There."

"I don't see it."

"I do," Bolot said.

Half a minute later Arkady saw it too. The helicopter was on its side like a stricken bird, half in and half out of the water where the impact had cracked ice.

How long had it been down? How hard had they hit? How deep had it gone?

Bolot rolled to a halt as near as he dared.

"Watch your footing," he said. "The ice will be weak where it's hit. You go under, you're not coming back up again."

Arkady nodded but he was already half out of the car. That Tatiana was still alive was the first thing he saw. She was still alive, and she was in the part of the cabin that was still above the waterline.

Her face was streaked with blood. Arkady could smell hydraulic fluid and gasoline. Kuznetsov was next to her, only just conscious. They had been in the back of the cabin, and the helicopter had gone into the lake nose first. Under the water, Arkady could see the bodies of those who had been farther forward. The crew and bodyguards were slumped, lifeless, and covered with blood.

Tatiana could not get out by herself.

Bolot was next to Arkady. He pointed to the ice between them and the helicopter. It was broken and slushy.

"Spread your weight," he said. "Walk like a crab."

"What about you?"

"I'll be behind you but at a distance. I don't want to put too much weight on the ice."

Arkady took a step toward the helicopter. His feet were frozen and numb. The ice moved beneath him.

"Wider," Bolot yelled. "Feet wider."

Arkady did so.

"Better."

"It feels wrong."

"Trust me."

Another step, legs so wide apart that Arkady could feel the strain on the insides of his thighs. And another.

"Left," Bolot said. "Take a step to your left."

"Why?"

"The ice in front of you isn't safe."

To Arkady, the two pieces looked alike, but he knew that when it came to ice, Bolot could see what he could not. He stepped to the left.

"Now straight ahead to the helicopter," Bolot said. "Slowly."

If it went wrong now, Arkady knew, he would go under. In these temperatures, that would be it. Worse, Tatiana would have no chance.

As he made it to the helicopter, the ice groaned. It rocked and settled.

Tatiana was near him, with Kuznetsov on the far side of her. She had her seat belt off. Arkady would have to use his bad arm as well as his good one to reach in and get her out. He moved to put his foot onto the sill of the helicopter for extra purchase.

"No!" Bolot yelled.

"Tatiana," Arkady said, "get yourself to me." They were a

meter apart, no more. She was wedged between her seat and the one in front, which had become detached from its mounting. "Can you do that?"

"I don't know. It hurts."

"I know it does. But you have to."

She pushed feebly against the seat back and cried in pain. "I can't."

Again a slight shift in the helicopter's position.

"You can do this," he said softly.

He saw the agony etched on her face as she summoned resolve. She twisted herself to get one leg free, and even in such cold she was sweating.

Arkady smiled, encouraging, reaching out to her. Tatiana pulled at her other leg. It didn't move. Arkady looked closer.

"Twist your foot," he said. "It's stuck against the seat strut."

Tatiana looked down, as though her foot were an alien entity. She twisted it and this time her other leg came free.

The helicopter lurched. A movement of half a meter, maybe more. Frigid water splashed against Arkady's shins.

It was about to go, Arkady knew. Lusud Khan was about to pull its prey all the way down.

Tatiana faced him.

"Jump," Arkady said. "Tatiana, jump to me."

Tatiana's eyes focused with fear and determination. Arkady held his arms out and she jumped.

There was a great rush as the helicopter finally lost its balance and plunged fully into the lake with Kuznetsov still in his seat.

Arkady lay flat on the ice with Tatiana on top of him. Bolot pulled them both away from the gaping, swirling hole made by helicopter's descent.

Arkady looked back.

Kuznetsov was beneath the surface, looking up through ice and water. He moved suddenly, striking hard for the surface. He broke into open air with a gasp as loud as a scream. His hands scrabbled for a solid edge in the ice. His head went under once more as he dunked to give himself momentum, and then he was up and out and standing on the ice. His face was flushed with pride and resignation, defiance and acceptance, and that was how they watched him die.

42

Saying good-bye to Saran was like saying good-bye to a child.

"Can we sit over there?" Arkady pointed to the couch in the corner.

Saran moved from behind her desk.

She looked at his travel bag. "Will you ever come back?"

"Yes, but not for a while."

"That means never, right?"

"No, it doesn't mean never. Would you ever leave your mother's mahjong parlor and come to Moscow?"

"I think I'd rather go to Paris," she said wistfully. "Anyway, you're already taken."

"That doesn't mean we can't be friends."

"Yes it does."

"We can talk on the phone and you can send me stories you write."

"Maybe." Her eyes brimmed with tears. She touched the scar on his forehead as if to capture it before it faded. "I wish you could slay a dragon for me."

"I would if I could."

She hugged him tightly and then broke away.

Bolot was waiting outside the hotel to take Arkady to the airport where Tatiana would meet him.

"I thought Aba was coming with us," Arkady said.

"No, he's staying a little longer. He's in the middle of an epic poem. On the scale of Pushkin, he says."

"Why not?"

Arkady didn't know how he was going to say good-bye to his friend and factotum, a man who had saved his life more than once.

"I'm too useful," Bolot said. "You need someone like me to keep you out of trouble, especially if you meet a bear."

"On the streets of Moscow, that's usually not a problem," Arkady said.

"What about the prosecutor? What kind of reception will he give you in Moscow?" Bolot asked.

"He wouldn't dare reprimand me. After all, I know about his Cuban mistress."

Bolot cackled. "You wouldn't use that against him again."

"No, but he doesn't know that."

· · ·

Arkady would miss his factotum, but he imagined them climbing Olkhon Island again. They would pick up at the exact point they'd left off. Arkady could almost hear the murmur of the drums.

MOSCOW

43

Back at their apartment in Moscow, Arkady found a note from Zhenya saying that he and Sosi would come back later that afternoon. He had left pastries on the kitchen table for Arkady and Tatiana. They made tea and sat across the table from each other. She reached for his hand and traced the lines on his palm.

"Do you believe in this sort of thing?" she asked.

"More all the time."

"I wish I could remember which line will tell me if you still love me."

"I couldn't stop even when I wanted to. I never will stop."

"It's hard to believe after all I put you through."

"I'm incorrigible."

He walked around the table, lifted her up, and wrapped his arms around her. He kissed her mouth, her cheek, and forehead. He kissed her again in the warm well of her neck and set her back down in her chair. She sat dazed.

Finally she said, "We need to visit Obolensky and drop off the article."

"Are you sure?" he asked.

"I promised him I would."

They walked along the Moscow River as swallows darted around the crenellations of the Kremlin wall.

"Did you finish reading the article?" Tatiana asked.

"I thought it was good. It reminded me of *Monsters of the Deep*, one of Saran's books."

"Other than that," she said.

"I would say that your prose floated as softly as blini."

"Don't tease."

"Okay, then I have to say it was excellent and will get you in a great deal of trouble. You're going to need a bodyguard."

"That means it is good."

"Yes."

They stopped on the Moscow Bridge to watch ice break and grind in the water below. At the far end of the bridge, protesters gathered with party horns and paper crowns in an ironic tribute to the latest coronation. With a fourth term secured, Putin now reigned longer than any ruler since Stalin.

ACKNOWLEDGMENTS

I am a lucky man surrounded by friends. The kind of work I do is exhausting and, without the help of these friends, impossible. My thanks go to Nell and Nelson Branco, who were willing to read my manuscript again and again; to Luisa Smith, my invaluable travel companion with a magic camera; to Don Sanders for his help in making the Siberian trip happen; and to Sam Smith for his great moral support.

Where do these people come from? Arkady Persov from Irkutsk generously entertained us while showing us his city and the natural wonders of Lake Baikal. Sean Manning, my editor at Simon & Schuster, came up with excellent ideas for the book and patiently encouraged me to take the time I needed. Lyuba Vinogradova has been my brilliant translator and research assistant for more than twenty years. She traveled from Mozambique to Siberia to be part of the team. Finally, there is

Andrew Nurnberg, my loyal friend and agent for almost forty years. He has traveled with me on research trips to Siberia, Moscow, Tver, Berlin, and Havana and always kept his sense of humor.

These friends buoy me up and keep me on my feet.

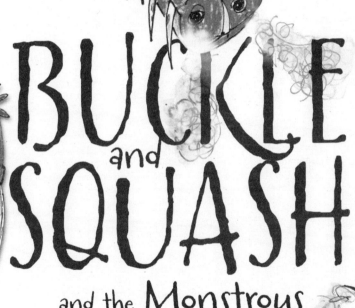

BUCKLE and SQUASH

and the Monstrous Moat-Dragon

SARAH COURTAULD

MACMILLAN CHILDREN'S BOOKS

First published 2014 by Macmillan Children's Books
a division of Macmillan Publishers Limited
20 New Wharf Road, London N1 9RR
Basingstoke and Oxford
Associated companies throughout the world
www.panmacmillan.com

ISBN 978-1-4472-5555-0

Text and illustrations copyright © Sarah Courtauld 2014

The right of Sarah Courtauld to be identified as the
author and illustrator of this work has been asserted by her in
accordance with the Copyright, Designs and Patents Act 1988.

All rights reserved. No part of this publication may be
reproduced, stored in or introduced into a retrieval system, or
transmitted, in any form or by any means (electronic, mechanical,
photocopying, recording or otherwise), without the prior written
permission of the publisher. Any person who does any unauthorized
act in relation to this publication may be liable to criminal
prosecution and civil claims for damages.

1 3 5 7 9 8 6 4 2

A CIP catalogue record for this book is available from
the British Library.

Printed and bound by CPI Group (UK) Ltd, Croydon CR0 4YY

This book is sold subject to the condition that it shall not,
by way of trade or otherwise, be lent, resold, hired out,
or otherwise circulated without the publisher's prior consent
in any form of binding or cover other than that in which
it is published and without a similar condition including this
condition being imposed on the subsequent purchaser.

For Eliza and Beatrice

BRISTOL CITY COUNCIL
LIBRARY SERVICES
WITHDRAWN AND OFFERED FOR SALE
SOLD AS SEEN

SALE
WITHDRAWN AND OFFERED FOR SALE
SOLD AS SEEN

Once upon a time, when the world was full of princes and princesses, knights and damsels, dragons and lady dragons, it was also full of mud.

Squelchy, squishy, gurgling, sticky, stinky, endless, mud-coloured mud.

To the two young girls cleaning out their goat pen, it seemed as if there was an infinite supply of mud in the field behind their old tumbledown farm, which was called Old Tumbledown Farm, in their village in the middle of nowhere, which was called The Middle of Nowhere, in a forgotten corner of the kingdom, which was called The Forgotten Corner of the Kingdom, deep in the realm of Squerb.

I said that they were both cleaning out the goat pen, but that wasn't totally true. Eliza was inside the goat pen, shovelling the mud, while her older sister Lavender was *outside* the goat pen 'supervising' her (if by 'supervising' you mean 'reading an enormous book of fairy tales, while wearing a pointy princess hat'). Occasionally, Lavender put the book down and burst into song:

'Ooh, Prince Charming
How handsome you are!
With a steed so shiny
And your hair so shiny
And your teeth so shiny
And your nose so shiny
Oooooh, Prince Charming . . . you are a prince.'

Inside the goat pen, Eliza gritted her teeth.

She was used to the way her sister's songs rhymed 'prince' with 'prince', 'shiny' with 'shiny', and 'princess' with 'bucketful of hens'. But that didn't mean she liked it. As Lavender started on the second verse, Eliza stopped shovelling mud and stuck her spade into the ground.

'You know, ever since you got that book of fairy tales,' she said, 'you've been unbelievably—'

'Princess-like?' said Lavender. 'I know! When I learn French, I'm going to sing all my songs *en français*, and then they'll sound even better.'

Eliza exchanged a look of despair with Gertrude, their goat, who was sitting at the other end of the pen, quietly chewing.

Admittedly, Eliza didn't really know what Gertrude was thinking. But she was pretty sure they understood one another.*

Then, for one beautiful moment, Lavender's singing stopped.

You could almost hear the grass growing, the sun shining, and the moles playing Snap underground.

* What *was* Gertrude thinking really? Was she thinking: 'I couldn't agree more. Lavender is the worst singer since Sister Margaret released her album *Songs for Phlegmy Voices*'? Or was she thinking: 'I am a magical time-travelling goat from outer space and, WOW, do I regret landing here rather than my intended destination in the year 215346B, where goats are worshipped and float around on silver cushions in the sky'?

Or was she just thinking 'Yum' because she had just gobbled one of Eliza's socks off the washing line?

We'll never know.

It didn't last.

'A knight!' Lavender cried, looking out across the field. 'A knight upon the high road! I may faint!'

Eliza looked up, and saw a small, bald man ambling down the path towards them from the direction of their local village, The Middle of Nowhere.

'That's not a knight,' said Eliza. 'That's Bob.'

'It is a knight, riding upon a steed!'

'No, it's Bob. Carrying some post.'

'It *is* a knight,' Lavender hissed. 'I'm going to faint!'

As Bob ambled along the path past Old Tumbledown Farm, he whistled at Eliza and chucked her a scroll. And, true to her word, Lavender sighed and fell to the ground at the sight of him, as if she had just been tapped on the head by a large, invisible spoon.

'Well?' Lavender whispered to Eliza, as she lay sprawled on the grass with her eyes firmly shut. 'How would you rate my faint? Out of ten?'

'I thought you had fainted,' said Eliza.

'I have!' Lavender hissed back. 'I'd just like some

feedback, that's all. How was the faint, overall? Out of ten? Maybe a seven? Do you think that yonder knight is in love with me?'

Eliza looked at her sister, and then looked at Bob, who was walking away down the path, scratching his bum.

And she knew the scroll she was holding in her hands was only going to make things worse.

'He's probably in love with me,' said Lavender. 'I must compose him a poem, telling him how sad I am to reject his love, for I am destined to marry a prince.'

Eliza *really* didn't want to give her sister the scroll in her hands. She knew it was only going to encourage her. Perhaps if she just quietly gave it to Gertrude, Gertrude would gobble it up, and Lavender would never—

'What's that? Is it for me?' said Lavender, springing to her feet and plucking the scroll from Eliza's hands. She broke the seal, and the scroll sprang open.

'Oooh – Prince Rudolph!'

As Eliza had predicted, it was a portrait of a prince. Lavender already had seven in her collection.

'Lavender,' said Eliza. 'Do you think you could just help me clean out the goat pen? Because after we do that, we need to feed the chickens. And then the pigs. And then we have to cut the grass . . .'

But Lavender had already skipped into the house to stick the prince's portrait to her bedroom wall. She spent the rest of the afternoon there gazing at it and daydreaming about her destiny, which was almost certainly going to feature a handsome prince.

And Eliza spent the rest of the day working in the fields, daydreaming about *her* destiny. *She* wasn't

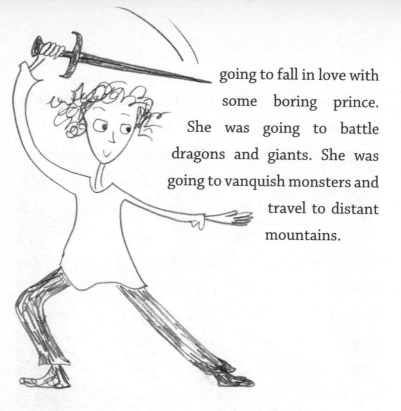

going to fall in love with some boring prince. She was going to battle dragons and giants. She was going to vanquish monsters and travel to distant mountains.

And she was going to solve mysteries like: *Who ate all the food in the pig pen?*

And:

Is the incredibly haunted forest really incredibly haunted? Or is it just moderately haunted?

And:

What really happened to Grandpa Joe?

Ever since that terrible day of calamity, the day which no one ever talked about, the day when Eliza and Lavender's parents had dressed up as trees for the village festival and been accidentally eaten by a bear, Eliza and Lavender had been looked after by Grandma Maud and Grandpa Joe.

Every day, Grandma Maud fed the pigs and the goat, and then sat in her sitting room, telling people's fortunes, while Grandpa Joe sat next door, where he worked as a tailor, making his warm and sometimes unusual clothes. Until one day, when Grandpa Joe went out to get some milk.

And then he came back with the milk.

And then he went out to get some air.

And then he came back with the air.

And then he went out to get a paper.

And *then* he never came back.

And no one knew what had happened to him, least of all Grandma Maud. Whenever Eliza asked her, she just said, 'Oh, who can say? Perhaps he fell into the Chasm of Infinite Darkness, from which no living soul has ever returned. Or perhaps he just got lost on the way to the shops. I suppose we'll never know.'

As Eliza worked, she imagined her way out of The Middle of Nowhere. She imagined slicing the heads off fire-breathing dragons. She imagined bopping wild beasts on the nose and making them cry. She imagined climbing down into the Chasm of Infinite Darkness and finding her grandpa.

And while Eliza imagined, Gertrude spent the rest of the afternoon sitting in her pen, chewing over *her* destiny. And who *knew* what that would involve?

That night, the two sisters were tucked up in bed while Grandma Maud read them a soothing bedtime story. Like many of Grandma Maud's bedtime stories, this one began with the fact that someone called William owed her fifteen silver pieces, and ended with every single symptom of the Black Death.

'And from that day on, he was covered in spots,' she said serenely. 'And then came the lumps. And then his skin started to wither. And then he collapsed. And then his fingers fell off. And then his legs fell off. And then he died.' She smiled. 'The end. Would you like another story?'

'No thanks, Grandma,' said Eliza.

'Wonderful!' said Grandma Maud. 'How about *The Tale of the Little Boy and the Very Deep Well*? Or how about *Young Alexandra and the Pirates Who Completely Murdered Her*? Of course there's always *Lamby the Lamb and the Delicious Sunday Lunch* . . .'

'NO THANK YOU, Grandma,' said Eliza and Lavender.

'Oh well. Suit yourselves,' said Grandma Maud, heaving herself out of the chair and shuffling over to the door. 'Goodnight, sleep tight, and don't let the Black Death get you in the night!'

'We won't!'

'Or the Shrinking Lurgy!'

'We won't.'

'Or the Incredibly Fatal Hiccups!'

'We WON'T,' said Lavender and Eliza.

'Or just the Fatal Hiccups. Of course, there's nothing you can do, if they do come.'

She shrugged, bent down to blow out the candle and shut the door behind her.

'Night, Lavender,' yawned Eliza, curling up under her covers.

'Night,' said Lavender, leaping out of bed and lighting the candle again.

Lavender gazed up at all her portraits of princes on the wall. There was:

Prince Fabian the Bold

Prince Arjuna the Italic

<u>Prince Alan
the Underlined</u>

'Goodnight, **Prince Fabian**,' Lavender began. 'Goodnight, *Prince Arjuna* . . .'

'I AM TRYING TO SLEEP,' said Eliza.

'Goodnight, <u>Prince Alan</u>,'

'Did you hear what I said?'

But Lavender carried on, right through the list.

'And goodnight to you, Prince Rudolph the Unusual!' Lavender said finally. 'I may not be able to see your face, but I still love you.'

Prince Chlknklkgkfj the Unpronounceable

Prince Orhan the Orphan

Eliza sat up in bed. This was too much.

'Lavender?'

'Yes?'

'You do not love him. You don't *know* him! You've never met him! You don't even know what he looks like!' She jumped out of bed. 'Nobody does! Look at that picture! He's holding a hawk in front of his face!'

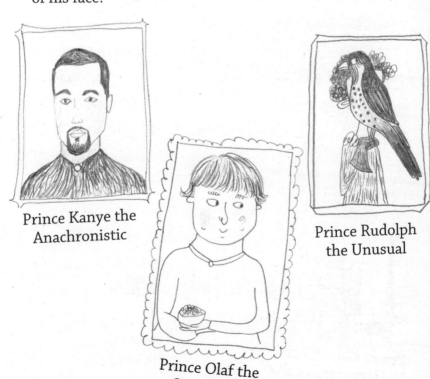

Prince Kanye the Anachronistic

Prince Olaf the Simply Fat

Prince Rudolph the Unusual

'Well,' said Lavender, 'it's not *his* fault his mother was married to his uncle, who was also a horse. He is a prince, and one day I'm going to marry a prince. And—'

'Look,' said Eliza. 'You have to face it. You're never going to be rescued by a prince. We live on a farm. We're just ordinary people. We're not noble ladies. Grandpa didn't even have a coat of arms.'

'Yes he did!' said Lavender.

'All right,' said Eliza. 'He did have a coat of arms. But that was just because his designs were . . . a bit . . . unusual. I think maybe he was ahead of his time.'

'Not *that* coat of arms. *This* one!' Lavender ran over to the very, very dusty wooden box in the corner. It had an old coat of arms painted on it, and you could make out the words 'Buckle and Squash' written across it.

'Here we go,' said Eliza.

'You *see*,' said Lavender. 'We come from a noble family. *Bouclay et Squash*!' (Lavender pronounced Buckle 'Bouclay'.) 'That is our family motto. Which clearly refers to the noble family Bouclay, and the Squash, which is, of course, the vegetable of the Royal Family of Squerb.'

Eliza folded her arms and frowned. 'No it isn't!' she said. 'That's not what Buckle and Squash means! Firstly, you don't even know where that comes from. Secondly, our ancestors were outlaws.'

'Outlaws?'

'They stole from the rich and gave to the poor. Their motto was "Buckle and Squash", because that was how they fought.'

'That makes no sense whatsoever.'

'Of course it does. "Buckle" stands for the buckle of a sword belt, *obviously*. And "Squash" is a highly advanced fighting technique, where you defeat your enemy by sitting on top of them.'

'Well, I think you made up that whole story.'

'Well, I think you made up everything about the noble vegetable.'

And so the argument went round and round and round until it became quite dizzy and had to sit down. Because the only person who knew where the coat of arms *really* came from was Grandpa Joe, and unfortunately there was no way of asking him.

Or was there?

No.

'Even if you *did* come from a noble family – which you don't,' said Eliza. 'Even if you *were* right about the coat of arms, which you're not, how would you even meet a prince, anyway? We live in The Middle of Nowhere. And all the princes live thousands of miles away. Look at the map!'

She pointed to the dog-eared *Map of These 'Ere Parts* on the wall.

'But we *do* live near the Forest of Dragons!' said Lavender. 'And everyone knows that princes love dragon-hunting!'

'But the princes all go hunting in the Forest of Scary-Looking but Surprisingly Sleepy and Stupid Dragons,' said Eliza. 'We live near the Forest of Toothy, Vicious and Flatulent Dragons, where no prince in his right mind would ever go! So no more talking about getting rescued by a prince! We're never going to meet any princes, and THAT is the end of it.'

'Fine,' said Lavender.

'Fine,' said Eliza.

'Fine,' said Lavender.

'Fine,' said Eliza.

'Can we stop saying "fine" now?' said Eliza.

'Fine,' said Lavender.

So Eliza blew out the candle, curled up again, and was soon fast asleep. But Lavender lay awake, her mind buzzing like a swarm of overexcited bees who have just eaten all their own honey.

Because Eliza had given her a brilliant idea.

'The Forest of Toothy, Vicious and Flatulent Dragons, where no prince *in his right mind* would ever go . . .' she had said. Which meant that a prince *who was not in his right mind* . . . might easily go there!

Very, very quietly, Lavender snuck out of bed,

picked up her book of fairy tales and her favourite pointy princess hat, peeled the map off the wall and tiptoed from the room.

Chapter Three

In which the villain Mordmont is introduced.

Early the next morning:

We would like to apologize for the delay to this chapter, which has been caused by the villain, Mordmont, not doing anything particularly villainous at this time. All he's doing at the moment is eating a slice of cake. He is expected to return to his usual villainy as soon as possible.

ANNOUNCEMENT

We would like to apologize for the further delay
to this chapter. Mordmont is now having his post-
breakfast nap. He's not really doing anything
very villainous at all. Unless you count snoring.
And dribbling. Delays to his villainy are expected
to continue throughout the day.

Chapter Three Again

In which Mordmont will probably still be snoring.

I wouldn't bother reading it if I were you.

'Violet? Violetta! Breakfast time, Violy Wioly!'

Inside the castle, Mordmont was now awake. In fact, he was more than awake, he was up and skipping like a slightly evil hare, through his bedroom, down the stairs and into his kitchen. He had cake in his stomach, curls in his moustache and joy in his heart.

Today is going to be a wonderful day, he thought to himself as he flung open the kitchen window and looked out at the moat.

'Breakfast!' he roared as he flung his dragon's breakfast – two Scotch eggs, one Welsh egg, four pieces of ham and three used handkerchiefs – out through the window and into the moat.

Violet didn't stir. Used handkerchiefs were among her favourite snacks, but she wasn't in a rush to collect her breakfast. She didn't usually listen too hard to what Mordmont had to say. Which wasn't surprising, since she was at least six times taller than him, 34,567 years older, infinitely more intelligent, and didn't particularly appreciate being called 'Violy Wioly Willykins'.

'Hmmmn. No Violy Wioly this morning,' Mordmont muttered to himself as he stared down at the still surface of the water, slightly disappointed. 'And none of the little Violettas either.'

Mordmont sighed. Nothing in the world cheered him up as much as the sight of Violet's blood-stained teeth. He cherished all the sweet things she did for him – like that enormous birthday cake that she'd set fire to and turned into a pile of ashes.

His heart was cheered by the sight of some of her many, many dragon children, tearing around the moat and playing games like 'Hide and Seek and Gobble and Crunch'.

Bless.

He decided to go outside to see if Violet or the rest of her brood would wake up if he chucked enough stones into the water. But as he got to the front door, he stopped short. His eyes boggled. He gasped. Because the letterbox was stuffed with ten of his least favourite objects in the whole wide world. Bills.

'Bonnet??' he shrieked. 'Bonnet??? BONNET! BONNET!!'

Mordmont was pale and quivering like a jelly in an earthquake

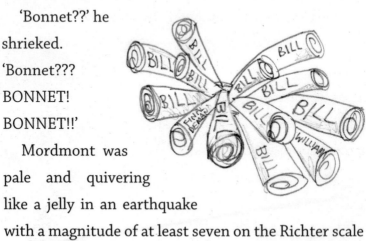

with a magnitude of at least seven on the Richter scale

by the time that Bonnet, his pudding-shaped servant, arrived panting at his side.

'WHAT. ARE. THESE?!' Mordmont gasped, pointing at the bills with a quaking finger.

'They're bills, sire,' said Bonnet, stooping to pick them up. As he did so, Mordmont snatched them out of his hands and started to open them.

'One hundred pieces of silver for a stuffed owl? Four hundred pieces of silver for a pair of solid gold shoes? *Six* hundred pieces of silver for a pair of gold shoes for a stuffed owl? Bonnet! WHO has been spending all this money on this USELESS RUBBISH?'

'Um . . .' said Bonnet. He coughed. He never liked giving bad news. 'I suppose that would be you, sire.'

'That is absurd!'

Mordmont said, glancing down at his feet and noticing for the first time that his shoes were remarkably heavy. And looked, well, definitely . . . quite . . . goldy.

He frowned. 'No doubt these were all necessities. And they shall be paid for. Fetch me the chest of silver from the East Wing.'

'I, er, I can't,' said Bonnet in a small voice.

'Can't?' said Mordmont. '*Can't?*'

'Well, er, the thing is, sire, you lost it, sire. In a bet. Playing poker, sire.'

'The *entire* chest of silver?' Mordmont asked.

'No, sire. The East Wing, sire,' said Bonnet. 'Your friend Lord Tartiflette had it removed this morning.'

'Oh,' said Mordmont. 'I see.'

Mordmont paced around the room. He did dimly remember playing poker with his friend Lord Tartiflette.

'So, there's no money left at all?' said Mordmont sadly, slumping to the floor.

'Not exactly, sire,' said Bonnet. 'Cake, sire?'

Bonnet held out a beautiful porcelain plate, with a large slice of lemon cake on it. Mordmont nodded, and mournfully stuffed it into his mouth.

'I'm a broken man,' he said between mouthfuls. 'I'm as broken as this plate.' He threw the plate across the room and it smashed against the wall. 'I don't suppose I won anything at the poker game, did I?'

'Er, only that priceless Chinese plate, sire,' said Bonnet.

Mordmont sighed again. He had spent all his money. He had gambled away half his castle. He wasn't even eating his favourite kind of cake. Life had gone badly wrong, and it was time for some clear thinking.

'I'm a man of simple pleasures,' he said. 'All I ever wanted was a castle, my own pride of lions, a jewelled crown, a choir of elves singing me awake each morning, sainthood, the power to make gold, the best moustache in Europe, a Jacuzzi, an elephant from the Indies, another one to be its friend, a singing giraffe, the power of invisibility, Magical Cheese Powers, a tiger with the feet of a lamb, the head of a lamb and the body of a lamb – basically, a lamb – power over the sea, power over the letter C . . .'

DEAR READER,
THIS IS JUST A NOTE TO SAY, I CUT THE NEXT 4,235
OF MORDMONT'S SIMPLE PLEASURES, BECAUSE REALLY
THEY WEREN'T THAT NECESSARY. OR SIMPLE. AND
BECAUSE I LIKE TO SAVE PAPER WHERE I CAN.
LOVE,
SIDNEY THE TREE

'. . . and a meringue that speaks Japanese,' Mordmont said finally. 'Is that really too much to ask?'

'Yes! No! Gorilla trousers! What?' Bonnet spluttered as he awoke from a small nap.

'It is clear that I must do a terrible thing,' Mordmont went on. A look of pain crossed his face, turned left at his ear, left again, and then crossed back over his face. 'I'm going to have to take you to the market and sell you as a slave.'

'Yuwhh?' said Bonnet.

'Oh, I know what you're thinking,' Mordmont sighed. 'How will I cope? Who will make my breakfast cake? Who will sing "The Loveliest Sheep" to me when I can't sleep? But don't think of me. I'll just have to get by without you.'

And Mordmont strode off to brood on the difficulties of his life. Mordmont was fond of brooding. He knew how handsome it made him look.

Unfortunately, as he brooded his way through the hallway, he tripped over a scroll, crashed into a lamp, fell over his own feet . . . and landed sprawled on the floor like a spider, with his nose pressed into that morning's copy of *The Squerb Times*. Inside it was the solution to all his problems.*

'YEAOOOOOW!' Mordmont shrieked as he read the front page. 'Bonnet – that's IT! Look!'

* Unfortunately, he didn't read that bit.

36

He jumped up, bolted back into the kitchen, and thrust the paper into Bonnet's face. 'Look! Read! Look!'

So Bonnet read out the headlines:

'The Black Death: Not As Much Fun As We Thought . . . Women: They're Just Wrong, Says Pope . . . Latest Tonsure Styles for Spring . . .'

'No – not that. This!' said Mordmont. He snatched the paper back, and read:

> **Princess Esmerelda of Vablinsk, kidnapped by notorious villain Deadly Oswald, was returned to her family last night after a ransom of one thousand silver pieces was paid to the dastardly criminal.**

'That's it!' Mordmont said as he danced a little jig. 'Don't you see, Bonnet, don't you see? One princess equals one thousand silver pieces! I don't need to sell you! Besides – how much would you have really fetched anyway? I mean, look at you. The Smallest Giant in the Kingdom. What are you worth, really? A bag of flour? Half a cabbage and a small glass of milk?'

'Thank you for not selling me,' said Bonnet quietly.

'Oh, Bonnet, I wasn't really going to sell you. You're basically worthless! All we need to do now is find a princess and kidnap her. Snap her up. Then bingo – Bob's your uncle!'

'But Bob's not my uncle,' Bonnet whispered as Mordmont danced around him.

'The ransom will be ours! That is – mine! And then all my troubles will vanish – just like that ridiculous owl!'

And walking over to the windowsill, he picked up a large stuffed owl (which was wearing a pair of gold shoes) and kicked it out of the window.

SPLASH!

'Present for you, Violet!' Mordmont shouted out of the window, although Violet did not reply.

'But . . . how are you going to kidnap a princess?' asked Bonnet.

'Ha!' Mordmont laughed. 'I'm not – that would be incredibly hard work, and really far too dangerous. No – you are!'

'I am?' said Bonnet.

'Yes. Not alone, of course. Alone, you couldn't kidnap your own eyebrows. No. You'll just have to find the princess. But you'll need someone's help to catch her. Someone big and strong . . .'

Please don't say Clive, please don't say Clive, please don't say Clive, thought Bonnet.

Of all the things in life Bonnet was scared of (and there were 87,564 at his last count), the thing at the top of the list was . . .

'Clive,' said Mordmont.

The next morning was bright and lovely. The birds sang. Dawn rose. Then she went back to bed. Luckily Dawn isn't part of this story. She didn't really get up to that much.

Eliza, however, was up early. She fed the chickens, cut the grass and washed all her clothes . . . while Lavender lay in bed snoring.

Eliza didn't mind that her sister was fond of staying in bed for hours 'practising being Sleeping Beauty'. She didn't *mind* doing all the work on the farm by herself. And if it just so happened that she chopped a few more logs than necessary . . .

. . . that was just a coincidence, and nothing to do

with her sister spending the entire morning in bed. But at lunchtime, when Lavender still hadn't appeared, Eliza decided she'd had enough.

'Lavender. Lavender. Lavender. LAVENDER!' she shouted, standing over her sister's bed. 'Are you planning to stay there for a hundred years? Lavender! Lavender?'

And she pulled back the covers, to see the gentle, sleepy face of . . .

'*Gertrude???!* Get out of there! Wait! Then . . . where's Lavender?'

While Gertrude skittered outside, Eliza stomped off to find her sister. She knew all Lavender's favourite spots.

But Lavender wasn't down by the pond, collecting frogs, just in case one of them turned out to be the Frog Prince.

And she wasn't gazing into her mirror, covering her face in flour, so she'd be just as pale as Snow White.

And she wasn't in the kitchen, dressed up as Cinderella, *pretending* to sweep the floor while singing a song.

Lavender had vanished. It was a mystery, even more mysterious than the mystery of Eliza's missing socks.

So Eliza went to ask Grandma Maud if she knew where Lavender had gone.

'Ooh, I expect she's been taken by the Black Death, dear,' said Grandma Maud as she sat in her rocking chair, examining a pebble.

'Er, I don't think she has,' said Eliza with a frown.

'That's the thing with the Black Death, dear,' said Grandma Maud. 'You never expect it. First you see the spots. And then the lumps. And then your skin withers. And then you faint. And then your fingers fall off. And then your legs fall off! And before you know it – *POOF*! You're gone!'

'I really don't think she's been taken by the Black Death,' said Eliza. 'She wasn't even ill.'

'Could be the Fatal Hiccups then,' said Grandma Maud. 'When they come, they come lightning quick.'

Eliza sighed. She clearly wasn't going to get any more sense out of Grandma Maud, so she went and sat down on her bed and frowned.

Everything's fine, she thought to herself. *Lavender will turn up. It's not as if she's taken the map and run away or anything . . .*

'ARGHHHHHHHH!!!!!!' yelled Eliza, who had sat on one of her sister's hairpins.

'ARGGHHHHHH!' she yelled again, when she looked up and noticed that the *Map of These 'Ere Parts* had vanished.

'Lavender, where HAVE YOU GONE?!'

Meanwhile, Bonnet was on his way to kidnap a princess, with Clive.

Clive, who had the shoulders of a bear and the neck of an ox (he kept them in his bag and liked showing them to people sometimes).

Clive, whose favourite hobbies were:

1) Poking Bonnet.

2) Poking Bonnet.

3) Poking Bonnet.

4) ~~Illuminating manuscripts~~ Poking Bonnet.

With his craggy face, his deep gravelly voice, his spade-shaped head and his head-shaped spade, Clive looked like a violent criminal – which he was. Bonnet, on the other hand, was dressed in a bonnet, and a long green dress, and looked like a high-born lady – which he wasn't.

Together they set out on the path to kidnap the princess. Or rather, Bonnet set out, and Clive lay back in the cart, chewing bits of straw and going over the plan.

'So,' said Clive. 'How do you identify a princess?'

'One,' Bonnet wheezed, 'she will walk in a dainty way. Two, she will either be picking flowers or dancing. Three, she will be wearing a pointy princess hat. Four, she will almost certainly be singing.'

'And when we locate her?'

'I will engage her in ladylike conversation,' gasped Bonnet, a little bit out of breath from dragging the cart, and Clive, along. 'I will impersonate a princess.'

'And on what topics will you converse with the said princess?'

'Princessy topics,' wheezed Bonnet.

'And what would they be?'

'Measles and France,' said Bonnet.

'Excellent,' said Clive. He knew a lot about ladies, having had a lot of girlfriends,* and he was pretty sure that that's what they liked talking about.

'Now. Just tell me again, one more time. Just to be sure?'

So, between wheezes, Bonnet told him all over again.

'Sorry, Bonnet, I was just listening to a chaffinch,' said Clive. 'Just tell me again?'

And so Bonnet told him the plan again. He *knew*

---

* If by 'a lot' you mean 'zero'.

that Clive knew what the plan was. He knew Clive just enjoyed seeing him drag the cart, and not trip over his dress, and talk, all at the same time. But he did it anyway, gritting his teeth.

And, in the back of the cart, Clive gritted his teeth too.

(How else do you think he got that deep, gravelly voice?)

All day they roamed across the countryside. They searched high and low, and at medium height, and they only stopped once, for a quick nap at lunchtime. And nothing much happened while they were asleep.

But they didn't find a single princess. Finally, as the sun was setting, Clive looked around and noticed that the cart was no longer on a road.

'Bonnet,' he said. 'Where are we?'

'Er . . . Quite near The Middle of Nowhere, I think,' said Bonnet.

'The Middle of NOWHERE!'

'Er, I think so. Not far off.'

'Well this is *perfect*,' Clive roared. 'You know what? You really *are* a giant. A GIANT EEJIT! If we have to go back to Mordmont without a princess, he is going to kill me. And after he's killed me, I am going to kill *you*!'

50

Bonnet nodded. 'Let's stick to that order,' he said.

'If I see a princess out here, in the middle of nowhere, I'll eat my hat, and then I'll eat *your* hat. And then I'll eat Mordmont's hat. That's right, that enormous big furry one, and who knows what that'll do to my digestion—'

'Shhh!' said Bonnet suddenly.

And they both heard it.

The sound of singing. Really terrible singing.

In the next field, a small girl was dancing, picking flowers, wearing a pointy princess hat, and singing:

'Oooh, Prince Rudolph, with your lovely chin (or chins)
They're so very handsome, what do you keep them in
     (when you're not wearing them)?
I would like to be saved by you and/or him
(by which I mean one of the other Princes) –
Oooh, Prince Rudolph,
You are . . . a Prince.'

51

'That,' Lavender said to herself, 'will sound wonderful in French.*'

And as she wandered through the field, Bonnet followed behind her on tiptoe. And inside the cart, Clive stood up and tiptoed too, just to be extra quiet.

Which didn't really work that well, as the cart itself creaked loudly as it rolled along.

They tiptoed closer and closer and closer.

* This has been tested. It doesn't.

In front of them, the princess picked flowers, and twirled, and sang, and soon arrived at the edge of a tall, dark, forbidding-looking forest . . .

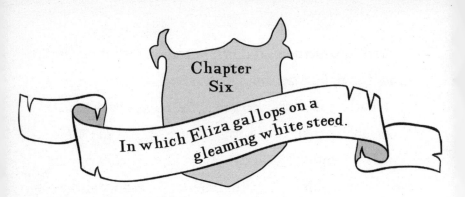

Chapter Six

In which Eliza gallops on a gleaming white steed.

Meanwhile Eliza was racing through the countryside to rescue her sister on the back of a gleaming white steed. She was riding like the wind, riding so fast her eyes streamed and – oh, wait. No she wasn't. She wasn't even riding like a light breeze. Because Eliza didn't have a gleaming white steed. What she *did* have was a grumpy brown goat.

'Come on, Gertrude!' she said. 'Let's GO!!!'

She was sitting on the back of Gertrude, in Gertrude's pen.

'Mnnnnhrr,' shrugged Gertrude.

'Come *on*! Don't you care about Lavender AT ALL? Don't you want to hear her singing ever again?'

At this, Gertrude sat down, rested her head on the ground and shut her eyes.

'What if she's lost and she never comes back? Just think about that!' Eliza said, and in reply Gertrude started to snore, with the ghost of a smile on her face. It was fair to say that Gertrude didn't always enjoy spending time with Lavender. Only last week, Lavender had decided to put on a play of *Cinderella*, and had made Gertrude and Eliza dress up as the Ugly Sisters.

The week before that, she had dressed Gertrude up as her fairy godmother.

The week before that, she had dressed her up as her 'delightful French handmaiden Lucille'.

It seemed as if Gertrude was going to need a little bit of persuading. But then Eliza had a brilliant idea. She dashed into the house, and in two minutes she was back with one of Grandpa

Joe's old fishing rods and the smelliest sock she could find. As if by magic, Gertrude opened her eyes and leaped to her feet. They were on their way.

So Eliza and Gertrude trotted along through fields,

and valleys, and fields, and then more fields, and then some more fields, and then a couple of fields, and after that some more fields. It was a farming area. And everywhere they went, Eliza asked: 'Have you seen my sister, Lavender? Sort of annoying? Sings a lot? Wears a pointy hat?'

But everyone said: 'No', 'No', 'No', 'No', 'No' and, 'We're a leper colony, run away while you've still got legs!'

Chapter Seven

In which there really are dragons.

At the edge of the forest, Lavender was smiling. *At last!* she thought to herself. *The Forest of Toothy, Vicious and Flatulent Dragons!*

She stopped to read the sign:

> THIS IS THE FOREST OF TOOTHY,
> VICIOUS AND FLATULENT DRAGONS.
> DO NOT ENTER.

And, ten steps behind her, Bonnet and Clive stopped too.

'What if she turns round?' hissed Bonnet, suddenly frightened. 'I'm not ready yet! She'll see us!'

'Don't worry,' Clive hissed back. 'If she turns round, we'll just pretend to be sparrows.'

'Oh, OK then.'

But Lavender didn't turn round. She started to walk into the forest, and beamed as she read the next sign.

SERIOUSLY. RUN AWAY
BEFORE YOU GET EATEN.

And the next one:

WHO DO YOU THINK IS WRITING THESE SIGNS?
THE ONLY VEGETARIAN DRAGON
IN THE WHOLE FOREST!

And the next one:

FINE. IGNORE ME. GET EATEN IF YOU LIKE.
I'LL JUST GET BACK TO MAKING MY QUILT.

Lavender kept smiling as she walked deep into the dark, gloomy forest. Before long, she had found exactly what she was looking for: a cave. She checked it against the picture in her book of fairy tales. It was perfect.

It had piles of bones strewn around the entrance, and low purring sounds coming from inside it, as if the cave was full of cats – giant cats who had giant claws and who smoked a hundred cigarettes a day.

So she tied herself to a nearby rock, placed some assorted meats on the ground next to her and decided to wait patiently until she was attacked by a dragon – because then she knew she would be rescued by a prince.

As she waited, she read another fairy tale, which reassured her that a handsome prince would be on his way to rescue her very shortly. Soon, she was so excited that she started to sing.

> 'I can't wait to be rescued by a prince,
> If he is bonkers, I won't mind!
> If he's a prince he will be kind
> And handsome and lovely
> And handsome and good
> He'll have arms and legs,
> Just as he should,
> And ankles and feet,
> And he won't be made of wood . . .
> He will be a PRINCE!'

Inside that dark, mysterious cave, a dragon pricked up her ears.

In fact, there was more than one dragon inside the cave. There was a mother dragon and, snoozing on her head, was a baby dragon. Here they are:

How sweet, you might think. But then you'd be an idiot.

BECAUSE THEY WERE DRAGONS.

After three weeks of her child's fire-breathing tantrums, the mother dragon had *just* managed to get her baby to sleep. *Peace. Finally, a moment of peace*, she thought. It had been a long three weeks. When her baby dragon cried, his flaming tears set fire to things. When he sneezed, his flaming snot set fire to things. When he was sick, his flaming vomit set fire to things. And by 'things', I mean 'his mother'.

The only time that the baby dragon wasn't setting fire to 'things' was when he was asleep. And now, finally, he was. *Peace*, the mother dragon thought again. *Lovely, quiet, flatulent peace.* For, apart from the low burble of dragon farts, and the peaceful sound of dragons sharpening their teeth and snacking on the occasional traveller, the forest was lovely and quiet.

And then she heard a terrible sound.

Was it a bear sitting on a hedgehog?

Was it an elephant weeping over his maths homework?

Was it a rhinoceros being forced to watch *Swan Lake*?

Whatever it was, it had to be stopped. NOW. Before it woke her baby up.

So, as softly as she could, the mother dragon put her baby down, slipped out of the cave, and saw, tied to her favourite rock, a small, strange creature in a tall pointy hat, making the most truly terrible sound that she had ever heard.

Meanwhile, outside the Forest of Toothy, Vicious and Flatulent Dragons, Clive was making a slight change to the plan. 'I'd love to go into the forest with you, Bonnet. Love to. But I can't.'

'Er . . . why not?' asked Bonnet.

''Llergic to dandelions,' said Clive with a shrug.

'Oh,' said Bonnet, looking down at Clive's feet, and the large clump of dandelions on the ground beside them. And then looking at the large yellow dandelion in Clive's hat.

'*Forest* dandelions,' said Clive. 'It's my sinuses. It's a shame, cos I'm very fond of dragons. Some real characters you meet in the dragon world. A lot of my best friends are dragons. Oh well. You run along into the forest – we don't want to lose her.'

'Right,' said Bonnet weakly. 'I'll just . . . go in there . . . on my own . . .'

He looked into the darkness and shuddered.

'Oh, you'll be fine, with your giant strength,' said Clive, giving Bonnet a small, friendly clap on the shoulder, which knocked him straight to the ground. After dusting himself off, Bonnet got up again.

'Here I go,' said Bonnet. 'I mean, what's the worst that could happen?'

'Ooh – getting eaten alive, I'd say,' said Clive. 'Or maimed. But you'll be fine.'

So Bonnet went shuffling off into the mysterious, stinking forest.

'I'm a giant,' he muttered quietly to himself. 'I am a giant. Quite a small giant. Not a huge giant. But . . . I'm still a giant. I'm a giant. I am a giant. I am a g—'

He stopped short. In the clearing ahead of him, he

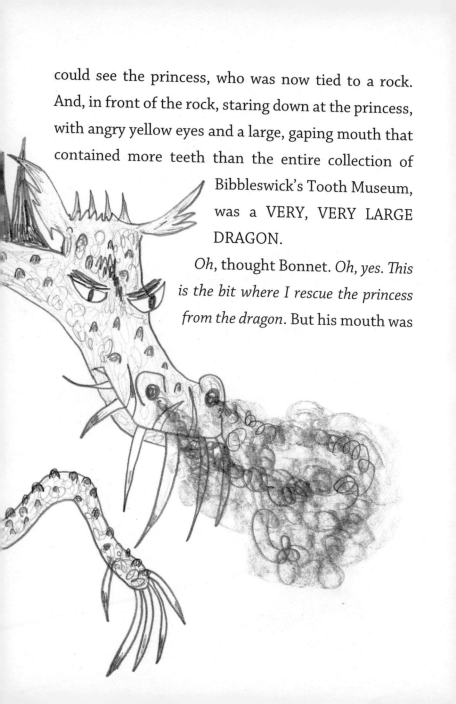

could see the princess, who was now tied to a rock. And, in front of the rock, staring down at the princess, with angry yellow eyes and a large, gaping mouth that contained more teeth than the entire collection of Bibbleswick's Tooth Museum, was a VERY, VERY LARGE DRAGON.

Oh, thought Bonnet. *Oh, yes. This is the bit where I rescue the princess from the dragon.* But his mouth was suddenly dry and his feet seemed to be glued to the spot. So he just stood and stared, as Lavender, opening her eyes, came face to snout with the dragon, and the dragon breathed a thick cloud of purple smoke into her face. Here's a closer look at the cloud:

32% moss

27% beetles

2% Don't even ask

13% Rodney the Hermit

26% other Hermits

As the smoke cleared, Lavender looked up into two unblinking yellow eyes and she managed to do what she'd been trying to do for so long.

She fainted.

With a grunt, the dragon picked her up by the tip of her pointy princess hat. She whirled Lavender around in the air, tossed her up and down a couple of times and shook her a little from side to side. Then she threw her up in the air and caught her by her feet.

I really should do something, Bonnet thought to himself. *I really should. Move, feet, move!* And suddenly, as if by a miracle, his feet did move, and he started to run. Away from the princess, away from the forest, and away from the enormous dragon.

Poached princess? Princess pie? the dragon thought as she whirled Lavender absent-mindedly in the air. All of a sudden, the dragon froze, as she heard a familiar sound.

'WAAAARGHHHHHH!'

My baby! Must not wake! Must not cry! No time for cooking! Dashing back into the cave, she tossed the princess and her pointy hat high into the air.

She soared over the trees, just as Bonnet stumbled out of the forest and arrived, panting, at Clive's side.

'I'm sorry,' he gasped, 'I'm sorry I'm sorry I'm sorry I'm sorry – ooohhhh – duck!'

They both stared with wide-open mouths as the princess came soaring through the sky, and landed with a WHUMPH on the soft straw in the cart.

'Hmmmn,' grunted Clive, looking at Bonnet in a whole new light. 'Not bad for an oversized dwarf.'

Lavender opened her eyes and gazed up at the two faces peering down at her.

'My rescuers!' she murmured.

'Yep,' said Bonnet, looking at his feet.

'So, which one of you is the prince?' Lavender asked.

Clive cleared his throat.

'We are neither rescuers nor princes,' Clive explained. 'We are kidnap—'

'RESCUERS!' said Bonnet, elbowing Clive. 'We're *rescuers*. That's why . . . we . . . rescued you.'

Clive blinked at Bonnet.

'Yes,' said Clive. 'That's right. My name is Clive, and I am an Organized Criminal and Princess Rescuer.'

He decided, since he had met a princess, he had better make some polite, princessy conversation with her.

'So, er, do you have the measles?' he asked.

'Um, I don't think so,' said Lavender.

'I'm Clive's assistant,' said Bonnet.

'He's a giant,' said Clive unhelpfully. 'And a lady. He's a lady giant.'

At this, Lavender frowned. She couldn't remember quite what happened in this part of the fairy tale, but she was pretty sure it wasn't supposed to go like this.

'I'm not a lady,' said Bonnet. 'But I am a giant. My parents were giants. I'm just not a very, er, big giant. For a giant.'

'I see,' said Lavender, who didn't.

'We have rescued you on behalf of the great Prince Mordmont,' said Clive. 'If you so desire it, we shall accompany you to the Prince's castle for your permanent incarceration.'

Lavender's head was spinning. Prince? Palace? She

didn't exactly know what a 'permanent incarceration' was, but she thought it sounded wonderful. Suddenly, everything was beginning to make sense.

'Just one thing,' said Clive. 'You *are* a princess, aren't you?'

There was a pause.

Then there were some paws. (That was just a nearby rabbit, sniffing around and looking for carrots.)

'Er . . . Yes!' said Lavender.

'Your name?' asked Clive.

'Princess . . . Fahalahalahalaha,' said Lavender. And then, because she wasn't sure if her name was impressive enough, she said:

'Princess Fahalahalahalaha Mimsford Lovelynose Cakey McSmith.'

'Princess Fahalahalaha Mimsford Lovelynose Cakey McSmith,' said Clive. 'Of the House of . . . ?'

'Um . . . er . . .'

'Of the House of Ummer! Delighted to meet you. Right you are, Bonnet. Let us now take fair

Princess Fahalahalaha—'

'Actually,' said Lavender, 'it's Fahalahalahalaha, not Fahalahalaha.'

'Fahalahalahalaha, not Fahalahalaha,' Bonnet repeated.

'That's right,' said Lavender. 'Fahalahalahalaha, not Fahalahalaha.'

'Well then, fair princess . . . fair princess,' Clive said. 'Let us set off at once for Mordmont's most luxurious and inescapable abode. Full steam ahead!'

So they all trundled off through the countryside.

As they travelled, Lavender burst into ~~a thousand pieces~~ song. All her dreams had come true! She just couldn't help it. She sang song after song after song. Songs about her prince, songs about the forest, songs about her rescuers, songs about lasagne. And as she sang, it was as if nature responded to her voice. Some nearby squirrels became unexpectedly depressed. Badgers started hitting each other over the head with rocks in order to make themselves deaf. And a whole swarm of wasps became incredibly angry and took out all their rage on some perfectly innocent strangers.

And every once in a while, when Lavender wasn't looking, Clive nailed a piece of parchment to a tree, which read:

THE INCREDIBLY ANNOYING,
CONSTANTLY SINGING
PRINCESS FAHALAHALAHALAHA
OF THE HOUSE OF UMMER
HAS BEEN KIDNAPED.
SHE WILL ONLY BE RELEESED IF
ONE THOUSAND SILVER PIECES ARE SENT TO:
MORDMONT'S CASTLE, THE VAGARIES,
OX5 FGL.
PS THE PRINCESS IS BEING HELD IN A
SECRET LOCATION.
DEFINITELY NOT AT:
MORDMONT'S CASTLE, THE VAGARIES,
OX5 FGL.

IMPORTANT MESSAGE:

DEAR READER,
THE NEXT CHAPTER CONTAINS IMAGES OF VIOLENCE
AGAINST TREES, WHICH SOME READERS MAY FIND
UPSETTING. PARTICULARLY IF THEY HAPPEN TO BE
TREES.
LOVE,
SIDNEY THE TREE

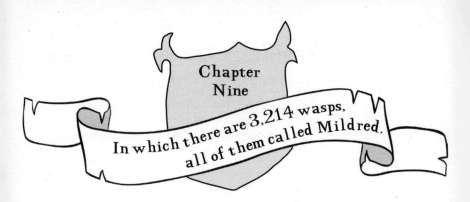
'OW!' screamed Eliza as she got stung by yet another

angry wasp. It was fair to say that the quest to rescue

Lavender was not going well. Before

the wasp attack, she had already

had to counsel several

depressed squirrels.

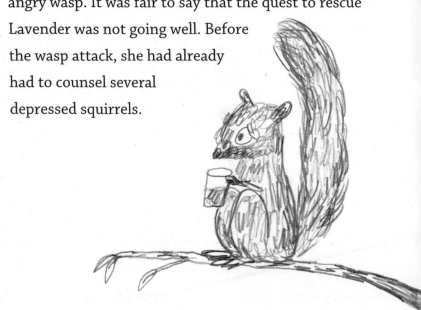

And she and Gertrude had only just escaped from a badger battle that involved an entire clan of badgers hurling rocks at each other . . .

And now this. A cloud of furious wasps swarming madly around her head.

'Come on!' she yelled, and she held on as tightly as she could as Gertrude raced away from the wasps, running so fast that the world around them seemed to blur. Gertrude ran and ran, until the wasps had been left far behind, and when she finally stopped, they found themselves in the middle of a dark and gloomy forest. They were totally lost.

Eliza looked around. There wasn't a soul or a tourist information point in sight. 'Hello?' she called, but no one answered. Probably because they were squirrels.

So they walked on, and on and on, through the dark and lonely forest. They walked over ground that was littered with piles of bones, and past caves with eerie, crunching noises coming from inside. They passed a pile of assorted meats, and a rope that looked strangely familiar, but there was no sign of Lavender anywhere. Until they trotted past a sign that read:

THE INCREDIBLY ANNOYING,
CONSTANTLY SINGING
PRINCESS FAHALAHALAHALAHA
OF THE HOUSE OF UMMER
HAS BEEN KIDNAPED.
SHE WILL ONLY BE RELEESED IF
ONE THOUSAND SILVER PIECES ARE SENT TO:
MORDMONT'S CASTLE, THE VAGARIES,
OX5 FGL.
PS THE PRINCESS IS BEING HELD IN A
SECRET LOCATION.
DEFINITELY NOT AT:
MORDMONT'S CASTLE, THE VAGARIES,
OX5 FGL.

That is NOT how you spell 'kidnapped'! Eliza thought. *Or 'released'! Stupid kidnappers, can't they even spell?*

So they trotted on.

'WAIT! Gertrude – reverse!' Eliza yelled.

79

Gertrude reversed.

Incredibly Annoying? Constantly Singing?

Eliza frowned at the piece of parchment again.

'LAVENDER! What have you done?' Eliza shouted to no one in particular. 'Lavender, you – grrrh!'

And in her frustration, she kicked the nearest tree.

'OW!' said the tree, kicking the nearest squirrel in his frustration.

'OW!' said the squirrel, kicking the nearest snail in his frustration.

'OW!' said the snail, kicking no one at all in his frustration, because he didn't believe in violence.

'Lavender, Lavender, Lavender,' Eliza huffed. 'First, I am going to find you. Then I am going to rescue you. And then I am going to KILL YOU!'

ANOTHER IMPORTANT MESSAGE:

DEAR READER,
HELLO. IF YOU FOUND ANY OF THE ISSUES RAISED IN
THIS CHAPTER DISTURBING, PLEASE CALL OUR LOCAL
BRANCH ON: 0800-LEAF-LEAF-LEAF. THAT'S MY
NUMBER. I'M ALWAYS AROUND IF YOU'D LIKE TO HAVE
A NICE CHAT OR A BUN.
LOVE,
SIDNEY THE TREE

As darkness fell, and the wind whistled an annoying tune through the treetops, Eliza and Gertrude trotted valiantly along. They had found an overgrown path, and so they followed it, until they came to a fork in the path, which was confusing. And then they came to a spoon in the path, which was even stranger. And then, just as they passed a ladle in the path, three wizards stepped out in front of them.

'Halt! What do you seek?' they boomed.

In a quavering voice, Eliza told them of her quest to find Mordmont's Castle. And the first wizard replied: 'Ooh, that rings a bell. I do know that castle. It's definitely near here. If it's the one I'm thinking of. Is it, Peter?'

'No, I don't think so. That's the wool shop you're thinking of, Nigel.'

'Oh, you're right, Peter. It *is* the wool shop I was thinking of. Sorry, love.'

'Thinking of, thinking of, thinking of . . .' added the third wizard, Frank, who was the wizard in charge of echoes.

'But we can help you on your quest,' said Peter. 'For we have many weapons in the fight against villainy.'

'And all of them are made from wool,' added Peter.

'Wool, wool, wool,' echoed Frank.

'Yes,' said Peter. 'We have swords of wool. Shields of wool. Ships of wool. Even horses of wool, such as those that we are riding . . .'

'This is Irene, this is Irene, this is Irene,' said Frank, holding out his horse.

'. . . and also beards of wool. Umbrellas of wool. Most precious of all, vials of wool, containing magical ointments that heal all wounds.'

'Well, they used to, used to, used to,' echoed Frank. 'But then they sort of leaked, sort of leaked, sort of leaked . . .'

'Silence!' said Peter. 'Child, please choose a magical item to help you on your way.'

'Er, have you got any gloves?' asked Eliza.

'Gloves! Don't be ridiculous. Gloves made of wool? Whoever heard of such a thing! You may have a hat and a beard.'

'Er, all right,' said Eliza as he handed her the woolly objects.

'May these aid you on your quest, and never make you itchy. And now we must be on our way. For trials and darkness lie before us, and the wool shop shuts at five o'clock.'

'No it doesn't,' said Nigel. 'It shuts at five thirty.'

'Yes, but you know that I like to look at all the different types of wool before I decide what to buy,'

Peter hissed. 'Farewell, young traveller, and good luck.'

'Do I have to keep echoing? Do I have to keep echoing? Do I have to keep echoing?' echoed Frank. Then there was a flash, and all three wizards vanished from sight, for they had disguised themselves as leaves floating on the breeze. Except for Frank, who had disguised himself as a bowl of grapefruits.

That evening, as the sun was setting, and Bonnet was sweating, the cart rumbled to a stop.

'Princess Fahalahalahalaha,' said Clive proudly, 'we have arrived!'

And Lavender looked up to see the castle of her dreams . . .

. . . and kept looking.

And kept looking.

And looking . . .

Then she tried some gazing . . .

. . . and squinting . . .

But she couldn't see *anything* that looked like the castle of her dreams. She checked in her book of fairy tales just to make sure, and she was right. All the castles in her book of fairy tales had tall, elegant turrets and tall, elegant people wandering through their tall, elegant gardens, saying things like:

'Goodness, how elegant and tall we are!'

And: 'Thanks, Mama, for giving me Switzerland for Christmas. It's lovely!'

But before her was a green, bubbling moat, and in the middle of it was was a grey castle, slumped dangerously to one side, like Grandma Maud when she'd had too much brandy.

'Welcome to Prince Mordmont's Summer Residence!' Clive announced. 'And also his Spring Residence, his Autumn Residence, and his Winter Residence.'

Lavender gulped.

'Are you sure this is it?' said Lavender, suddenly feeling worried.

'Oh yes,' said Clive, putting a large, beefy arm around her.

The castle's rickety drawbridge lowered across the

moat, the portcullis rattled upwards, and they crossed over the stinking bubbling water.

'Look out for Violet,' said Clive.

'What's that?' said Lavender.

'Violet, the moat-dragon,' said Clive. 'And her many, many children. There must be – I don't know – a hundred of them swimming around in there. Charming creatures. I'm sure you'll see them when they're hungry.'

Lavender looked down into the green water and was pretty sure she saw something moving under the surface. She shuddered. She'd never heard of a prince with his own dragon before, and she'd never heard of a prince's castle that had a bag of rubbish outside the door and smelt a bit like Grandpa Joe's oldest socks, the ones he'd inherited from his great-grandfather.

But there was no time to think, because a moment later they had arrived in the courtyard of the castle, and the front door burst open.

'The prince!' Clive announced.

'The prince!' Lavender gasped.

'The prince!' said the prince, leaping through the door.

Lavender was prepared to be amazed. But . . . Wait! He didn't look anything like the princes in her book of fairy tales. For a start, he wasn't wearing a crown, or long, flowing robes. He wasn't holding a rose, or a slipper. And he didn't have a calm yet gentle face, glowing with a quiet nobility.

No.

This prince was wearing a crumpled pink dressing gown, which seemed to have half a piece of cake stuck to it. He had eyebrows that looked like caterpillars, a long oily moustache and a beard you could hide an otter in. He was only wearing one shoe. And on his shoeless foot, his toe poked through a hole in his sock, and it was incredibly hairy and also a bit yellow. And instead of processing, or bowing, as princes usually did, he was skipping up and down and clapping his hands.

'You've done it! You've actually done it!' he shouted.

'An actual live princess. A real specimen! This is the happiest day of my life!'

'This,' said Clive grandly, 'is Princess Fahalahalahalaha. Of the House of Ummer. Princess Fahalahalahalaha, your gracious host, Prince Mordmont.'

'Princess Fahalahalahalaha! Enchanted!' said Mordmont. '*Enchanted! Welcome to the family pile!*'

Mordmont pointed to a small pile of pebbles in the middle of the courtyard, as Clive whispered something in his ear.

'Princess Fahalahalahalaha, it is an honour to have you here. Really, this is a quite magical experience for me. Welcome, fair princess. I do hope you enjoy the cell . . . the celebration – which we are holding in your honour in just a few days' time. Now, let me show you to your quarters. It's so wonderful to have a captive . . . audience.'

With that, he turned and pranced into the castle. And, not knowing what else she could do, Lavender followed him.

'Mind the puddles!' Mordmont shouted as they walked along a dark, cavernous corridor. 'It's just this roof, I'm afraid. These old houses are a real curse. Come along, come along!'

And as Lavender hurried along behind him, Mordmont led her past the ballroom . . .

... the scullery ...

... the pantry ...

. . . and through another gloomy corridor and up a stone spiral staircase. At the top, Lavender stopped and looked at the strange sight in front of her.

Instead of a normal door, the door was barred, like the door to a prison cell. And instead of a bed, there was a pile of straw on the floor, like you might find in a prison cell. In fact, thought Lavender, the whole thing looked very much like . . .

'The guest suite!' said Mordmont. 'With en suite bathroom, of course,' he said, pointing to a small bucket in the corner.

'But . . . I don't understand,' said Lavender, stepping through the door. As soon she stepped into the room, Mordmont slammed the door behind her, plucked a key from his pocket, and turned it in the lock.

'Aha!'

He put his head through the bars, and grinned.

'A ha, ha, ha, ha, ha. Well, Princess Fahalahalahalaha, I do hope you have a very enjoyable kidnapping.'

'Kidnapping?' said Lavender.

'Kidnapping.'

'*Kidnapping?*'

'Yes, kidnapping!' said Mordmont, who didn't have all day to spend just repeating the word 'kidnapping'. He had new trousers, and new debts, to get into.

'You have been tricked by my evil plan!' said Mordmont proudly. 'You were brought here under false pretences. And now you, Princess Fahalahalahalaha, are my prisoner!'

'But, you can't just keep me here!' said Lavender.

'Look, I know I might look beastly to you,' Mordmont replied. 'But underneath, I'm just a dastardly villain. This is just what I do. When the ransom arrives, you will be free.'

'The ransom?'

'One thousand silver pieces. Until it is paid, you will be trapped. As trapped as my wind,' said Mordmont grandly, shifting in his breeches. 'And like my trapped wind, you will never be free – unless the ransom is paid!'

'I . . . I think there's been a mistake,' said Lavender quietly. 'I'm afraid you'd better let me go. You see . . .' She gulped. She felt as if she might be sick, and her voice suddenly sounded very, very small. 'I'm not . . . I'm not *really* a princess! I was just . . . pretending.'

Mordmont looked shocked. 'Oh, well then, you must leave immediately,' he said in a grave voice before exploding with laughter. 'Not a princess? Not a PRINCESS?! Nice try! But I can see your pointy princess hat, and I won't be fooled that easily, Princess Fahalahalahalaha of the House of Ummer.'

'But—' said Lavender.

'Oh, don't look so miserable. If this all works out, the ransom will be here any day, and then you can run along home to your castle and do whatever it is you princesses like to do. You can talk about measles and France to your heart's content. And you'll never see this beastly face again!'

And he skipped off back down the stairs, leaving Lavender looking around her cell and shuddering.

'Forests aren't scary,' Eliza said to Gertrude as they picked their way through the darkness. 'Forests are just trees. And what's scary about trees?'

'Nothing, really,' said Sidney the Tree, who they happened to be passing.

'Exactly,' said Eliza. 'There's nothing to be scared of. And anyway, Lavender's probably fine. Maybe she's been kidnapped by a nice kidnapper who just wants to practise French conversation. Or play cards. Or learn how to faint. Everything's fine. There's no reason to be scared . . .'

'Halt!' said a voice from out of the darkness.

'Er, hello?' said Eliza.

98

'I am Boris the Wise,' said the voice. 'I know what you seek, and I can help you.'

'You're not another wizard, are you?' said Eliza.

'Certainly not,' said the voice as a lantern appeared in the darkness, and Eliza saw a figure crouched next to a large black cauldron. She had a face as wrinkled as a raisin that's been in the bath for a really long time. Like Eliza, she had bright red hair. It sprang out of her head in all directions, as if it was quite embarrassed to be there in the first place, and was trying as hard as it possibly could to leave. As Eliza stepped closer, she deduced that Boris the Wise had not washed in a while, as she smelt a little bit like a stagnant badger.*

'I'm looking for Mordmont's castle,' said Eliza.

'I can help you, but my wisdom comes at a price,' Boris replied with a crooked smile on her face.

'What do you want?' asked Eliza.

'Only . . . your knees,' said Boris.

* Eliza was quite wrong about that. Boris had bathed in some pigeon poo only yesterday.

'My knees?'

'Your knees. Just for a day or two. For I am trying to fix my roof, and you should try getting up there with these knees. Do you accept?'

'Um . . . no?'

'Excellent,' muttered Boris. 'She agrees.'

She gazed down into her cauldron, stirring it with a large spoon and mumbling strange words under her breath. Words like 'gimbleskimbletillytumtickleflub' and 'halibut'.

Eliza crept closer and gazed into the cauldron too. But all she could see in it was some watery soup and a single, sad-looking turnip.

'I SEE IT NOW!' Boris suddenly shrieked. 'THE TURNIP OF DESTINY! HEARKEN! IT WILL COME TO YOUR AID! DO NOT FORGET! – There, the vision fades. Fades. Fades. Fades . . . It's gone. Ooh – it's coming back! No, that's just an advert. It's gone.'

She sighed, and then fixed Eliza with a steely look. 'Be gone, child. It is over! Get thee hence!'

But Eliza didn't go anywhere, possibly because she didn't know where 'hence' was. She looked down into the cauldron, and then up at Boris again. 'Are you quite sure that was the Turnip of Destiny?' she said. 'Only I was looking into the cauldron, and the turnip in it . . . Well, it looked just like an ordinary turnip to me. I don't really think you deserve my knees. And you haven't told me where to find Mordmont's castle.'

'Child, you know less than nothing! That is the TURNIP OF DINNER. What *I* saw in my vision was the TURNIP OF DESTINY. They are completely different turnips. And if you can't tell the difference between a real turnip and a visionary turnip, that is not my affair. Now, get lost! Go on! Scram! No – not that way! The castle's the other way! That's right. Just over the hill, and then turn left! Be gone!'

So Eliza and Gertrude rode off.

Silly old bat, thought Eliza. *As if she could borrow my knees. What a completely ridiculous idea.*

She looked down at her legs.

'Aaarrrggghhh!'

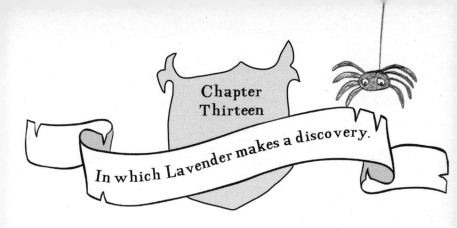

Locked in her cell, Lavender stood and shivered.

She stared at the damp pile of straw in the corner, and the spiders' webs hanging from the ceiling, and she felt like the ground beneath her might be about to give way. (And since she was in a badly built castle, on an island floating in the middle of a moat, that might well have been true.)

I'm trapped! she thought. *The ransom is never going to arrive. I'll be locked here until I'm really old . . . like, twenty-two . . . or even older!*

103

Since she couldn't bear thinking about it, she curled up on the damp straw bed and opened up her book of fairy tales.

The page fell open on the tale of *Beauty and the Beast*:

Moments earlier, the man in front of her had been a hideous beast. But as she kissed him there was a flash of light. Before her stood the handsome prince she had been dreaming of.

'A wicked fairy put a curse on me,' he told her. 'She turned me into this hideous beast. Only by finding true love could the curse be broken. Your kiss has broken the spell forever . . .'

Suddenly, everything fell into place. Lavender slammed the book shut, jumped up and started to pace around the tiny room.

She thought of Mordmont's yellow teeth – teeth that looked like they belonged to a warthog. And of his wild, wiry eyebrows that looked like they belonged to a warthog. And of his warts, which also looked like they belonged to a warthog . . .

warthog

warthoggy eyebrows →

hairy ears →

wart →

yellow teeth →

Of course!

MORDMONT
WAS THE BEAST!

Lavender thought of everything he had said to her, from his very first words: 'Enchanted! . . . A real curse! . . . Soon, my life will be transformed! . . . This is the happiest day of my life! . . . I might look beastly to you. But underneath, I'm a lovely prince!'*

Mordmont really IS a handsome prince after all! Lavender thought. *He's just trapped by a terrible curse, which has transformed him into a beast and turned his beautiful castle into this hideous ruin!*

And what did her book say could break the spell?

True Love's First Kiss!

That's it, she thought to herself. *Only true love can break the spell! I just need to see Mordmont as the handsome prince he really is. And see this room as the beautiful room it surely is . . .*

That stool in the corner was probably a beautiful dressing table. The pile of straw was a beautiful four-poster bed. That large, hairy spider was probably just an unlucky footman called Graham, trapped by an evil curse.

* Mordmont didn't actually say that last bit.

106

'Poor Graham,' Lavender said, and she stroked the spider's hairy back. 'Don't worry, Graham, it's all going to be all right,' she whispered, before breaking into song:

'*Once the spell is broken*
My prince will be revealed,
All handsome and kind
and polite and refined
And I'll be wined and dined
I can see in my mind
That he's one of a kind,
In my heart he's enshrined
And our stars are aligned
For our fates are entwined
Now I've found peace of . . .'

'... Rind?' said Bonnet, appearing at the door.

'Oh – thank you!' said Lavender, whirling round, her eyes glowing with happiness.

'Rind soup,' said Bonnet as he handed her a bowl of thin, grey soup through the bars.

'It looks delicious!' Lavender replied, for she knew that the food was enchanted. If only she could see it as it really was, it would be something like a slice of double dark chocolate fudge cake (with extra chocolate ice cream). It just *looked* like thin, grey soup. But Lavender could imagine how gooey and delicious it looked, and how sweet and delicious it tasted. With all the different layers of chocolatey deliciousness just stacked on top of each other ...

'This must have taken hours,' said Lavender.

'Er, not really,' said Bonnet.

'Well, you're very kind.'

'Oh, thank you, Your, er, Highness,' said Bonnet shyly, his heart melting. (Not literally melting, you understand. That would have been disgusting.) 'It was the least I could do,' he said with a shrug. (Which was true. It really was the least he could have done.)

Bonnet trudged off down the stairs, thinking how kind and polite princesses were.

I wish I could help her. But I'm only a tiny giant. What can I do? Bonnet thought to himself, absent-mindedly swinging the keys to Lavender's cell.

Chapter Fourteen

In which Mordmont reveals the secret sweet side that no one knew he had.

Chapter
Fifteen

In which there is a kiss.

That night, before Lavender got ready for bed, she decided to practise for True Love's First Kiss by kissing Graham the Footman. He didn't seem to mind, although she did wonder if it would be a bit awkward when the spell was broken, and he became a human and stopped being a spider. Then, just as she was curling up to go to sleep, there came a crash, and a bang, a tumble, and in through the window came . . .

'Eliza?!!!! GERTRUDE! What are you doing here?!'

'Quick!' said Eliza. 'Come on! I've come to rescue you!'

'How did you even get up here?'

'Gertrude can climb anything. Now, come on. I think the guard spotted me! Let's go!'

'Eliza,' hissed Lavender. 'I'm not going anywhere!'

'What?' said Eliza.

'Look, you can't rescue me. I've already been rescued! It's too complicated to explain.'

'Come on! We have to go, before someone comes and everything's ruined!' Eliza said.

'No, YOU have to go, before someone comes and everything's ruined!'

'Wait: you don't *want* to be rescued?' said Eliza, her eyes nearly popping out of her head.

'No!' said Lavender. 'Of course not! I've found my prince. I'm living in a beautiful castle. Once the spell is broken you'll understand. But if you want me to be happy, you should leave. Right now!'

'I should *leave*?!' said Eliza. 'After I got lost in the woods, got attacked by wasps, survived a badger stampede and climbed all the way up this tower?'

'Exactly!' said Lavender. 'That's exactly what I'm saying!'

'Have you completely lost your mind?' Eliza asked.

'No, I have completely found my prince. And if you weren't so jealous, you'd be happy for me. Isn't that right, Graham?'

'Who's Graham?' asked Eliza.

'Graham,' Lavender said primly, 'is a very nice footman, who has been transformed into a spider by an evil enchantment.'

'Right,' said Eliza. 'You're talking to a spider. And you want me to leave.'

'Yes!'

'You don't want to be rescued.'

'No! Now go away, before anyone sees.'

'Sees what?' said the deep, gravelly voice of Clive, jutting his spade-shaped head through the bars.

'Sea . . . sea . . . *I do like to be beside the seaside,*' sang Lavender uncertainly. 'I'm just doing my evening singing,' she went on as Eliza ducked behind the pile of straw.

'You sure everything's all right in there?' asked Clive. 'Thought I heard a bit of a commotion.'

'No, no, everything's perfect!' said Lavender.

'Everything's perfect?' said Clive, a little surprised.

'Everything's PERFECT?' said the pile of straw.

'What was that?' asked Clive suspiciously.

'Echoes!' said Lavender. 'Funny things. Really, I'm fine in here. Never been better.'

'Hmmmmn,' said Clive, smelling a rat.

He put the rat back in his pocket. He just liked the smell of them really.

Clive looked around, sighed and frowned.

'Well, keep a lid on the singing,' he growled. 'When you're in your own castle, you can sing to your heart's content. But for now, you're Mordmont's prisoner, all right?'

'Of course,' said Lavender.

And Clive trundled off back down the stairs.

'Eliza?' said Lavender, waiting for Eliza to come out of her hiding place. 'Gertrude?'

But there was no reply.

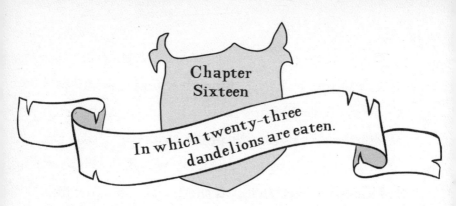

Chapter Sixteen

In which twenty-three dandelions are eaten.

Meanwhile, with Eliza on her back, Gertrude skittered, hopped and climbed as delicately as she could down the outside of the tower, which was not very delicately at all, as she lost her footing, fell, and landed on Eliza's head.

OW.

After Eliza's head stopped spinning, she and Gertrude picked themselves up and began to step across the stones that helpfully stretched across the moat.

Hmmmn, thought Eliza as she hopped on to the first stone. *The bump on my head must have confused my brain. I'm sure these stepping stones were in a different place a minute ago. It almost feels like they're moving under us. And they do seem quite spiky, for stones.*

But she kept hopping from one stone to the next as Gertrude reluctantly followed her. Gertrude didn't like water at the best of times. But she particularly didn't like unknown water in the dark. Her hoofs trembled as she jumped across the stones.

Then, just as they were about to step off the last stone and on to the bank, the stone underneath them slid sideways through the water. And opened its eyes.

'Ayyee!' shouted Eliza as quietly as she could, which was not quietly at all. 'It's alive! Jump!'

The stepping-stone-with-eyes was now rushing through the moat at quite a pace. Gertrude's eyes were as big as saucers. Her teeth chattered. Her hair stood on end. Eliza leaped, and then Gertrude shut her eyes, and with a terrified bleat she jumped high into the air.

Phew!

They made it by a whisker and landed on the bank in the most elegant manner possible, which was in a tangled heap.

This time, Eliza landed on Gertrude's head. Which sort of evened things out a bit.

'Oh,' said Eliza. 'Look at that.' As she looked back, she noticed that all the stepping stones were moving rapidly through the water. And each one had a pair of brightly glowing, violet eyes.

'Gertrude,' she hissed. 'I think it might be time to leave.'

And she started striding back towards the forest, with the trembling Gertrude running along behind her.

'That is *it*!' said Eliza as they stomped through the forest. 'Not only does Lavender *not* allow us to rescue her, she also doesn't warn us at all about the incredibly dangerous creatures in the moat! No "Oh, you might want to look out because the stepping stones are alive". No "Oh, by the way, mind the MONSTERS ON YOUR WAY OUT"!'

'Hrumph,' sighed Gertrude, who was still trembling from nose to hoof.

'Well, if she doesn't want to be rescued, she's not going to be rescued!' Eliza said. 'That's FINE with me. I don't need to risk my life breaking into castles and escaping monsters! She can just stay in her prison cell and talk to spiders, and I DON'T CARE.'

'Hrumph,' Gertrude said again, apparently in agreement. But before they got very far, Gertrude stopped. And began to munch on some dandelions.

'Gertrude? Come *on*! We're going home!'

At this, Gertrude sat down. The trip across the moat had terrified her to the bottom of her goaty soul, and she hadn't had as much as a paper bag to eat for hours. When she saw the dandelions, she decided that was it. She wasn't going to move another inch.

'Oh, don't look at me like that!' said Eliza. 'Lavender's just going to have to stay there. I'm going home. On my own. I'm going to look after the whole farm, on my own. And I'm going to listen to Grandma Maud's stories about the Black Death ON MY OWN. Come on. Let's go.'

Gertrude didn't move.

'Come on!' said Eliza.

These dandelions, Gertrude was discovering, were *much* tastier than the dandelions around Old Tumbledown Farm.

'Well, what am I supposed to do now . . . just stand around waiting for my sister to realize she's trapped?'

'Harrkkkkh,' croaked Gertrude.

'Or I suppose I could just find a thousand silver pieces and hand over the ransom?'

'Krrr,' Gertrude replied.

'Wait,' said Eliza. 'So, what you're saying is . . .'

'Chhhhrrrrrrr,' rasped Gertrude. (She had a bit of dandelion leaf stuck in her throat.)

'And then, if I . . .'

'Kaaaarrrrrr,' said Gertrude. The leaf really was stuck.

'And then I . . .'

'Errrr . . .'

Gertrude was now properly choking, not that Eliza had noticed.

'That's it! I could – just maybe . . .'

'Haaaakkkaaaaaaar!' wheezed Gertrude, toppling over on to her side and slowly turning blue.

'A brilliant plan!'

'Krruuugghhhh!' went Gertrude, desperately trying to breathe.

'I just need a disguise!'

'Yarghhhhhk!' rasped Gertrude, finally coughing up the leaf.

'Yes!' said Eliza. 'Gertrude, you are brilliant.' She gave Gertrude a friendly pat. 'That's *exactly* what I'll do!'

Chapter Seventeen

In which there is giddiness.

The next morning, Lavender was skipping around her tiny cell. Today was THE DAY! She could feel it in her bones. Today they were going to share True Love's First Kiss. She had brushed her hair. She had put on her pointy princess hat. She had dabbed flour on her face and stuck on one of her beauty spots.

She was ready.

When Mordmont strode into the cell, Lavender leaped up to greet him.

'My little prisoner,' Mordmont said. 'You're looking very . . . happy this morning.'

'How could I not be happy?' said Lavender, swaying from side to side. She felt almost giddy with joy. 'Soon I hope I will be able to bring you the greatest happiness.'

'Very generous of you to see it like that. Of course, my happiness *is* the most important thing,' Mordmont replied.

'It is to me,' said Lavender. She sighed and gazed at the beast before her. She looked at that horrible moustache, drooping beneath Mordmont's nose like a soggy weasel's tail. And at his yellow teeth . . . and his straggly swamp of a beard . . . and his horrible warts . . . And she thought of the terrible curse that had transformed him into this hideous beast, and her heart went out to him. (Not literally. That would be disgusting.)

'I have one small favour to ask of you,' he said.

'Anything,' said Lavender.

'Please shut your eyes,' said Mordmont.

Shut my eyes? This is the moment! Lavender thought. *The moment I've been waiting for. True Love's First Kiss!*

So she shut her eyes. And waited. And heard a *snip*. And then heard the door clang shut.

When she opened her eyes, the room was empty.

Poor Mordmont. How shy he is! Lavender thought. And then, looking down, she saw some strands of her hair glinting on the floor and realized what had happened.

He has taken a lock of my hair for safekeeping! How romantic! She sighed.

Meanwhile, Mordmont skipped down the steps feeling very pleased with himself. *Take one lock of her hair*, he thought, *and send it to the House of Ummer as a dreadful warning.* That should get the ransom on its way soon enough.

For the rest of the day, Lavender waited patiently for True Love's First Kiss.

She waited.

And waited.

And waited.

It was evening before Mordmont returned. This time Lavender was sure that he was about to kiss her, because he kept saying romantic things like 'When I get my hands on the ransom, I'm going to get some incredible gold trousers', and 'I'll be so rich, no woman will be able to resist me', and 'I do hope that athlete's foot hasn't come back again'.

Lavender smiled at her prince. How shy he was! How sweetly he tried to declare his love for her. In fact, she was pretty sure he was about to kiss her – because now he was picking something long and green out of his teeth – when Bonnet burst into the room, waving a piece of parchment in the air.

'For you, sire!' he said. 'It's worked! It's coming!'

Mordmont grabbed it, and feverishly read it out loud:

To the Dread Villain Mordmont,

Release Princess Fahalahalahalahalaha at midnight and you shall receive your ransom.

Do NOT bring any weapons if you do not wish to be harmed.

From The Squire of The Royal House of Ummer.

For a moment, Mordmont froze. Then he leaped into the air.

'It's happening!' he shouted. 'It's truly happening!

Bonnet, I could kiss you!'

'Please don't, sire,' said Bonnet.

'Fine, I'll kiss you instead,' he said, turning to Lavender. And so Lavender was completely taken aback and unprepared for Mordmont to plant . . .

True Love's First Kiss!

on her cheek. But he did. When she opened her eyes again, that haddocky smell would be gone! Those whiskers would have disappeared! The soggy moustache would vanish forever! The yellow teeth would disappear! The swampy beard would be gone for good!

Lavender could feel the cold wetness of Mordmont's lips. And the prickliness of his moustache. But in another moment, Mordmont the Beast would be gone, and in his place would be the lovely, handsome, perfect prince of her dreams.

There was a crash. There was a bang.

That was just Bonnet, tripping over himself as he fell backwards down the stairs.

'Don't you just love it when a plan comes together?' said a voice. 'I am going to look so incredible in those gold trousers. Of course, there are bills to pay. But I really do need more trousers. I wonder how many princesses there are in this kingdom?'

Lavender opened her eyes and saw . . .

Mordmont.

With the same horrible moustache and beard.

The same revolting warts.

The same pink dressing gown.

The same unfortunate yellow trousers.

The same unfortunate yellow teeth.

The same haddocky breath.

Mordmont sighed and looked at her.

'It's as if all my dreams have come true!' he said, grinning at her.

'And it's as if mine . . . haven't,' said Lavender.

'Well, no, of course not. But I mean, who really cares

about you? Not to be rude or anything. But this is the Tale of the Dread Villain Mordmont, and his Rise to Become the Most Dreadful Villain in the Kingdom.* You're not exactly a significant character.**'

With that, he skipped out of the cell, slamming the door behind him.

Lavender slumped to the floor.

'What a horrible mess,' she said, to nobody in particular. 'I would really like to go home now, please.'

I'm all alone, she thought. And, as if to prove her wrong, Graham the Footman – or, to use his more usual name, 'a spider' – crawled all the way up her leg. Which did not make Lavender feel better. At all.

* No it isn't.
** Yes she is.

Chapter Eighteen

Which is bathed in a silvery light.

As the clock struck midnight, the moon shone a silvery light over the castle and its surroundings. Clouds raced across the sky, and one of them won and was given a medal. As Mordmont lowered the drawbridge, a dark, shadowy figure appeared at the other end of it, seated on the back of a noble steed.

'He's here,' whispered Bonnet. 'The squire from the House of Ummer!'

'Greetings, Squire!' Mordmont called into the darkness as he stepped on to the drawbridge, with Lavender by his side. 'I am Mordmont! Hand over the ransom, or I'll throw you in the moat and you will be at the mercy of my moat-dragons!'

This was greeted with silence.

'Come on. Be quick about it! Clive, fetch the ransom!'

But as Clive started to pound his way across the drawbridge, the shadowy figure said, 'Come no further! First, the princess must be freed.'

'Not until we've seen the silver,' Mordmont called back. 'Just hand over the ransom, and Bob's your uncle.'

'Bob's not my uncle,' the squire replied. 'He's my third cousin.'

Lavender looked into the darkness and wondered who the mysterious figure could be. Was this, perhaps, her true prince?

'The ransom is in this sack,' the squire called, holding up a large, bulging sack. 'Look!'

The squire flicked a coin through the air, which bounced near Mordmont's feet and plopped into the moat.

'Sorry,' called the squire. 'I'll just try that again.'

A second silver coin came skittering along the drawbridge, and rolled most of the way to Mordmont's feet before it dropped off the edge and into the moat.

'Sorry!' said the squire again. 'Listen, I can promise you this – the ransom is genuine. As genuine as my own beard. It is every bit as real as the House of Ummer – on that you have my word.'

'What word?' asked Mordmont.

'What?'

'What word?' asked Mordmont again.

'Um . . . "geranium"?' said the squire.

'I accept,' said Mordmont, who was so pleased about getting the ransom he probably would have accepted almost any word, even quite a boring one like 'spade'.

'Princess Fahalahalahalaha,' Mordmont announced, 'you are free to go.'

So Lavender started to walk across the drawbridge towards the mysterious squire, while the mysterious squire got down from his steed and began to walk towards Lavender, holding out the bulging sack.

Unfortunately, the squire was not to stay shadowy or mysterious for long. For, as he came closer, the wind whistled by and whipped off the squire's beard.

'Yarghhhh!' the squire shouted as the beard, which was made of wool, blew away in a gust of wind.

As the squire reached out to catch it, he dropped the sack, which split and sent silver coins rolling everywhere.

'The ransom!' shrieked Mordmont. 'Quick! Bonnet! Clive!'

Mordmont raced after the coins as they went rolling and skipping and flying off the drawbridge in all directions. He picked up as many as he could, stuffing them into his pockets . . . and then suddenly he stopped, and looked at the coin in his hand. All right, it looked silvery, in the silvery light of the moon.

But it wasn't, in fact, a coin. It was a pebble.

And so were all the others. His very own pebbles.

'My family pile! You stole my family pile!' Mordmont seethed.

Then, looking up, he gasped.

Lavender gasped too.

Bonnet wheezed.

Clive grunted.

Because, without his beard, the squire wasn't a squire at all.

'You came back!' Lavender shouted to Eliza.

'Came back?!' shrieked Mordmont.

'I'm sorry!' Lavender was shouting. 'What do I do?'

Uh-oh, thought Eliza. She hadn't planned this bit. 'Run!' she yelled.

So Eliza and Lavender began to run across the drawbridge, towards Gertrude, who was standing on the bank with hope in her eyes and a dandelion in her mouth. But, before they reached the end of the drawbridge, Clive reached the pulley, and the drawbridge started swinging up into the air.

As Eliza and Lavender scrambled to the edge, they found themselves high above the murky, stinking waters of the moat, where strange shapes swirled back and forth below the surface.

'I think this is the bit where we, er . . . jump.'

'We jump?' said Lavender. 'I can't jump!'

'We have to,' said Eliza. 'We have to swim for it.'

'I can't!' said Lavender. 'It's too high.'

'Listen, take my hand. One, two, thr—'

But before they could jump anywhere, Clive gave one final tremendous pull on the pulley, and the drawbridge went swinging upward with such force that they were thrown backwards through the air.

Whumph! They landed on the ground as the drawbridge shut with a horrible thud.

'Got you!' said a deep, gravelly voice.

And Lavender was once more gazing fuzzily up into the face of Clive. Except that this time she knew that he was definitely *not* her rescuer.

'What a horrible mess,' Lavender said, because she could see that they were now in even more trouble than before. And because she could see all the way up Clive's nose.

urggh

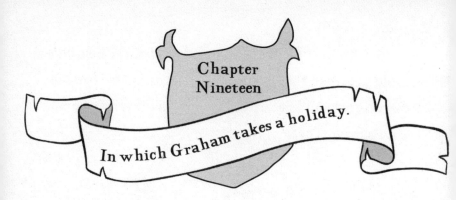

Before long, Eliza and Lavender were sitting back in the cell, which looked gloomier and more frightening than ever.

'Now, my little princesses, don't even *think* about trying to escape this time,' said Mordmont, poking his head through the bars and grinning at them.

'We're not princesses,' said Eliza.

'And don't *even think* about pretending not to be princesses,' Mordmont replied. 'Two sisters. Two princesses. Two thousand silver pieces! It couldn't have worked out better. Soon I'll have more money than brains!'

'Soon?' muttered Eliza.

'One little letter to the House of Ummer, and two thousand silver pieces will soon be mine!' Mordmont went on. 'Do you have any more sisters?'

'No,' said Eliza. 'And we're *really* not princesses. We live on a farm—'

'Yes, yes, with a goat called Gertrude – as if anyone would ever believe that,' said Mordmont. 'But I know that you are Princess Fahalahalahalaha, and Princess—'

'Trahelehelehelehe,' said Eliza sarcastically.

'Ha! Caught you off-guard there. Princess Fahalahalahalaha and Princess Trahelehelehelehe, from the House of Ummer. Do you have any brothers?'

'Oh yes. Prince Troholoholoholoho,' said Eliza.

'Prince Troholoholoholoho. Very interesting,' said Mordmont. 'Now, if you're planning to escape, I would just take a moment to consider the lilies. And Violet. Both of which are highly dangerous. Both of which are in the moat.'

'Violet?' said Eliza. 'The colour violet?'

'Violet, my moat-dragon. And all her many children. I've put her on a strict diet.* So she is ravenously hungry. If you want to try and escape across the moat, go ahead.'

And with that, Mordmont was gone. He went tripping down the stairs, thinking about how he was going to spend two thousand pieces of silver. Of course, it didn't need to stop there. *This is only the beginning!* Mordmont thought. *This could be the making of me. I've found my vocation. Kidnapper extraordinaire.* Soon, he was so excited that he began to sing.

> *'I'll have hundreds of princesses,*
> *Each one will have her nook,*
> *I'll borrow her and give her back*
> *Just like a library book.*
> *And "happily ever after"*
> *Will live everybodeeeeee*
> *If by everybody you mean . . . me!*

* Mordmont had forgotten to feed her.

And I will kidnap princes,
And I will kidnap kings,
King Harold, Queen Matilda
And all their diamond rings!
I'll be such a dreadful villain
That no one will resist
And anyone who's anyone
Will want to be . . .
Will queue to be . . .
Will fight until they're blue to be . . .
The very lucky kidnappee
Who's next upon my list.'

Sitting on the cold, damp floor of the cell, Lavender and Eliza listened to the echoes of Mordmont's singing, until he finally stopped. (He had been distracted by an incredibly handsome-looking face that he'd spotted in the mirror.)

'Well,' said Eliza.

'Well,' said Lavender.

'Well,' said Eliza.

'Maybe if *I* sang a song . . .' Lavender began.

'Please don't.'

'What if I grew my hair, just like Rapunzel, and then let it down out of the window, and—'

'Lavender!' said Eliza.

'What?'

'No more fairy tales,' said Eliza with a scowl.

'Sorry,' said Lavender. 'What if I pretended to be asleep, and then a prince would come and rescue me—'

'LAVENDER,' said Eliza.

'Or what if there's a frog in the moat who's really a cursed prince, and he's just waiting for me to dive in and kiss him? I suppose I would have to kiss every frog in the moat, and the toads too, to be safe—'

'LAVENDER!' said Eliza.

'Sorry,' said Lavender.

'What did I just say?'

'Er . . . Lavender?' said Lavender.

'NO MORE FAIRY TALES!' said Eliza, and she picked up the book of fairy tales and hurled it out of the window. It landed in the moat with a splash, and was never seen again.

'Eliza!' said Lavender.

'What?' scowled Eliza.

Lavender paused.

'Thanks for trying to rescue me,' she said in a very small voice.

'Twice,' said Eliza.

'Thanks for coming to rescue me, twice. I'm sorry about everything. It really is all my fault,' said Lavender.

'Yep,' said Eliza.

'You were just trying to help me.'

'*Rescue* you—'

'But I made a mess of everything,' said Lavender.

'Yep.'

'And now everything's ruined.'

'Yep,' said Eliza. 'Although my plan didn't exactly work either,' she added quietly, staring at her fingernails. She hated admitting she was wrong. 'I could have had a better disguise. And I suppose I did drop the ransom. I made a mess of everything too.'

'Well, you tried,' said Lavender, putting an arm round her sister. 'At least we're together, that's the most important thing.'

'You're right,' said Eliza. 'That *is* the most important thing.'

'This is a bit cheesy,' said Bonnet, pushing open the bars to their cell, and setting down two bowls of soup.

'Cheese and turnip soup,' he explained.

'Thanks, Bonnet,' said Lavender.

'It was the least I could do,' said Bonnet. 'I hope you are quite comfortable?'

'Not really,' said Eliza. 'We'd like to go home.'

'Of course,' said Bonnet. 'I only wish there was something I could do to help.'

'You could help by giving us the keys,' said Eliza.

'The keys?' asked Bonnet innocently.

'Yes, the keys in your hand.'

'Oh,' Bonnet replied. 'Those keys.'

For a moment he stood there, his mouth opening and shutting like a slightly confused trout. 'Hmmmmmnnngh,' he said. 'I'll . . . er . . . I'll . . . yes, I see . . . let me just . . . um . . . yes.'

'All you need to do is give them to us,' said Eliza, staring at him hard. 'It's quite simple.'

'You're right,' said Bonnet, flushing pink. 'Well, here you are.'

Bonnet held out his hand.

'Bonnet?' said Eliza.

'Yep?'

'Those aren't the keys. That's a piece of paper, with a picture of some keys on it.'

'Is it? Oh. So it is. Er, my mistake. I'll, um . . . I'll . . . just . . . er . . .'

And without finishing his sentence, Bonnet edged backwards, locked the cell, and went quickly down the stairs.

I really should help them, Bonnet thought. *They're innocent, after all. And Princess Fahalahalahalaha sings such beautiful songs. Of course I will help them. I must.*

He turned round and started walking back up the stairs.

But then, what about Mordmont?

As Bonnet reached the top step, he came to a halt, turned, and ran back down the stairs again. And he was almost at the bottom of the staircase when another thought popped into his head.

But what will become of the princesses?

So, very slowly, he started tramping back up the stairs again. He was almost at the princesses' cell when a very vivid image popped into his head.

Clive!

Which made him run all the way back down the stairs again.

An hour later, Bonnet was exhausted and dizzy and still holding on to the keys. *What a horrible mess I'm in,* he thought. *But what can I do? I'm only a tiny, cowardly giant.*

And, in an effort to cheer himself up, he decided to go and eat an egg in the bath. He hated being a villain's sidekick's sidekick. It was even worse than his previous jobs, which were:

- A laughing stock.
- A human bowling ball.
- Really missing his parents.
- Crying.*

Back in the cell, Eliza was trying to force down some of the disgusting soup. It was cold, and as sticky as glue.

'We have to get out of here,' said Eliza.

'I know,' said Lavender. 'Ugh! What happened to your knees?'

'Just . . . don't even ask,' said Eliza. She had almost forgotten about her incredibly knobbly old-lady knees. Here they are again, just in case you missed them the first time:

---

* Those last two weren't really jobs. They were just things he'd done quite a lot of.

'They're so lumpy and hairy and withered! They're disgusting!'

'I know,' said Eliza. 'I just had to lend my knees to a witch . . . Oh, never mind.'

'You *really* shouldn't have done that,' said Lavender unhelpfully. 'You don't know what she'll do with them. And those knees won't help us get rescued, will they?'

'Thanks for pointing that out, Lavender,' muttered Eliza. 'Look, there has to be a way out. I'm sure we can think of something.' She shut her eyes tight to help herself think.

And then there was a silence.

It was long.

R e a l l y   long.

It was longer than the world's longest animal. (A Mongolian Death Worm, since you ask.)

'Well?' said Lavender. 'Eliza? Eliza, are you *asleep*?'

'Put them in the sheep basket,' murmured Eliza.

'Eliza. You *are* asleep!' said Lavender, prodding her sister.

Eliza opened her eyes.

'You're supposed to be working out our escape plan!' said Lavender.

'Sorry,' said Eliza. 'Let's both think.'

So they both thought.

There was another silence, longer than *two* Mongolian Death Worms.

'Maybe we'll think of something in the morning,' said Lavender, stifling a yawn.

'Yeah. Maybe,' said Eliza.

So they both curled up on the damp straw bed, and shut their eyes, trying not to think about the possibility that they might never escape Mordmont's castle.

'I hope Gertrude's all right,' said Eliza.

'I know. And Grandma Maud,' Lavender whispered. 'She's probably worried sick about us.'

In fact, Grandma Maud wasn't doing too badly. Here's what Grandma Maud was doing at that very moment:

'I wonder what she would do if she was here,' whispered Lavender.

'She'd tell us a story about the Black Death,' Eliza said. 'With spots . . .'

'And lumps . . .'

'And withered skin . . .'

'And fingers falling off . . .'

'Wait!' they both said at the same time.

'Are you thinking what I'm thinking?' said Lavender.

'I don't know,' said Eliza. 'Are you thinking what I'm thinking?'

'I don't know. Let's both say what we're thinking at the same time!'

So they did.

'Let's pretend we've got the Black Death!' said Eliza, at the same time as Lavender said, 'Let's sing a song about Grandma Maud!'

Eliza looked down at the grey, gluey cheese and turnip soup, and remembered the words of Boris the Wise. Maybe the turnip could help them after all . . .

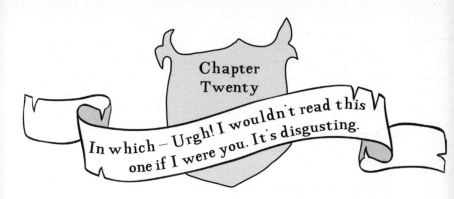

Chapter Twenty

In which – Urgh! I wouldn't read this one if I were you. It's disgusting.

The very next morning, Eliza and Lavender were awake at the crack of dawn.

'How many stick-on beauty spots have you got?' whispered Eliza.

'Um . . . seventy-three,' said Lavender.

'Seventy-three?!!' said Eliza.

'And a bag of flour to make myself look like Snow White. It's always good to be prepared.'

'And how much sticky soup do we have?'

'Two bowls,' said Lavender. 'Full of bits of turnip.'

'And we've got all these cobwebs . . .'

'Yep,' said Lavender.

They took the flour and rubbed it into their skin

until they looked as white as ghosts. Then they took Lavender's stick-on beauty spots, and covered themselves with those. They got the cold, gloopy soup and covered their arms and legs with sticky bits of turnip.

Then they took all the spiders' webs from the ceiling and wrapped them around their fingers to make their skin look withered.

'This is the most disgusting thing I have EVER, EVER done,' said Lavender. 'I do not like this.'

'You should try cleaning out Gertrude's pen more often.'

'Hmmmmm,' said Lavender, frowning. She did not appreciate being made to look disgusting. 'If I meet a prince like this, I am going to kill you,' she said.

'It's not that likely,' said Eliza.

At last they were ready.

'We really are in a horrible mess,' Eliza said with a grin.

At about this time, Mordmont sprang out of his bed feeling particularly pleased with himself. 'Two thousand silver pieces!' he said. 'Two thousand silver pieces! All for ME!'

He danced through the hall, waltzed through the pantry and skipped up the staircase to check on his prisoners.

'Good mor— Ughhh!' he yelped, looking into the

cell. 'What is the meaning of this?!' he gasped.

'Oh, it's nothing really. We've just got a few spots,' said Lavender in a weak, quavering voice. (Lavender had an amazing sick voice. She had used it many times before to get out of cleaning Gertrude's pen. But it had never had such a dramatic effect as it did now.)

'*Spots?*' said Mordmont.

'Only fifteen or so,' said Eliza.

'I've got twenty-three,' Lavender croaked proudly. 'But then she has got more lumps. Would you like to see them?'

'A thousand times, no,' said Mordmont very quickly before he yelped again. 'What on earth happened to your knees?! They're so . . . withered!'

'Oh, er, I see what you mean,' said Eliza.

Mordmont shuddered and turned to Lavender. 'Princess Fahalahalahalaha, why is your hand in a bandage?'

'Oh, it's a bit embarrassing,' said Lavender. 'I . . . I . . . oh, oh dear . . .'

And then Lavender slumped to one side and collapsed on to the floor, in her most convincing faint ever.

'What is wrong with her?!' said Mordmont. 'What have you done to her! Why has she collapsed? What is going ON?'

'Er, a bit of her finger, sort of . . . fell off . . . in the night,' said Eliza apologetically. 'She's just feeling a bit peaky.'

And Eliza held up what looked a lot like a withered fingertip. (Although on closer inspection it looked a lot more like a withered turnip.)

'Spots,' said Mordmont, growing paler by the second. 'Lumps . . . Withered skin . . . Collapsing . . . Fingers that fall off . . . That can only mean one thing . . .

THE BLACK
DEATH!'

And then, as if his moustache had been set on fire, Mordmont started hopping up and down.

'OUT! GET OUT! OUT! OUT! OUT! OUT! GET OUT OF MY CASTLE!'

'Oh, are we free to go?' said Lavender, opening her eyes. 'That's very kind of you.'

And they both stood up to give Mordmont a grateful hug.

'DON'T TOUCH ME!' he shrieked. 'GET AWAY! GET AWAY! GET AWAY! GET AWAY! GO ON GO ON GO ON GO ON – GET OUT GET OUT GET OUT GET OUT!!!'

And he chased them out of the cell, down the stairs and through the pantry, the scullery, the ballroom, the hall and right out of the front door of the castle.

'BE GONE!!!!' he screeched. And with a last swift, powerful kick, Mordmont sent his horribly diseased prisoners flying through the air, to freedom!

If by the word 'freedom' you mean 'a stinking, deadly moat, full of monstrous moat-dragons'.

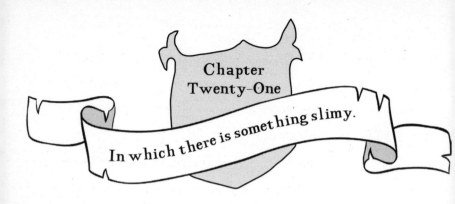

Chapter
Twenty-One

In which there is something slimy.

'Yaaaaaaaaaaaaaargh!'

The girls plunged straight into the yellowy-green slime, and were hit by a smell worse than Gertrude's morning breath.

'Gurgggghhhh,' said Lavender, surfacing with her eyes shut tight.

'Erghhhhhh,' said Eliza, doggy-paddling beside her, squinting and trying hard not to breathe in the fumes, as tendrils of moat weed wrapped themselves around her arms, and legs, and ankles. They were soft and they were everywhere, wrapping themselves around her like strands of witch's hair.

'Bleurghhhghhh,' coughed Lavender as she

accidentally swallowed a mouthful of moat water. It tasted like a seasick goblin's vomit. She pulled her chin as high out of the water as she could, shut her eyes and swam round and round in a circle.

'This way!' Eliza shouted. As they shrieked and swam and splashed and screamed, Bonnet, who was having a quiet nap in the kitchen, woke up and pattered over to the window.

And the moat-dragons, who were also having a quiet nap, deep in the moat, woke up too.

The prisoners! The prisoners have escaped! Bonnet thought. *They're free!* He smiled. And then he remembered the moat-dragons. *Oohhhh! Someone should rescue them. Really. Someone should really rescue them. Now.* Bonnet gulped as he looked out across the moat to the forest beyond. *Perhaps a knight will ride by. Or a prince? A prince on a bright white steed?* But no prince materialized. All Bonnet could see from his window was a slightly sad-looking goat nibbling flowers on the outskirts of the forest. *Hmmmmn.*

~

'*Ggg*-maybe the moat-dragons are *gg*-asleep!' gurgled Eliza.

But just as she said that, she heard a hissing. And then a snorting, snuffling sound. As Eliza turned her head, she caught sight of several pairs of bright eyes, staring back at her. The eyes glowed violet, and they belonged to three bright green heads, each topped with long, sharp spikes.

'YARGHHHHH!' screamed Eliza.

'ARGHHHH!' screamed Lavender. The two of them started swimming as fast as they could through the thick, treacly water. There's nothing like a horde of ravenous moat-dragons chasing you to make you zoom across a moat at an incredible speed.

Well, there are *some* things. Like magical powers, or a dolphin to ride on, or three wizards suddenly appearing and giving you a ship made of wool to sail away on. Any of those would have been great. Apart from the last one: that probably wouldn't have worked at all. But Lavender and Eliza didn't have anything to help them, apart from their fear. And that gave them a surge of energy and they swam as fast as they could.

As she swam, Lavender thought about the swooshing, rushing, snapping, gnashing sounds that were coming from behind her. They almost certainly weren't from moat-dragons, surging along in the water, getting more and more hungry and excited as they got closer to their prey.

No, she thought. They were probably just the sounds of lilies, floating on the moat. The lilies had probably always made those snapping, toothy, bitey, snarly, hungry sounds, only she had never really listened to them before.

And those sharp jabbing pains in her toes? They definitely weren't moat-dragons biting them because they felt like a cheeky little pre-dinner snack. Definitely not. Those pains were probably just some totally harmless bitey water.

Lavender and Eliza kept swimming, and swimming, with the dragons streaking through the water behind them. The girls' arms felt like lead, and their legs felt like lead, and it was lucky they weren't actually made of lead, because then they would definitely have sunk, or been used to make pipes. But soon they were almost at the bank, and beyond that was the forest. And standing under the trees, not far off, was Gertrude, looking wildly excited to see them after all this time.

'Done it,' Eliza gasped, 'we've done it!', as they both reached the bank and pulled themselves up and out of the water. A second slower and the dragons would have had them for dinner, and possibly tomorrow's breakfast as well, for now they were hissing and spluttering and snapping at the edge of the bank, but Eliza and Lavender were safe.

They caught their breath, and then threw it, and then caught it again, and wiped the weeds, slime and frogs off their faces.

'We got out,' said Eliza. But as she said those words she heard an enormous SPLASH, as if some huge and heavy object had just dropped from a great height, into the moat.

Which it had. For, in the middle of the moat, something was thrashing wildly in the water. And two pale white arms were flailing in the air.

'Bonnet?' said Lavender.

'I've – come – come – to – to – to . . .' Bonnet

gasped just before his head, and his bonnet, disappeared under the water.

'Bonnet!' Lavender screamed.

He bobbed up again.

'. . . to save you!'

He bobbed down again. As his head disappeared under the surface, Eliza realized that the snorting, snuffling, snapping moat-dragons were no longer swarming in the water at her feet. They had all suddenly slipped away.

'Oh no. No! No, no, no. I'm not going back!' said Eliza.

But what choice did she really have? They had to save the little giant or they'd never forgive themselves. They'd never be able to forget the sound of his terrified struggle, at least not until they were really old and could no longer remember each other's names, or what jelly was.

'We're coming!' they yelled as they dived straight back into the moat, back through the slime, back through thick weeds like witch's hair, and back towards the moat-dragons, which were now circling around Bonnet as he flailed and struggled in the water.

'Quick!' Eliza shouted. 'One. Two. Three . . .'

The two sisters took two huge gulps of air, and then dived down into the stinking green water. And Lavender, her eyes shut tight, reached out below her, and touched something slimy. And Eliza, plunging downwards, accidentally caught hold of the gnarled old leg . . .

. . . of a piano . . .

. . . tuner.

And they kept swimming down and down . . . until they grabbed on to Bonnet's ankles. But a fierce moat-dragon had already grabbed Bonnet by his bonnet.

Eliza and Lavender tugged upwards, as the dragons yanked downwards.

'GHHHHRR!' went Eliza.

'GHGHHGH!' went Lavender.

'. . .' went the moat-dragon. (He wasn't wasting energy making noise. He was concentrating on getting his dinner.)

And he dragged Bonnet and Lavender and Eliza down, and down, and down, as the water got even darker and murkier . . .

Soon Lavender and Eliza had completely run out of air, and they felt so dizzy that they didn't even know which way was up. They gave one final tug, just as the dragon gave one final yank, and tore Bonnet's bonnet off, and Bonnet, Lavender and Eliza all went shooting up to the surface.

'Gurghhh!' Bonnet burbled, before promptly fainting.

So while the moat-dragon tore Bonnet's bonnet to shreds – Bonnet had never washed it, so it was extremely greasy and delicious – Eliza and Lavender dragged the unconscious Bonnet to the edge of the moat. When they finally reached the edge, Eliza jumped out, and she helped pull out Bonnet and then Lavender, all of them blinking, and coughing, and spitting out mouthfuls of green moat water. Which, frankly, you shouldn't really call water, as it was made of weeds, algae, toads, old newspapers, shoes, hair-oil, broken plates, furniture and various liquids that come out of dragons.

As Eliza pulled a small snail out of her left nostril, Lavender turned to Bonnet.

'Bonnet, you saved me!' Lavender said.

'Um, really?' said Eliza. She was trying to raise an eyebrow, but no one noticed, because she still had weed all over her face.

'You came to rescue me!' said Lavender again. 'You're my hero!'

'Lavender, can we go now, please?' said Eliza.

But Lavender wasn't listening. She was gazing happily at Bonnet, and saying things that no one had ever said to him before.

Things like: 'You're so brave!' and 'Onomatopoeia'.

'Lavender, we really need to GO. Now,' said Eliza.

'. . . and you just jumped in and – ooh!' Lavender stopped. 'You've got a tiny moat-dragon in your hair – look!'

It was true. Clinging to a clump of
weed on Bonnet's head
was a baby moat-
dragon, no bigger than
a thumb.

'LAVENDER!' said
Eliza.

'What a sweet little moat-dragon!'
said Lavender. 'He's so tiny! I could
keep him as a pet. What shall I call him? I could call
him Moaty. Or Moatred. Or Moatle. Or maybe it's a
she. What do you think, Bonnet?'

Bonnet mumbled something indistinct. He was still
reeling from all the nice things that Lavender had said,
and he wasn't capable of together a sentence stringing
all at, no, no wasn't he no.

'LAVENDER,' said Eliza again.

'Or Moataria?' said Lavender.

'LAVENDER!'

'Or Moatvis? Did I say that already?'

'LAVENDER!!!!'

'What?' said Lavender.

As Lavender looked at her sister, she noticed that Eliza was looking very pale, and trembling. And that, oddly enough, Lavender was now standing in a shadow. Which was strange, because it was really quite sunny, and . . . Lavender turned round. And saw what Eliza was staring at. It was another moat-dragon. It was just like the teeny-tiny moat-dragon in Bonnet's hair. It was also the size of a thumb. IF THAT THUMB BELONGED TO AN INTERGALACTIC MONSTER WITH UNUSUALLY LARGE THUMBS.

'Ah,' said Bonnet, looking up at the beast that was staring down at them, growling. 'I wondered what had happened to Violet.' He cleared his throat. 'Hello, Violet. Um. Yes. You'll probably be wanting . . . this. S-s-sorry.'

Bonnet stepped forward and, with pale, shaking hands, untangled the baby dragon from his hair before dropping the wriggling creature into the moat. There was a tiny splash, and it swam away and disappeared.

'Sorry, Violet,' Bonnet gulped. 'No – harm intended.'

He patted his pockets. 'Would you like a piece of cake? Or maybe an egg? No?'

Violet stared down at Bonnet, and Lavender, and Eliza, and growled.

'Well, nice to see you,' said Bonnet.

'I think we should go now,' hissed Eliza.

'Unless there are any princes nearby?' whispered Lavender.

'Lavender. It's time to go,' said Eliza in a strained voice.

So Bonnet and Eliza and Lavender started to shuffle backwards. As they backed slowly away, Violet continued to stare down at them. What was she thinking? Was she thinking: *These are just poor innocent humans, and why not say live and let live*? Was she deciding whether or not to help them escape by letting them climb up on to her back, and then soaring into the air and flying straight over the forest, back home to Old Tumbledown Farm, where she would leave them safely behind and they would watch her go, with tears in their eyes?

Frankly, no. She was just deciding who to attack first. And the answer that she came up with was: *All three of them at the same time.*

Chapter Twenty-Two

In which it is revealed that Lavender's singing has unusual powers.

Violet roared, and sent a huge ball of fire towards them, then swiped at them with her enormous claws, and snapped at them with her enormous teeth.

'RUNNNNNN!' shouted Eliza. All three of them ran headlong towards the forest, but it was no use. With one scoop, Violet picked Eliza and Lavender up in her claws.

This was definitely not part of the plan. Lavender shut her eyes. She froze like an ice cream. 'GRRRRR!' said Eliza. She was pummelling Violet as hard as she could with her fists, as she tried to prise herself out of the moat-dragon's grasp, but it was impossible.

'Violet!' shouted Bonnet from the ground. 'Over

here!!' He jumped and waved to get Violet's attention. He clapped his hands. He did a dance. But Violet was much more interested in the two small girls in her claws.

'I know,' gasped Lavender. 'I've got it! I'll charm her with a song!'

'Is that a JOKE?' said Eliza, still kicking and punching

and whacking Violet as hard as she could, although her attack seemed to be about as effective as pelting a whale with marshmallows.

'Whatever you do, don't sing!' Eliza yelled. 'It will just make her more angry!'

But Lavender took no notice. A moment later, Mordmont heard the unfortunate sound, and came running outside, astonished to see that the two princesses were still alive.

He lowered the drawbridge, and soon he was nearly at the dragon's side, staring, amazed, at Violet and at Lavender, who was singing at the top of her voice.

'Ooh, lovely Violet, you've got a lovely face,
You've got such pretty fangs, and what a lovely
    place . . .'

'Stop!' said Eliza. 'STOP!!!' Because the more Lavender sang, the more violently Violet shook them from side to side. And now the moat-dragon's head began to sway and clouds of purple steam started pouring out of her ears.

'Ooh, lovely Violet, you've got a lovely smile,
You've got a lovely, very slightly homicidal style.

Ooh, lovely Violet, please please don't eat us for
　　your tea
Cos I taste worse than Brussels sprouts, and she
　　tastes worse than me . . .'

'Lavender, stop – your
singing is making her
crazy!' Eliza yelled. 'It's
driving her bonkers!
It's sending her over the
edge!'

　It was true. Dragons
have very sensitive
hearing. To any
human who
was listening,
Lavender's song
would have sounded incredibly painful. But to any
dragon, her song sounded incredibly, incredibly,
incredibly, incredibly, incredibly, incredibly,

incredibly, incredibly, incredibly painful. All Violet's children had fled from the castle to get away from the terrible sound. But the noise had affected Violet so badly that she didn't even *try* to escape. She just reeled and writhed in pain.

> '*Ooh, lovely Violet, you've got such lovely hair,*
> *You could be on the cover of* Dragony Fair.
> *Ooh, lovely Violet, you've got such lovely ears,*
> *And oh, what lovely screams, and oh, what lovely*
>   *tears . . .*'

'Wait! No – don't stop!' said Eliza. 'Keep going! This could be our chance to escape! Keep singing! Louder! Higher! She can't cope!'

So Lavender kept singing.

> '*Ooh, lovely Violet, oh what a lovely smell!*
> *A hint of vintage vomit and some deep-sea snot as*
>   *well . . .*'

'MORE!' screamed Eliza. 'More!'

Violet was flailing around so violently now it was hard for Lavender to breathe, let alone sing. But still she kept going. As she went up an octave, Violet's violet-coloured eyes turned orange. Her tail crashed and thrashed and thumped on the ground. She started to wail.

'Someone should make a perfume and call it after you: Eau du Violent Violet, Fragrance de Poo . . .'

That was it. As Lavender hit a top C, and windows in a nearby century shattered, Violet shut her eyes and keeled over. As she fell to the ground, her claws opened, and Eliza and Lavender went tumbling out on to the grass.

A moment later, they started to run towards the forest, with Bonnet bumbling along behind them. They didn't stop until they reached the trees, where Gertrude was overjoyed to see them.

And if they were worried about Mordmont chasing them, they needn't have been. Because when they looked back, they saw him standing beside Violet with a look of amazement on his face. As they watched, Violet lifted up her head, groaned, shook herself, and got to her feet.

Next to her, Mordmont had begun to dance.

'Violet. Violet, Violet, Violet, I have been such a fool!' he roared. 'To think it was here all along. Staring me in the face! My fortune! Right here in this moat! Don't you see?'

It was unclear whether or not Violet *did* see. But still Mordmont carried on, his moustache quivering with excitement.

'It is quite simple. The princesses escape from the castle, completely riddled with the Black Death . . .

Then you, Violet, pick them up. And what happens to them? Where are the boils? The bumps? The lumps? Gone! GONE! It's you! You, Violet, are a miracle, a medicinal dragon! With one touch you cured those pestilent princesses! Which means each little dragon in this moat is worth a small fortune! All I have to do is sell them at the market, and there we go – a fortune for me! Who needs princesses?'

And because Mordmont was so wildly excited by the vision of his vast fortune, and his new collection of silver, gold and platinum trousers, he did not notice the low growls coming from the dragon beside him.

'Now,' he said, bending over the moat, 'where are they all? Come my little Violy Violettas! Come to Mordy-Wordy! Come on, come – urgh!'

Mordmont yelped and blinked. It seemed that the moat was rushing away from him. Wait! . . . No. It was *he* that was rushing away, up into the air. He craned his neck around, to see that Violet had picked him up by the loop of his dressing gown, and was now dangling him over the moat.

'Violet. Stop that!'

She began to swing him back and forth.

Swish. Swish.

With every swing, Mordmont became paler and paler.

'That's enough now, Violet. Put me down, there's a good dragon.'

His gold shoes fell off into the water.

Kasplosh!

'Come on now, Violet! I was joking! Joking! Of course, I would never do anything to harm you or—'

WHOOSPLUSH!

Mordmont never got to finish his sentence, as his dragon dunked him in the moat.

KASPLISH!

She did it again.

Then she took off into the air, flew up over the castle and dropped him into the moat from a great height.

And, as she flew past the castle, Violet gave it a resounding thump with her tail, which sent the entire building tumbling into the water.

BOOM!

Lavender, Eliza and Bonnet stood on the edge of the forest and stared, open-mouthed, until Bonnet cleared his throat.

'Well, bye then,' he said quietly. 'I suppose you'd best be going home.'

'Bye then,' said Eliza.

'Bye,' said Lavender. 'You were so brave, Bonnet,' she added. 'Thank you.'

She planted a kiss on Bonnet's cheek.

'So, where are you going now?' said Lavender.

'Oh, I've made a plan,' said Bonnet.

'And what's your plan?'

'I thought I might just sit under that tree for a bit,' said Bonnet.

'Hmmmn,' said Lavender. She wasn't sure if that was really such a great plan. 'Which tree?'

'That one over there,' said Bonnet.

I could describe it to you, but really there was nothing remarkable about it. It was just your standard tree: branches, a trunk, leaves, that sort of thing.*

'Well,' said Eliza. 'Do you want to come with us instead?'

Bonnet hesitated. Of course, he wanted to say 'YES PLEASE, I WOULD LOVE TO DO THAT, more than I love sunshine and velvet and cheese and jumping up and down'. But he was a bit shy. So he just said, 'Um, yeah, all right.'

* Actually, it was Sidney's cousin, Dave.

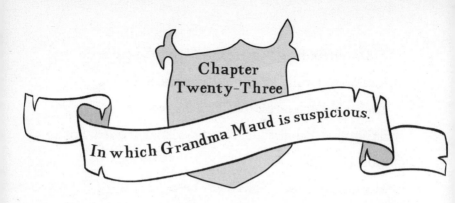

Several hours, thirty-two dandelions, three wrong turnings, one asthma attack, five arguments, fourteen owls, two hundred and thirty-two songs, twenty-eight burst owl eardrums, thirty-one huffs, seventy-four puffs, four calling birds, three French hens, two turtle doves, and countless pained looks on the face of Gertrude later, Eliza, Lavender, Gertrude and Bonnet arrived back at Old Tumbledown Farm.

'Get away, get away, you horrible little man!' said Grandma Maud, who couldn't see very well in the dark and thought Bonnet was Old Mr Nettles, trying to sell her nettles again. But when she realized that her grandchildren had returned, she was overwhelmed.

'My grandchildren!' she said. 'I don't suppose you picked up any milk on the way home, did you?'

Then she welcomed Eliza and Lavender with open arms, and welcomed Gertrude with an open bottle of brandy, and welcomed Bonnet with an open look of suspicion and hostility.

'This is Bonnet, Grandma,' said Eliza.

'He's our friend,' Lavender added. 'He's a giant.'

'Oh, I'm sure he is,' said Grandma Maud, looking Bonnet up and down and not sounding sure at all. Then they all sat by the fire, and Eliza and Lavender told Grandma Maud the whole story.

'Well,' said Grandma Maud when they had reached the end. 'I must say, I was sure you had been taken by the Black Death.'

'No,' said Eliza.

'Or the Fatal Hiccups.'

'Nope.'

'Or the Shrinking Lurgy.'

'Nope.'

'Or Spontaneous Combustion.'

'No . . .'

'Or Unexpectedly Lethal Itchy Leg.'

'No . . .'

'Or Wandering Teeth.'

'No . . .'

'Or Inexplicable Brain Melt.'

'No . . .'

'Or Deadly Yellow Bottom.'

'No . . .'

'I was so sure it was one of those,' said Grandma Maud, sounding only a little disappointed. 'But it wasn't to be.'

'No,' said Eliza. 'We're fine.'

'For now you are, dear,' she replied, patting Eliza's head. 'For now.'

~

So everything went back to normal at Old Tumbledown Farm. Gertrude stood in her pen, thinking mysterious thoughts. Eliza cleaned out her pen while Lavender 'helped'. Except now Bonnet helped out too, with things that he was good at. Like tripping over, and apologizing.

The following night, Lavender and Eliza were tucked up in bed while Grandma Maud read them a story.

'. . . And then they all lived happily ever after,' she said soothingly, 'until they were completely murdered. Well, goodnight then.'

'Goodnight,' said Lavender and Eliza.

And so Grandma Maud blew out the candle, and shuffled off to bed.

'Night, Lavender,' Eliza said sleepily. 'It's good to be home.' She yawned. Then she curled up, picked a bit of moat weed off her skin and hugged her knees to her chest.

'My knees!' Eliza said suddenly, sitting straight up in bed.

'What's that?'

'I've got my knees back,' Eliza explained. She was quite happy to have them back. From the feel of them, they were a little bit scuffed, but otherwise they seemed to be in good condition. She thought they'd probably gone back on the correct legs too. Although it was hard to be completely sure.

'Nice to have my own knees,' Eliza said drowsily, and soon she was drifting off to sleep . . .

. . . and then drifting back awake again, as she heard her sister whispering:

'Goodnight, **Prince Fabian**, Goodnight, *Prince Arjuna* . . .'

'Lavender. Lavender. LAVENDER!' hissed Eliza.

'Mnnnn?' said Lavender innocently.

'Lavender, have you not had enough of princes yet?'

'Oh, was I sleep-talking?'

'No, you were not sleep-talking,' Eliza replied through gritted teeth. She sat up in bed. 'You were *talking*-talking. Did all that kidnapping, imprisonment and escaping from dragons not teach you anything?'

'Of course it did!' said Lavender. 'It taught me lots of things. It taught me how spiders are not always your friends. And how sometimes my singing is so beautiful it can make people – or dragons – quite overwhelmed with emotion. Which can be bad for their health—'

'Yes, that's *exactly* what happened,' said Eliza.

'And it taught me that if you're going to get rescued by a prince, you should really make sure that he's a true prince.'

There was a pause. A pause in which Eliza's face expressed some deeply felt emotions. But, since the room was dark, Lavender couldn't see them.

And so, very quietly, Lavender whispered goodnight to the rest of the princes.

'Goodnight, Prince Rudolph the Unusual. Goodnight, Prince Chlknklkgkfj the Unpronounceable. Goodnight, Prince Olaf the Simply Fat . . . Goodnight, Fair Bonnet, who *might* be a prince . . .' Lavender whispered.

'Goodnight, *who*?' said Eliza, sleepily.

'Hmmmn? Nothing. What? I'm asleep. I'm babbling. Tomato,' said Lavender unconvincingly. 'Goodnight.'

Lavender gazed up at the portrait of Bonnet that had mysteriously appeared on her bedroom wall. Beside her, Eliza was already fast asleep, dreaming of their next adventure.

About the Author

Sarah Courtauld lives in London, where she writes sentences with all sorts of words in them – nouns, verbs, adjectives – occasionally even her favourite word, 'parcel'. She owns more pencils than is strictly necessary and can often be found drawing the goats in her local park. Her favourite cheese is 'all of them'. This is her first children's book.

Goth Girl

and the Ghost of a Mouse

CHRIS RIDDELL

COSTA BOOK AWARDS **Winner 2013**

Meet Ada Goth.
She lives in Ghastly-Gorm Hall with her father, Lord Goth, lots of servants and at least half a dozen ghosts, but she hasn't got any friends to explore her enormous, creepy house with.

Then, one night, everything changes when Ada meets a ghostly mouse called Ishmael. Together they set out to solve the mystery of the strange happenings at Ghastly-Gorm Hall, and get a lot more than they bargained for . . .

RODDY DOYLE
BRILLIANT

Gloria and Rayzer must save their Uncle Ben. The black dog has got him. That's what they heard their granny say anyway. And, she says, it's taken Dublin's funny bone too.

Gloria and Rayzer are really brave, but the black dog is scary and they can't fight it alone. Soon Dublin's children are helping . . . And then the animals in Dublin Zoo . . . And some cheeky seagulls as well. But could the biggest help of all be an ordinary word shouted – as loudly as possible – by all the kids together?

MY BIG FAT ZOMBIE GOLDFISH

MO O'HARA

THIS FISH JUST GOT NASTY!

When Tom's big brother dunks Frankie the goldfish into toxic green gunge, Tom zaps the fish with a battery to bring him back to life! But there's something weird about the new Frankie – he's now a BIG FAT ZOMBIE GOLDFISH with hypnotic powers . . . and he's out for revenge.

TWO BIG FAT FISHY STORIES THAT WILL KEEP YOU HOOKED AND MAKE YOU LAUGH OUT LOUD!

VISIT THE **GOBSTOPPERS** WEBSITE FOR

AUTHOR NEWS · BONUS CONTENT
VIDEOS · GAMES · PRIZES ...
AND MORE!

MACMILLAN
Children's Books